Dark Shadows
Resurrected

Dark Shadows Resurrected

BY JIM PIERSON
FOREWORD BY DAN CURTIS

POMEGRANATE PRESS LTD.
LOS ANGELES   LONDON

This is a Pomegranate Press, Ltd. book.

Dark Shadows Resurrected

Copyright 1992 by Jim Pierson.

Library of Congress Catalog Card Number: 92-064167

Hardcover Edition ISBN: 0938817-24-8
Tradepaper Edition ISBN: 0938817-23-X

First Printing: October 1992

FOR POMEGRANATE PRESS, LTD.

Publisher/Editor: Kathryn Leigh Scott
Creative Director/Book Design: Benjamin R. Martin
Book Cover Design: Heidi Frieder
Typography Consultant: Leroy Chen

Printed and bound in Korea

POMEGRANATE PRESS, LTD.
Post Office Box 8261
Universal City, California 91608

Dedicated To
Those Who've Kept
The Dream Alive

𝔄𝔠𝔨𝔫𝔬𝔴𝔩𝔢𝔡𝔤𝔪𝔢𝔫𝔱𝔰

A special thanks to the following who helped make this book possible:

Lysette Anthony, Dennis Baker, The Black & White Works, Barbara Blackburn, Deena Burkett, Linda Campanelli, Michael Cavanaugh, Dave Chamberlain, Marc Chamlin, Bob Cobert, Ben Cross, Dan Curtis, *Dark Shadows* Festival, Jim Fyfe, Lori Gerson, Joanna Going, Jeff Goldberg, Tom Gunn, Matthew Hall, Heather Hills, Meg Hoffman, Ruth Kennedy, Bud Klotchman, Veronica Lauren, Joseph Gordon-Levitt, Lisa Magdaleno, Cindy Marvin, Armand Mastroianni, Paul McGuire, Metro-Goldwyn-Mayer, Bob Meyer, Bill Millar, Gayle Mnookin, M.M. Shelly Moore, Dusty Morales, Debbie Nodella, Adrian Paul, Mary Phipps, Ely Pouget, Kim Reed, Bryan Ryman, Jean Simmons, Mark Sobel, Barbara Steele, Roy Thinnes, Rosalie Wallace, Michael T. Weiss, Ann Wilson.

Table of Contents

Dan Curtis

Foreword

by Dan Curtis

After a quarter of a century, no one is more surprised than I with the devotion that *Dark Shadows* still commands. I can't believe that it's been going on all these years. When the original daytime series ended in the spring of 1971 and we finished the second theatrical film shortly thereafter, I figured that *Dark Shadows* was a thing of the past.

As the years passed, it became apparent that *Dark Shadows* was much more than just a fond memory. The undying fascination and loyalty for the series was astonishing, and in 1990 I found myself back in the dark corridors of Collinwood, producing a new incarnation of *Dark Shadows* for primetime, weekly television.

I never intended to do *Dark Shadows* again, but the show refused to die, kept alive by legions of passionate fans. Although the new series was only given a network life of 12 episodes, I think we were able to recreate and reinvent the magic that first enthralled viewers so many years ago.

I had no idea that a dramatic serial combining Gothic romance and supernatural horror would endure with such intensity. *Dark Shadows* is a romantic fantasy. It's not really a horror film. It's certainly got scary elements, but it's a strange kind of dreamlike, unique thing. That's why no one could ever copy it. It's a very tough show to do.

I'll always feel a great sense of fondness for both of my *Dark Shadows* eras, and the many talents that helped bring the mysteries of Collinwood to life. I can see now that *Dark Shadows* will remain eternally "undead."

Jim Pierson

Introduction

In 1965, when novice television producer Dan Curtis literally dreamt the story of a young governess aboard a train on her way to a forbidding New England mansion, little did he know that over twenty-five years later his nocturnal vision would be reborn as a primetime TV series.

The *Dark Shadows* saga is a unique chapter in television history. Originating as a Gothic daytime soap opera for ABC-TV, the show debuted on June 27, 1966 with former Hollywood movie star Joan Bennett heading the cast of performers. Housed in a small New York studio, the show, initially taped in black and white, was a relatively tame melodrama focusing on romance, revenge, and murder.

It wasn't until ten months into the series that, in an attempt to salvage the program from impending cancellation, a vampire named Barnabas Collins was introduced and *Dark Shadows* became a *bonafide* phenomenon. Portrayed by Shakespearean actor Jonathan Frid, the vulnerable vampire Barnabas became the series' trademark character and kept the show alive for a total of 1,225 episodes and two feature-length motion pictures (*House of Dark Shadows* and *Night of Dark Shadows*).

Dark Shadows revolutionized daytime television by becoming the first soap opera to attract a sizeable young audience as well as the traditional housewives. At its peak in 1969, *Dark Shadows* was ABC's most popular daytime attraction, commanding an audience of nearly twenty million viewers. But after five frenzied years, the spooky serial eventually ran its course. Upon leaving the airwaves on April 2, 1971, it appeared that *Dark Shadows'* days in the sun were over.

Although the second *Dark Shadows* film was released that fall, several months after the cancellation, no additional motion pictures based on the original series were produced. Dan Curtis was ready to move on to other things. However, unbeknownst to Curtis or anyone else, *Dark Shadows* had made a lasting impact on a nation-wide audience that refused to allow it to fade away.

In 1975, *Dark Shadows* made television history by becoming the first daytime serial to be sold in syndication. Reruns of the original episodes, beginning with the arrival of Barnabas, began to appear in several dozen cities across the United States. Unfortunately, only one year's worth of shows was released for rebroadcast, and the show again vanished from view.

However, by the early 1980s, the rampant growth of independent stations and the increased need for programming fueled the reappearance of *Dark Shadows*, and prompted the release of more original episodes into syndication. Also at this time, Public Broadcasting Service stations, in an effort to broaden their audience, started experimenting with cult TV shows on their schedules. The intense viewer loyalty for *Dark Shadows* helped make the series a PBS staple in several markets.

During this period, a group of dedicated supporters of the show formed the *Dark Shadows* Festival fan organization and invited actors and production personnel from the series to participate in conventions. The Festivals also served as fund-raisers for the PBS outlets airing *Dark Shadows* reruns.

In 1989, *Dark Shadows* again proved its remarkable longevity by being the first soap opera to be released in its entirety on home video, a process that would take MPI Home Video over five years to implement.

As revivals of classic television series became a successful trend throughout the 1980s (*Star Trek: The Next Generation, The New Leave It To Beaver*), fans often speculated on the possibility of a new *Dark Shadows* movie or series. However, at the time Dan Curtis was in the midst of his decade-long involvement with two monumental mini-series based on the renown Herman Wouk World War II novels, *The Winds of War* and *War and Remembrance*.

Although Curtis had established himself as a top-flight producer of thrillers with such TV films as *The Night Stalker, Trilogy of Terror, The Turn of the Screw*, and *Bram Stoker's Dracula*, he had moved away from the horror genre, further proving his stellar filmmaking abilities by directing, producing, and co-writing the most ambitious and expensive mini-series in TV history, *War and Remembrance*.

War and Remembrance brought Curtis a spate of prestigious accolades; The Emmy, The Golden Globe, Directors' Guild, People's Choice, American Film Institute, and numerous other awards. The unparalleled achievement of *War and Remembrance* clearly represented the pinnacle in Curtis' esteemed career. With the accomplishment of a lifetime under his belt, Curtis seemed ready to return to his roots — and the dream that would not die.

Author Jim Pierson served as an assistant to the writing and publicity staffs of the 1991 Dark Shadows.

The Dream That Would Not Die

O ver the years, Dan Curtis has received numerous requests to resurrect *Dark Shadows*. In the mid-1980s, ABC-TV mulled over the possibility of bringing it back once again as a daytime soap. Several filmmakers have also expressed interest in producing new film versions. Following the success of the horror spoof *Beatlejuice,* one major studio even considered filming a campy *Dark Shadows* movie. But, without a doubt, *Dark Shadows* is and always will be Dan Curtis' creative vision; and he knew that if the show would ever be brought back, it must happen under his guidance.

After spending ten years traveling the world and constructing his herculean pair of mini-series, Curtis was ready to reactivate his production company. Upon completing *War and Remembrance* in the spring of 1989, Curtis' longtime friend, National Broadcasting Company's Entertainment President Brandon Tartikoff, convinced him that the time was right for a return to Collinwood. It had been a year since Tartikoff had first approached Curtis with the idea of bringing back the series. Curtis now figured that a *Dark Shadows* revival might not only make commercial sense but also provide some light entertainment and welcome relief following his all-consuming World War II epics.

As part of Curtis' development deal with Metro-Goldwyn-Mayer Television, NBC commissioned a two-hour *Dark Shadows* pilot movie in October 1989. Curtis was drawn to the project knowing that NBC's enthusiasm virtually guaranteed a series commitment.

In sorting out his thoughts on how to bring back *Dark Shadows* two decades later, Curtis decided that too many years had passed to retain the original cast in their previous roles. Recalling the gruelling story demands from the daytime version, he also felt that the new *Dark Shadows* should be a retelling of the original story. The 1990s *Dark Shadows* would not be a sequel or a reunion; it would be the first actual remake of a television series.

With a new *Dark Shadows*, Curtis saw a rare opportunity to redo an entire television series, using the luxury of hindsight and a multi-million-dollar primetime budget to make the mysteries of Collinwood bigger and better than before. He would remain faithful to the show's flavor but revise the original stories by trimming and tightening the plots. Some storylines were dropped altogether, and a number of characters and their relationships would be reworked in an effort to strengthen and modify the series for a weekly primetime format.

As Curtis pored over the twenty-year-old *Dark Shadows* scripts to formulate the new incarnation, he called upon original series writer Sam Hall to assist him in the effort. Not only had Hall written several hundred episodes of the original show, but his wife, the late Grayson Hall, had also starred on the daytime version as Dr.

Julia Hoffman. On board as technical adviser for the pilot was Sam's and Grayson's son Matthew, who as a young boy had grown up hanging around the Manhattan ABC-TV studio where the daytime series originated. New writing blood was also provided by Bill Taub and Hall Powell and by supervising producer Steve Feke as well as Curtis himself.

Curtis' easiest decision regarding the updated storyline involved the elimination of the daytime series' first year of shows prior to Barnabas' arrival. Curtis realized that the script for the 1970 theatrical film, *House of Dark Shadows*, would make an ideal adaptation for the new series' launch. The film had, in fact, borrowed heavily from the original TV series by compressing parts of the Barnabas story into a ninety-six-minute motion picture. The main difference between *House of Dark Shadows* and the daytime series was the characterization of Barnabas. In the movie, Barnabas' evil qualities were more heavily emphasized, particularly since the vampire was killed off in the finale. As Curtis came to rely on *House of Dark Shadows* for much of the plot structure in the new series pilot, the 1990s Barnabas would similarly emerge as a bit more sinister than before, but also more romantic.

When word of the project was announced to the media in late December 1989, *Dark Shadows* fans across the nation were spellbound with unrelenting excitement and agonizing curiosity. Many veteran devotees were devastated at the news that their beloved original series actors would be replaced, and indeed a considerable degree of skepticism rapidly spread among the fans. Fond of the daytime series' cast and sensitive to their popularity among the fans, Curtis declared that he intended to bring back original members in new roles on the primetime version. But initially, the featured characters would be composed of an all-new cast.

With filming of the two-hour *Dark Shadows* pilot set to commence in mid-March of 1990, Curtis and his casting team found themselves with only a few weeks to prepare for the return to Collinwood. Casting calls went out in Los Angeles, New York, and London in the search for a new Barnabas and the other inhabitants of Collinsport.

As with the original series, several young performers would receive their first regular national exposure with *Dark Shadows*. Among the first actors to be hired was Jim Fyfe as mischievous handyman Willie Loomis, a role that would be expanded to accommodate Fyfe's flair for comedy and Curtis' fondness for the underdog character. Horror film buffs were especially delighted by the selection of actress Barbara Steele for the pivotal role of Dr. Julia Hoffman. Steele had served as Curtis' producer on *War and Remembrance* but is best known for her starring roles in numerous 1960s horror films such as *The Pit and the Pendulum* and *Black Sunday*. Another familiar face, Roy Thinnes (TV's *The Invaders*), was chosen to portray Roger Collins.

Just as the 1960s version had featured a glamorous motion picture actress as matriarch Elizabeth Collins Stoddard, the updated *Dark Shadows* would enjoy the same distinction. Veteran screen actress Jean Simmons (*Spartacus*, *Guys and Dolls*) was secured for the role originated by the late Joan Bennett. An enthusiastic Simmons immediately admitted that she and her teenage daughters had been regular viewers of the first *Dark Shadows*.

As the starting date grew closer, the search intensified for the two central characters: Barnabas Collins and Victoria Winters. One of the major changes that Curtis had decided upon was to make the naive governess Victoria the focal point of Barnabas' affections instead of Collinsport waitress Maggie Evans, who had been Barnabas' obsession in the original *Dark Shadows*. Accordingly, Victoria would now be the one to resemble Barnabas' lost love from the eighteenth century, Josette Du Prés. The chemistry between the performers selected to portray Barnabas and Victoria would be crucial to the creative and commercial success of the *Dark Shadows* revival.

Ironically, the actress eventually chosen for the pivotal role of Victoria had been initially passed over during the early stages of auditions. But Dan Curtis instinctively realized that an oversight had occurred, and Joanna Going, an alumna from the daytime soap opera *Another World*, was hired to play the series' heroine in search of her past.

The singularly most difficult casting challenge lay ahead. With two weeks left before the start of filming, a new Barnabas had not been found. Dozens of actors had tested for the coveted role, and numerous others had been considered, yet Curtis knew the final choice could not be rushed. On Tuesday, March 6, 1990, noted British actor Ben Cross (*Chariots of Fire*) auditioned on videotape, reading lines from the *House of Dark Shadows* script. Upon viewing the performance, everyone concerned knew that the search for *Dark Shadows'* star vampire had ended.

The Resurrection

On Monday, March 19, 1990, filming began at 11:00 a.m. on the *Dark Shadows* pilot. With director Dan Curtis at the helm, the crew set up at Gulls' Way in Malibu to shoot the series' first scenes: Sheriff George Patterson (Michael Cavanaugh) visiting Professor Michael Woodard (Stefan Gierasch) at Woodard's seaside cottage.

Unlike the original daytime *Dark Shadows*, which featured location footage only on a limited basis in its early episodes, the 1990s version had the financial resources to venture outside a studio to broaden the exterior views of Collinsport. With the pilot budgeted at $4 million and the subsequent hour episodes on a $1.2 million budget each, the *Dark Shadows* revival could afford numerous luxuries never dreamed of by the daytime version.

After a full inaugural day, including an afternoon on the beach at Paradise Cove, the *Dark Shadows* company relocated to the Trancas Restaurant & Nightclub in Malibu, which would serve as the Three Gables Roadhouse. But, most importantly, the Trancas parking lot would be the location where, after sundown, Barnabas Collins would reemerge after twenty years.

That first night of filming would truly test the vulnerable vampire's stamina. Ben Cross, the new Barnabas, arrived for make-up at 4:00 p.m.; he was scheduled to report to the set two hours later. His scenes with Gloria (Hope North) and Muscles (Michael Buice) were to commence after dark. But with the inevitable first-day delays, Barnabas did not go before the cameras until the midnight hour, and filming continued in chilly temperatures until 3:30 the next morning. Television's most famous vampire was back in fittingly haunting fashion.

After two more days of location filming in the greater Los Angeles area, the *Dark Shadows* cast and crew settled into what would be their home for both the pilot and the subsequent series — the Greystone estate in Beverly Hills.

A majestic Tudor-style mansion built in the late 1920s by millionaire oilman Edward Doheny, Greystone sits on eighteen hillside acres of land accentuated by formal gardens. The 55-room structure has been featured in numerous television and film projects over the years and since 1965 has been owned by the city of Beverly Hills, which began operating the historic landmark as a public park in 1971.

Greystone would serve as the exterior for the ominous Collinwood estate as well as most of the Collinwood interiors, with the exception of the foyer, great hall, and drawing room. These would be specially built on Stage 6 at the Warner Hollywood Studios.

In a case of filmmaking trickery, Greystone would also function as the Old House exterior (from the front side only), and all of the Old House interiors, with the exception of Barnabas' bedroom which would be constructed on Stage 6. Other areas of the Greystone property to be seen in the pilot and series would be the stables, abandoned swimming pool, and the multiple levels of gardens.

An area of the basement was used to create the sheriff's office, while another section would later be turned into jail cells for the 1790 story. The building adjacent to the greenhouse was transformed into Maggie Evans' (Ely Pouget) studio apartment.

Large production trucks, vans, and trailers were set up in the parking lot at Greystone to house technical equipment, wardrobe, and dressing rooms. The normally vacant interior of the mansion was filled with antiques and other furnishings specifically for *Dark Shadows*. The mystical aura was complete once park rangers began to educate the cast and crew regarding Greystone's tortured past, including tales of alleged hauntings and mysterious deaths.

Although *Dark Shadows* had taken over virtually all of Greystone, the estate remained open to the public during regular park hours, 10:00 a.m. until 5:00 p.m. During those hours the crew kept filming areas roped off and guarded in an effort to keep curious visitors from interfering with the production. Since the public is not allowed inside the mansion, the interior filming was less problematic.

To create the illusion that a Beverly Hills mansion surrounded by palm trees was really an eighteenth-century New England estate overlooking the Atlantic Ocean, an elaborately detailed miniature of Greystone was designed and constructed specifically for use on *Dark Shadows*. As with the real house, the miniature would represent both Collinwood and the Old House. But unlike the actual Greystone, the miniature would be situated on a dark, jagged cliff at the edge of the ocean. In addition, the miniature would feature "fantasy" sections of the house, expanded portions that did not exist in reality.

Under the expertise of special effects master Bill Millar, the miniature was created at a cost of approximately thirty-five thousand dollars but was not actually built until the fall of 1990, months after the pilot was completed. "Miniature" is not the most accurate description for the elaborate model, which measured twenty-five feet along the front and fifteen feet deep.

The detail work on the miniature was extremely intricate so that it would appear realistic in close-ups. The structure was made of plastic and fiberglass instead of the usual paper and wood so that it could withstand effects such as rain, fog and snow. The miniature was seen depicting Collinwood on the main titles and in various establishing shots. It would be slightly altered for establishing shots of the Old House, with chimney pots and landscaping rearranged.

One special effect that was, literally, hard to swallow, was the smoke used on the set to give many scenes a foggy, hazy appearance. Upon being exposed to the airborne mineral-oil based smoke for endless hours, cast members found it uncomfortable, if not unhealthy, to breathe. Unlike the crew members, they could not wear protective breathing masks. After vigorous complaining, the offending mixture was replaced with an oil-free solution.

On the afternoon of April 5, 1990, the fourteenth day of filming the pilot, the cast and crew moved to Warner Hollywood Studios Stage 7, home of the basketball-court-sized interior of the Collins Mausoleum and secret room.

This would be the day for recreating handyman Willie Loomis' fateful unleashing of Barnabas from his 200-year imprisonment in a chained coffin.

The next morning, the company traveled to the woods of Fern Dell at Griffith Park to shoot exteriors intended to represent the cemetery surrounding the Collins Mausoleum. Along with artificial tombstones and statues, a false entry for the mausoleum was used. For the subsequent series episodes, the simulated graveyard would be situated on the front grounds at Greystone, while the mausoleum and secret room interior set would be relocated in Greystone's parking lot.

The fourth and final week of filming the pilot marked the unveiling of the majestic Collinwood foyer, great hall, and drawing room sets on Warner Hollywood's Stage 6. The cavernous great hall, two stories in height, represented one of the largest, most elaborate and costliest sets ever constructed for a television pilot, let alone for a series. With each section sporting four walls and a ceiling, being on the set gave the cast, crew, and visitors the feeling that they were really inside a genuine Gothic mansion.

After eighteen days of production, filming of the pilot wrapped up on Wednesday, April 11. Over the ensuing four weeks, Dan Curtis and his team of film editors assembled a preliminary version of the pilot to present to NBC.

Another original *Dark Shadows* contributor had joined the reincarnation effort, music composer Bob Cobert. Not only did Cobert write all of the music for the daytime *Dark Shadows* (including the popular standard *Quentin's Theme*), but he also scored nearly all of Dan Curtis' productions in the intervening years. With the revival, Cobert would rerecord a few of the original themes, but concentrate mostly on new compositions.

On May 16, the pilot was delivered to the network. Brandon Tartikoff and his colleagues would now view the completed project and decide if they felt the effort was worthy of being picked up as a new series for their fall schedule.

It would be a week before NBC officially announced their line-up for the 1990-91 season. But with the tremendous amount of publicity surrounding *Dark Shadows'* resurrection, the audition of the pilot appeared to be a formality. Yet, when NBC revealed their schedule, *Dark Shadows* was nowhere to be found.

Dan Curtis received an apologetic call from Tartikoff, who explained that *Dark Shadows* had narrowly missed being picked up. But Curtis wasn't prepared to give up without a fight. He expressed his dismay and disappointment to Tartikoff, pointing out that there had been an understanding from the beginning that the show was destined to get on the air. As a conciliatory effort, Tartikoff responded with an offer for five new *Dark Shadows* episodes to be put on NBC's schedule as a mid-season replacement. However, Curtis knew the abbreviated order was half-hearted as well as inadequate for a show of *Dark Shadows'* scope. It simply wouldn't be financially sound for Curtis and MGM to produce a minimum of five episodes. The expense and ambition of the show would require a commitment of at least thirteen hours. But Tartikoff declined, and Curtis notified the stunned cast and production members that Barnabas would not be rising from the dead after all.

NBC's rejection was unexpected, unsettling, and temporary. Two days after *Dark Shadows* was declared dead and buried, Tartikoff phoned Curtis with a reprieve; the network had reconsidered and was now prepared to offer a firm thirteen-hour order for *Dark Shadows* as a mid-season replacement. Tartikoff promised Curtis that the series would be given priority back-up status, assuring him that it would be inserted into the schedule as soon as an opening became available.

Curtis moved swiftly to assemble a full staff of writers and other production team members. In addition to Curtis and Steve Feke, Matthew Hall returned to write for the series along with the newly-recruited Jon Boorstin, M.M. Shelly Moore, Linda Campanelli, and William Gray. By midsummer when the series would go into production, nearly three months had passed since the pilot had been completed. Most of the crew members had gone on to other projects, but several key production personnel would return to participate in the series. Since NBC had ordered thirteen hours of the show, eleven additional hours, comprising episodes 2 through 12, were now to be produced to follow the two-hour pilot episode.

A unique and innovative production schedule was devised for *Dark Shadows* when it resumed filming on July 23, 1990, at Ports O' Call and Fisherman's Wharf in San Pedro, California. These waterfront areas would serve as settings for the village of Collinsport. Multiple episodes would be shot simultaneously to help curb high production costs. Dan Curtis would direct scenes for episodes 2, 3 and 4 intermixed over 27 days of filming, ending on August 28.

The remaining eight episodes would be divided up in sequential pairs among four additional directors. Armand Mastroianni, who would also become one of the show's producers, was brought in to direct episodes 5 and 6, covering 16 days of filming from August 29 until September 20. Paul Lynch was hired for episodes 7 and 8, also spanning 16 production days, from September 21 until October 15. Rob Bowman would direct episodes 9 and 10 over a 20-day shooting period covering October 16 through November 7. The final two shows, episodes 11 and 12, would be shot over 18 production days, November 8 through December 5, under Mark Sobel's direction.

In mapping out the storyline for episodes 2 through 12, Curtis and his writing staff continued to adapt the original series' major plots into a new framework. Recalling the immense popularity of the daytime version's flashback sequences, Curtis determined that the 1990s *Dark Shadows* would also delve into Barnabas' past and reveal how he became a vampire. Starting with episode 7, the original 1795 storyline would be reworked as the 1790 storyline and focus on the cursing of Barnabas by the beautifully wicked witch, Angélique (Lysette Anthony).

Unlike the 1960s adaptation, the new *Dark Shadows* would not feature entire episodes set in the past. Instead, the 1790 episodes would also contain scenes set concurrently in the present time of 1991.

With the decision to place most of episodes 7 through 12 in the eighteenth-century, costume designer Rosalie Wallace scoured theatrical wardrobe supply houses in New York and Los Angeles to locate appropriate period clothing for the cast. Wallace and the wardrobe staff created various apparel items that were unavailable, such as the men's shirts, jabots, and most vests, in addition to all of the children's clothing. Much of the women's costumes for 1790 were rebuilt versions of existing clothing. Certain items such as Josette's wedding gown were made especially for *Dark Shadows*.

Once production on the final six episodes was well underway, it became apparent that the elaborate requirements of the 1790s storyline were placing a strain on *Dark Shadows'* already sizeable budget. The extra time required for the special costumes, hair styling, and set dressing meant added production time and expense. In an effort to avoid further cost overages, MGM informed Dan Curtis and the production staff that all scenes in the remaining episodes must be shot at Greystone, with the exception of the Collinwood interiors and Barnabas' bedroom set at the Warner Hollywood studios.

As a result, set designer Bryan Ryman and his staff were faced with the challenge of adapting and disguising areas of Greystone to serve as completely new locations. Although a genuine ocean cliff in Malibu had served as Widows' Hill in the third episode, in episode 9 the location would have to be created on the Greystone grounds. This was accomplished by constructing an artificial rock formation, made of fiberglass, along the hillside adjacent to the driveway leading to

Greystone's parking lot. Utilizing wind machines, strategic camera angles, and stock ocean footage, it appeared as if Jeremiah (Adrian Paul) jumped off an actual cliff into the sea.

The design staff's ingenuity was also reflected in the transformation of the Old House drawing room into the courtroom interior for episode 11. After covering up the fireplace, certain windows and doorways, the room was filled with a judge's desk, witness stand, jury box, and spectator pews. Following this successful conversion, designer Ryman knew he could create virtually anything at Greystone.

Following a four-day Thanksgiving weekend break, *Dark Shadows* began its final days of filming during the first week in December. The practice of alternating the stories between the present time and the eighteenth century within the same episode had led to production delays. Although originally scheduled to finish filming on November 26, episodes 11 and 12 lingered before the cameras until December 5. To help bring production to a close, both Dan Curtis and Armand Mastroianni returned to direct with a second production unit while Mark Sobel completed directing other scenes. Among the material shot on the final day were retakes of the courtroom sequences under Curtis' direction.

On the night of December 5, a wrap party was held at the El Paso Cantina Restaurant & Bar in Hollywood. Most of the cast and production members joined Curtis to celebrate the end of filming, anxiously anticipating the series' broadcast debut, which was scheduled for the following month.

As an example of the massive publicity that would surround *Dark Shadows'* return, a *USA Today* entertainment section cover story was published on the day filming was completed. Starting in mid-December, NBC began running teaser promotional spots to inform viewers of the January debut of *Dark Shadows*. The network signed up Domino's Pizza as a promotional sponsor for the show. A nationwide radio contest with the theme "Don't Be Afraid of the Dark" was conducted in thirty major cities, offering prizes such as original *Dark Shadows* series videotapes, compact discs, *The Dark Shadows Companion* book, and specially made miniature wooden coffins. Grand prize winners were flown to Los Angeles for an advance screening of the pilot and a "*Dark Shadows* Vampire Slumber Party."

NBC's innovative marketing techniques also included the placement of theatrical style trailers for the show on monitors in United Artist movie theaters as well as Circuit City and Highland electronic stores across the country.

Special "sneak-preview" style theatrical screenings were held in Los Angeles, New York, and Chicago during the first week in January. NBC further hyped *Dark Shadows'* debut by scheduling the two-hour pilot for Sunday, January 13, from 9:00-11:00 p.m. PST, with episodes 2 and 3 placed back-to-back at the same time the following night. The network promoted these first four hours as a mini-series, with the actual series set to begin in its regular Friday night time period on January 18. As a result, five hours of the series would be seen in less than a week.

On Sunday, January 6, a press conference with Dan Curtis, Ben Cross, and Jean Simmons was held at the Ritz-Carlton Hotel in Marina Del Rey, California, as part of NBC's annual Press Tour. The nation's journalists were given a preview of the four-hour "mini-series" and the opportunity to interview the three representatives from the show. A press party with additional cast members was held that evening at Greystone.

When the pilot finally aired seven days later, it came in a solid second place in overall household ratings for the time period, receiving a 14.6 rating and 23 per cent share of the audience. But most significantly, it was the highest rated show in the time period for all young audience demographic categories, including women ages 18-34 and 25-54, as well as men ages 18-34 and 25-54. The show was also top- rated among teens and kids.

The critics' reviews were mostly favorable, and it was instantly apparent that the new *Dark Shadows* had won over not only the apprehensive original series' followers, but also a whole new legion of devotees. In addition to countless newspaper articles, features on the return of *Dark Shadows* appeared on numerous television magazine shows (*Entertainment Tonight, Inside Edition, The Today Show*) and in many prominent publications (*Newsweek, People, TV Guide*).

Monday, January 14, the second night of the "mini-series," (comprising episodes 2 and 3) also yielded encouraging ratings and demographics. But in a matter of days, an untimely international incident would inflict a fatal wound.

By the time the first regular hour-long presentation of *Dark Shadows* (episode 4) appeared on Friday, January 18, the Gulf War had begun, and the network's programming had been heavily pre-empted for the previous two days. NBC chose to delay *Dark Shadows* one hour past its scheduled 9:00-10:00 p.m. PST period so that the network's highly successful Thursday night block of comedies could be shown on Friday after being preempted the previous night.

Because these schedule changes were all made at the last minute, printed TV logs could not reflect the actual network schedules. As a result, confusion prevailed when viewers turned in to see *Dark Shadows* but found *Cheers* instead.

NBC ran intermittent promos that night announcing that *Dark Shadows* had been moved back an hour later, but clearly a majority of viewers had no idea what was going on. Although that night's show, episode 4, aired in the EST and CST zones, the West Coast feed was pre-empted by an NBC News update on the Gulf crisis.

The following Friday, January 25, NBC attempted to salvage the damage in the West Coast markets by scheduling the unseen episode 4 back to back with that week's new episode, number five. But the harm had already been done. *Dark Shadows'* momentum had been interrupted by the war, and the timing could not have been worse. The show's ratings had begun to fall.

On March 8, NBC moved *Dark Shadows* to a later time slot, from 10:00-11:00 p.m. PST, in the hopes of building the audience for the final three episodes of the season. Sadly, it was too little, too late.

Even though the show had maintained a strong audience composition of young viewers, the overall ratings were weakened by the fact that very few viewers over age 55 were watching. NBC was at least partially to blame since their early on-air promos for the show had stressed horror and the vampire theme instead of the more commercially appropriate romantic and fantasy elements.

When episode 12 aired on March 22, a slight increase in viewership occurred, offering a sense of encouragement. Everyone connected with the show knew that it would be a close call on whether or not *Dark Shadows* would return for another season. However, because of the high level of young viewers (the most desirable demographic groups among advertisers) and the enthusiasm NBC had exhibited for the series, those close to the show felt a return was more likely than not.

But just as the ill-timing of the outbreak of war had sabotaged the series' launch, the departure of Brandon Tartikoff from NBC also seemed to work against *Dark Shadows'* chances of survival. New network entertainment president Warren Littlefield simply didn't appear to possess enough faith to give the show a fair, second chance.

Aware that the *Dark Shadows* revival was in danger of extinction, the nation-wide network of fans quickly banded together to voice their fervent support.

NBC headquarters in Burbank, California, and in New York were flooded with calls and letters asking for the renewal of *Dark Shadows* and urging the network to rescue it from the void of Friday nights, where viewing levels are traditionally low. During this time, after receiving similar requests, NBC moved another Friday night victim and a Tartikoff favorite, *Quantum Leap*, to a more advantageous mid-week time period.

Dark Shadows reportedly equalled the 50,000 pieces of viewer mail that *Quantum Leap* generated, but as Tartikoff left NBC to move to Paramount Pictures, the network's interest in *Dark Shadows* appeared to be diminishing rapidly.

Realizing that *Dark Shadows* needed all the help it could get, the fans began to organize rallies to demonstrate their support. The first gathering was a peaceful demonstration outside NBC's Burbank studios on March 27. A similar picket line was formed outside NBC's Rockefeller Center offices in Manhattan on April 10.

Finally, on May 8, die-hard followers across the country organized "Save *Dark Shadows* Day," with rallies held outside NBC stations in eighteen cities, including Chicago, San Francisco, Philadelphia, Detroit, St. Louis, Los Angeles, and New York. Hundreds of fans thoughtfully demonstrated their support for *Dark Shadows* by carrying homemade picket signs. At the Los Angeles rally, series actors Roy Thinnes (*Roger Collins*), Lysette Anthony (*Angélique*), Michael T. Weiss (*Joe Haskell*), Ely Pouget (*Maggie Evans*), and Joseph Gordon-Levitt (*David Collins*) dropped by to thank the fans for their efforts.

The incredible outcry generated considerable press coverage, but when NBC released their schedule for the 1991-92 season, *Dark Shadows* was not among the living. The network had chosen to put a cancellation stake through Barnabas.

The verdict brought disbelief, disappointment, and devastation. Yet NBC's decision was not entirely surprising. Although the network had commissioned an outline of possible second season storylines and presented a specially compiled presentation reel to potential advertisers, NBC's commitment to the show seemed to fade when the series was not able to recover from the disastrous premiere week.

Upon disappearing from NBC, the thirteen hours of the new *Dark Shadows* were sold in numerous foreign countries and released on home video. The 1990s incarnation also spawned a subsequent array of merchandising, including T-shirts, model kits, wristwatches, posters, and comic books. Ironically, all of these were issued after the show was cancelled.

Despite its all-too-short network life, the 1991 *Dark Shadows* revival clearly reinforced the devotion of the original fans and made a lasting impact on millions of first-time viewers who became part of a new "*Dark Shadows* Generation." They have discovered for themselves the unique and timeless qualities of the dream that would not die.

The Critics Say It's Delicious!

"It's a heavily atmospheric romance with mythological flourishes and plenty of supernatural jolts... the show is more embedded in romantic fantasy than in the horror genre."
John Carman, SAN FRANCISCO CHRONICLE

"This new 'Dark Shadows' is slicker, sexier and, of course, more violent, with lots of gory special effects."
John J. O'Connor, NEW YORK TIMES

"As a creepy romantic saga, 'Dark Shadows' has all the elements to keep viewers coming back week after week."
Frances Katz, BOSTON HERALD

"... this gothic chiller is bound to enchant TV viewers who are swayed by a lovingly designed experiment in style and flavor... the vampire's kiss is irresistible."
Lynn Voedisch, CHICAGO SUN-TIMES

"... it's bloody good. Fans will get a rush from the new (series) because, in many ways, it's faithful to the original. And new viewers looking for something to sink their teeth into won't be disappointed either. Ben Cross (as Barnabas Collins) and Joanna Going (as Vicky Winters) are excellent."
Bush, DAILY VARIETY

"... played with clench-jawed earnestness by an impossibly gorgeous cast with oh-so-vulnerable necks, this resurrection of the cult super-natural soap is junky, clunky and altogether irresistible..."
Matt Roush, USA TODAY

"... dark, slick and expertly acted and executed... beautifully photographed... Cross is exceptional in his role as Barnabas."
Art Chapman, FT. WORTH STAR-TELEGRAM

"It's spooky and sexy... what a charming nightmare, in the person of Cross."
Jonathan Storm, PHILADELPHIA INQUIRER

"'Dark Shadows' remains resolutely—and delectably—the same... dashing style."
Diane Werts, NEW YORK NEWSDAY

"'Dark Shadows' has blood, bats, babes—everything! And in Ben Cross, as the elegant caped fangster himself, it has a grand Barnabas."
Howard Rosenberg, LOS ANGELES TIMES

"... a horror story that plays more like a gothic romance, one sure to lock in fans of the rather unique genre. Wonderful sets and stately surroundings complete the package here, making it a visual as well as a gothic treat."
Rick Sherwood, HOLLYWOOD REPORTER

Dark Shadows

Starring BEN CROSS   LYSETTE ANTHONY   BARBARA BLACKBURN   JIM FYFE   JOANNA GOING   JOSEPH GORDON-LEVITT   VERONICA LAUREN   ELY POUGET   BARBARA STEELE   ROY THINNES   MICHAEL T. WEISS and JEAN SIMMONS as Elizabeth Collins Stoddard   Executive Producer DAN CURTIS   Series Created by DAN CURTIS   Certain Characters Developed by ART WALLACE   Directors: DAN CURTIS   ARMAND MASTROIANNI   PAUL LYNCH   ROB BOWMAN   MARK SOBEL   Writers: HALL POWELL & BILL TAUB   STEVE FEKE & DAN CURTIS   SAM HALL   MATTHEW HALL   JON BOORSTIN   WILLIAM GRAY   LINDA CAMPANELLI & M.M. SHELLY MOORE
A DAN CURTIS TELEVISION PRODUCTION INC., IN ASSOCIATION WITH MGM/UA TELEVISION PRODUCTION GROUP, A DIVISION OF MGM-PATHE COMMUNICATIONS CO.

MGM/UA TELEVISION PRODUCTION GROUP, A DIVISION OF MGM-PATHE COMMUNICATIONS CO.
©1991 MGM/UA TELEVISION PRODUCTION GROUP, A DIVISION OF MGM-PATHE COMMUNICATIONS CO.

Quotes From Collinwood

Dan Curtis (*Series Creator/Executive Producer/Director/Writer*): I have a very strange imagination. I was never thinking about is this new or is this different. That never came into the equation. It's just what am I going to do next? And I would have to squeeze my head real hard and come up with these bizarre stories.

Ben Cross (*Barnabas Collins*): It has turned out to be one of the most challenging roles I have ever done. I spent the whole series taking pleasure in biting ladies' necks. Then there came a day when I was bitten. That rather turned me on. When I felt her [Joanna's] teeth on my neck, it was instant goose bumps.

Jean Simmons (*Elizabeth Collins Stoddard*): People are always fascinated with black magic or voodoo or vampires. Of course, I absolutely adored Barnabas.

Joanna Going (*Victoria Winters*): She [Victoria] knows he [Barnabas] has some kind of problem — he acts pretty peculiar...it is a romantic story, a tragic love story...What is exciting is the warm feeling out there from the people who really love this show.

Barbara Steele (*Dr. Julia Hoffman*): There's a compressed energy when everything is shot at a crisis level, which *Dark Shadows* was shot under. The appeal of *Dark Shadows* is that it is extraordinarily romantic and it allows this dark side to come through that we all have in ourselves. It is a metaphor for the duality in all of our natures.

Lysette Anthony (*Angélique*): Being as mean as I've been able to be playing Angélique, it's very liberating. My husband got very worried as week after week more terrible things were coming out of Angélique's closet, but I enjoyed those surprises.

Roy Thinnes (*Roger Collins*): I was hired to play Roger Collins, and about four weeks later Dan Curtis told me I was playing Reverend Trask. Anybody familiar with Trask knows what a wild man he is. As I put him together, he looks a little like the *other* Jean Simmons [Gene Simmons of the rock music group Kiss].

Barbara Blackburn (*Carolyn Stoddard*): I've always been obsessed with vampires. I've always wanted to travel to Rumania and hear all the legends. It's a myth that's had enormous appeal to me. I completely buy it. It's very cool to be a vampire slave.

Jim Fyfe (*Willie Loomis*): I wrenched my back pretty badly right before we shot the pilot. I was in constant physical pain the entire time, and I'm not exaggerating. It was only the excitement of making my first pilot and all the fun that I was having, that kept me from checking my sorry self into a hospital.

Veronica Lauren (*Sarah Collins*): I don't mean to be rude, but I didn't even hear of it [*Dark Shadows*] until I got ther part.

Michael T. Weiss (*Joe Haskell*): I was a huge *DS* fan as a kid. Everyday I'd race home from school to get my "nightmare fix." I still can't sleep with my hand dangling over the side of the bed. The fear of the unknown is frightening and tantalizing at the same time.

Ely Pouget (*Maggie Evans*): All the special effects, and the blood, and the fangs, and the screaming and yelling is a great thing to do on a weekly basis.

Joseph Gordon-Levitt (*David Collins*): Probably if I wasn't in it, it would be pretty scary to me. But 'cause I know all the people in it, it's cool.

Michael Cavanaugh (*Sheriff George Patterson*): Whenever I mentioned to people that I was doing *Dark Shadows*, I think that every single person I told said they had grown up running home from school to watch it [the original series].

Adrian Paul (*Jeremiah Collins*): It was great fun to work with Ben. He's a very professional actor, as were the rest of the cast.

Armand Mastroianni (*Producer/Director*): The biggest challenge was to maintain a consistency and style in the amount of time we had to shoot it. The story and the textures were so rich. I found a lot of women were turned on by the eroticism. The legacy of the story swept you away like an old-fashioned novel.

Mark Sobel (*Director*): We worked on a television schedule, but the production value was that of a movie. We were never on schedule; it was a constant catch-up process. I now feel like I can do anything — *Dark Shadows* was the ultimate challenge. I've done an epic.

Bob Cobert (*Music Composer*): This was even more exciting than the first time around. It's a much more sophisticated approach, and I've got bigger orchestras!

Bryan Ryman (*Set Designer*): Since parts of Greystone were Collinwood and parts were the Old House, the relationship of all the rooms was like an incredible jigsaw puzzle. The shows were so elaborate, it was difficult to keep costs down. But, it's amazing when push comes to shove, and an effect is needed and there isn't anymore money, you find a way.

Rosalie Wallace (*Costume Designer*): I never worked with such a wonderful, homogeneous group. They were just the best group of actors. They were fun, they were good, they were friendly. We were a group. We were a family. We all hung out together.

Bill Millar (*Special Visual Effects*): The most interesting effect was hanging Angélique in a harness twenty feet off the ground for six hours with an airplane propellor blowing on her. Lysette Anthony was fantastic — harnesses aren't comfortable.

Matthew Hall (*Writer/Technical Advisor*): It was a job I had wanted all my life. It was really a gas.

M.M. Shelly Moore (*Writer/Executive Story Editor*): My experience working on the show was the experience of working with Dan Curtis - that's why I wanted the job. I'm so glad I had the opportunity. I learned a lot of important lessons just by watching Dan.

Linda Campanelli (*Writer/Executive Story Editor*): When I was in the sixth grade, I remember running home from school every day so I wouldn't miss a second of *Dark Shadows*. I remember playing the soundtrack album while my friends and I had mock — well, we didn't think they were mock — séances in dark rooms. So when I started on the new series and found myself in a room with Dan Curtis, it was great.

𝕻𝖗𝖊𝖘𝖘 𝕮𝖔𝖓𝖋𝖊𝖗𝖊𝖓𝖈𝖊 𝕳𝖎𝖌𝖍𝖑𝖎𝖌𝖍𝖙𝖘

As part of NBC's annual January Press Tour, a *Dark Shadows* press conference was held at the Ritz-Carlton Hotel in Marina Del Rey, California, on Sunday afternoon, January 6, 1991.

Dark Shadows creator/executive producer Dan Curtis joined stars Ben Cross and Jean Simmons to answer questions for the nation's entertainment reporters. Highlights from the one-hour session follow.

Question: Mr. Curtis, for those of us who never saw the original, can you explain — is the tone of this the same as the original? And are these the same characters and the same basic premise?

Dan Curtis: Well, hopefully the tone is the same. The characters are the same. We haven't added any new characters yet. I don't know whether we plan to ever add any new characters...The goals of our main characters are the same. The vampire, Barnabas, hates his existence and is still in love with his Josette from two hundred years ago. And the difference between this and the old show is that the Victoria Winters character, the governess, is now the reincarnation of the Josette character, something we would have done then if we had known what the story was going to be.

Now we know what the story is going to be, so we're able to do some of the things we were unable to do. The basic parameters of the story are the same. The incidents within have all been replotted. So there are new and different ways of getting to some of the same places that we got to.

Question: Ben, there's something horribly romantic about this character. Would you give your opinion of what you think Barnabas' appeal is?

Ben Cross: I love that phrase, "horribly romantic." That's exactly music to my ears, because that, in effect, is exactly what I was trying to do. I have no idea. I can make certain, dare I say, intelligent guesses as to why.

I think one of the first things is the way a woman might view a vampire and a vampire tale, is somewhat different to the way a man would. We learn in the series — I mean, the series gets to a certain point where we simply have to go back into the past and find out exactly what went on.

And so we do go back. We see Barnabas as this really very, very nice guy. Very, very happy family. And it's really like a cautionary tale for married men. He actually has a — he has a fling with the wrong person. And the phrase of, hell hath — having no fury like a woman scorned, is absolutely true, because, in fact, she comes from Hell.

And so, in a sense, he makes a human mistake that a lot of people, if they're honest, have actually made. He regrets it, and then becomes himself a victim and becomes a vampire. So, in a sense, he is as much a victim of his own condition, in the way that the people he finds himself biting.

Question: Mr. Curtis, you've talked about how you've been able to plan this one compared to how you kind of worked the previous one out as you went along. Could you describe that a little bit?

Dan Curtis: Well, it [the daytime version] started off as an attempt at a Gothic romance/mystery. It was never intended to show or actively be involved with the supernatural. And there were a lot of conversations about locked rooms and howling in towers, but you never saw anything. The show was rapidly going down the tubes.

My kids, who were nine to ten years old then, said to me, "Daddy, if it's going to go off the air, why don't you at least make it scary?" And I said, "All right, why not."

We had a 26-week order, and this was right near the end of the 26 weeks. And I went in there and said to the writers, "Look, we're going to change this whole thing; let's scare the hell out of these people. And I put a ghost in. I just immediately changed the story...

The next rating period that came in, the numbers started to grow. And I said, "Well, let's stay with this a little bit longer. And we made it a little crazier...I decided I would find out how far we could go, what would the audience accept. Now, for me as a kid, the scariest thing was always a vampire. That was my personal scary monster. I decided I'll put a vampire on this show. And then we'll kill him off and see how far we can go with it...

We put the vampire on the show and we couldn't kill him off. He became an instant matinee idol. This guy was out there ripping throats out, he was doing everything awful. And they all went crazy over him. The women went insane. The kids went crazy. And now I had to deal with the biggest problem, how do I now perpetuate a vampire? So we made him a reluctant vampire.

Question: Jean, from a ladies' point of view, what do you find horribly romantic about the Barnabas character?

Jean Simmons: I think he's very vulnerable...You're sort of drawn towards him with absolute fascination. And of course I think he's terribly sexy. But he's a vulnerable vampire. You feel sorry for him at times because he can't help it.

Question: Will there be subplots with other kinds of stories in addition to the vampire threat? Will you have subplots like other serials?

Dan Curtis: It doesn't work on *Dark Shadows*. In the old days we would try to stick to normal, everyday plot devices and story devices. They don't work. They're always involved with the supernatural. And we learned that through a lot of trial and error, which makes this show terribly difficult to do, I might add.

It's very tough to squeak the door every week and to hold an audience in a suspenseful situation...this is the most difficult kind of material to do well.

Question: Are you using the same scripts from the original series?

Dan Curtis: No, we can't. We couldn't. I was hoping that we'd be able to use a lot of the script material from the original. But it hasn't worked out that way. Because they were very repetitious...

Question: Ben, this is your second time playing a vampire. What draws you to this type of character and are you at all concerned with typecasting?

Ben Cross: I've played three Jews in my life, I've played four priests, I've played various Middle Eastern gentlemen. I don't think I'm in any danger of being typecast per se because I've played two vampires. They were totally different...On the contrary, from my point of view I'm trying to make the character [Barnabas] as complex and as interesting, and as fascinating as I can on every single level, except Dan Curtis insists that he doesn't have a sense of humor, or if he does, he doesn't show it...

Question: Mr. Cross, you say that the vampire has no sense of humor, and yet, last night he described his career to someone as "all consuming." Was that unintentionally funny?

Dan Curtis: He has a slight sense of humor..a little irony when he lies.

Ben Cross: There are quite a few moments like that. Dare I say I put some in myself, some are the script like that one, and some I put in myself. There's one thing to be aware of a situation being funny, and it's another thing for my character to actually crack into a smile or laugh. So there is a fine area there.
I also have to be very careful. I don't want him to be flip — I'm sure you'll understand what I mean when I say in the James Bond sense. That punning on a situation which is kind of cute. There's nothing cute about Barnabas, and I wouldn't play him cute.

Question: Jean, were you a hard sell? Was it difficult to sell you on this project? What was your initial reaction when you were offered the role?

Jean Simmons: Well, I was one of the people that was a great fan of the old one. The children would come home from school and before homework, before tea, we would sit down and watch *Dark Shadows*. And when Mr. Curtis offered me to be part of it, I just wanted to kind of join the club.

Question: Mr. Curtis, is the fact that you had just done *War and Remembrance* and you'd spent all those years of your life doing these very serious dramas, very meaningful things, and then to come back into this — what is the feeling? Is it fun?

Dan Curtis: Yes, it's fun. It's a welcomed change of pace. I'm really having a good time. We're having a lot of laughs. It's great not to have to be very serious, and we're having a good time. We're not saying this is anything other than fantasy and fun, and it's a great change of pace for me. I'm surprised. I thought I might be unhappy, but I'm not.

Question: There seems to me to be a division between part one and part two, about how serious it was...Is there an intentional difference?

Dan Curtis: Well, I tell you something. You've pointed out something to me I wasn't aware of. So I don't know how to answer your question. I didn't intend it to be any different. Part one introduces the characters. You're bringing the people in, you're getting your story rolling. Maybe you can answer it, Ben?

Ben Cross: It has to be said that the first two hours we made in March, with a completely different crew and we were all terribly new. And then we came back I guess in June to pick up the rest of the series.

Dan Curtis: It's a continuation of the story, it's still the same.

Ben Cross: The story's the same, but there could be kind of subliminal differences that you picked up on, and how very astute you were...

Question: Well, I'd like to ask Ben, why were you attracted to this role? Why did you want to play it?

Ben Cross: Let me answer you in a roundabout way. Really, I had to make decisions about what I didn't like about this kind of project. And I'm more satisfied myself about things that I once viewed as negatives.

For instance, there was a question earlier: is each week kind of a complete story within itself that has a beginning, middle and an end, i.e. *Moonlighting* or something like that? And the answer's no. That was one of the key questions I was concerned about in the beginning, because if it was going to be like that, it would mean that we'd have, at the top of the show the guests starring every week who somehow or other would get fanged...I was really not going to be interested in any way, shape or form in that kind of series about a vampire...I felt that the time there were much more interesting areas. It's more like a psychological study, an exploration of the whole mythology of vampirism.

And when I was satisfied that it was going in that particular direction, it was fairly easy for me because it's an extraordinary story and an extraordinary character, and I can promise you I'm not exaggerating when I say it's really one of the most challenging roles I've ever played because I have to come up with something new every episode...

There's always some challenge because we are dealing in the supernatural and not the natural, and by the time we got to the end of the twelfth episode, I was very grateful because I felt just totally empty. I really had nothing more to give and I needed time to come away from it and hopefully gear up for the second season.

Question: Jean, a weekly series will be a change of pace for you, a change from the one-shot projects like movies and minis. Is it a different weekly pace? Are you enjoying it?

Jean Simmons: I'm having to do tremendous adjustments, coming from the old-time shooting movies into TV gradually with mini-series, and I have to make a lot of adjustments. I'm learning...the speed is really terrific, and the hours are very long. I am fortunate that I don't have to work absolutely every day, not like Ben has been doing.

Question: Mr. Curtis, how far can you go with this? I mean, as a mini-series it's really dynamite...But I'm wondering how far can you go weekly with a series where we know the man is a vampire?

Dan Curtis: Well, we did five years of the [original] show. We had a number of storylines that were very, very successful that I liked a lot. That's basically what we're going to stay with. We'd go far afield. We go into such things as parallel time. We go back in time.

There was a very popular story we did, which was the Quentin story. Two kids go into a room in a closed off wing of the house, they pick up an old telephone and they hear heavy breathing on the other end. It turns out to be Quentin coming from the past...

This is basically a fantasy, and there are all kinds of story twists and storylines and ideas that have appealed to me over the years in fantasy. When I was a kid I used to read *Fantasy and Science Fiction* all the time, the monthly magazine. I was always fascinated with time travel and parallel time. And I go back to the old days of thinking of the old horror stories, the werewolves, and of course the vampires, which carry this thing through. There's enough material here to last for about five years, and then hopefully we'll all pack it in and move away.

Picture Gallery

At Collinwood: Elizabeth Collins Stoddard (Jean Simmons), Barnabas Collins (Ben Cross), Victoria Winters (Joa Going), David Collins (Joseph Gordon-Levitt), Carolyn Stoddard (Barbara Blackburn), Roger Collins (Roy Thinr

r. Julia Hoffman (Barbara Steele) and Barnabas (Ben); Roger (Roy Thinnes) and Elizabeth (Jean Simmons); David (Joseph ordon-Levitt) and Victoria (Joanna Going); Willie Loomis (Jim Fyfe) and Julia (Barbara Steele).

At the Collins Family Cemetery: (above) Sarah Collins (Veronica Lauren); (below) Willie Loomis (Jim Fyfe); (opposite) Barnabas (Ben Cross).

Roger (Roy Thinnes); Julia (Barbara Steele); Mrs. Sarah Johnson (Julianna McCarthy); Sheriff George Patterson (Mich Cavanaugh).

In the mausoleum secret room: Willie, Barnabas, Julia.

Barnabas (Ben Cross) and Carolyn (Barbara Blackburn).

Barnabas (Ben Cross) and Victoria (Joanna Going).

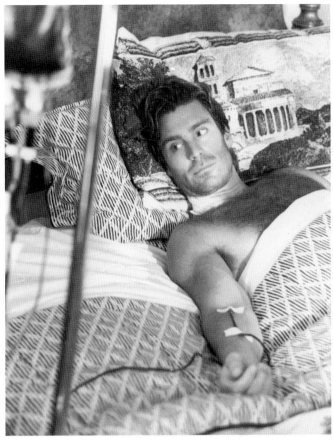

Joe Haskell (Michael T. Weiss) and Carolyn (Barbara Blackburn).

David (Joseph Gordon-Levitt) and Sarah (Veronica Lauren).

Elizabeth (Jean Simmons) and Roger (Roy Thinnes).

Victoria (Joanna Going); Carolyn (Barbara Blackburn); Maggie Evans (Ely Pouget); Daphne Collins (Rebecca Staab).

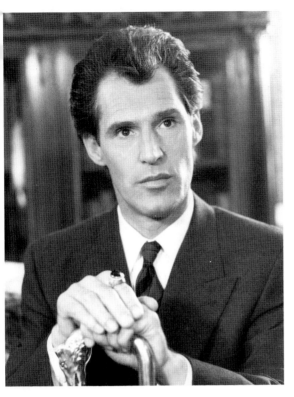

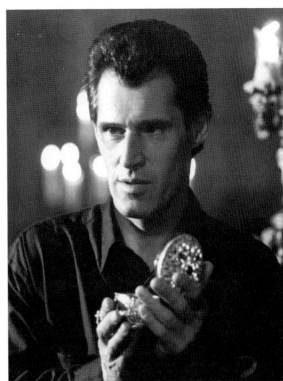

Barnabas (Ben Cross).

Elizabeth (Jean Simmons) and Barnabas (Ben Cross).

(Above) Roger (Roy Thinnes), Elizabeth (Jean Simmons), Dr. Hyram Fisher (Wayne Tippit), Mrs. Johnson (Julianna McCarthy), Julia (Barbara Steele); (below) Willie (Jim Fyfe), Barnabas (Ben Cross), Julia (Barbara Steele).

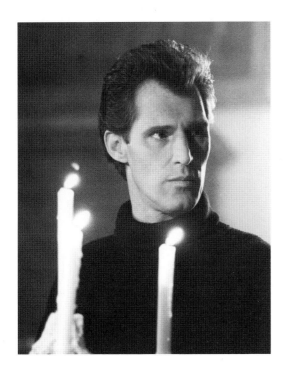 

Barnabas (Ben Cross) and Victoria (Joanna Going) at the Old House.

Willie (Jim Fyfe) with Mrs. Johnson (Julianna McCarthy) and Victoria (Joanna Going); (opposite) The Collinwood grounds.

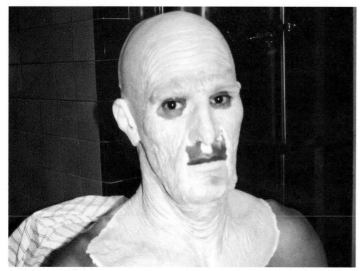

The aging of Barnabas.

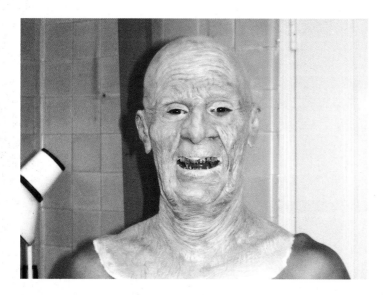

Julia in her lab.

Victoria finds Sarah's Grave.

Daphne's Funeral.

The First Séance; Phyllis Wicke (Ellen Wheeler); (opposite) Dan Curtis directs Barbara Steele and Ben Cross.

1790: Barnabas (Ben Cross) with Naomi (Jean Simmons) and Natalie (Barbara Steele).

1790: Angélique (Lysette Anthony) and Barnabas (Ben Cross).

1790, The Duel: Barnabas (Ben Cross), Ben (Jim Fyfe), The Referee (Chris Eguia), Peter (Michael T. Weiss), Jeremiah (Adrian Paul).

1790: Jeremiah's Funeral.

1790: Trask (Roy Thinnes); Millicent (Barbara Blackburn), Angélique (Lysette Anthony), Abigail (Julianna McCarthy); Ben (Jim Fyfe), Daniel (Joseph Gordon-Levitt), Peter (Michael T. Weiss); André (Michael Cavanaugh) and Joshua (Stefan Gierasch).

1790, Victoria's Trial: Trask (Roy Thinnes); Victoria (Joanna Going); Joshua (Stefan Gierasch), Naomi (Jean Simmons), Peter (Michael T. Weiss), Natalie (Barbara Steele).

1790: Angélique (Lysette Anthony); Barnabas (Ben Cross); Ben (Jim Fyfe); Naomi (Jean Simmons).

1790: Barnabas (Ben Cross) and Sarah (Veronica Lauren).

1790: Barnabas (Ben Cross); Abigail (Julianna McCarthy) and Naomi (Jean Simmons).

Roger Collins (Roy Thinnes); Elizabeth Collins Stoddard (Jean Simmons); Willie Loomis (Jim Fyfe); Dr. Julia Hoffman (Barbara Steele).

Maggie Evans (Ely Pouget); Joe Haskell (Michael T. Weiss); David Collins (Joseph Gordon-Levitt); Carolyn Stoddard (Barbara Blackburn).

Daphne Collins (Rebecca Staab); Sheriff George Patterson (Michael Cavanaugh); Professor Michael Woodard (Stefan Gierasch); Mrs. Sarah Johnson (Julianna McCarthy).

Collinwood: The 1991 Costume Party.

Victoria; David; Barnabas; Sheriff Patterson and Elizabeth; Julia and Barnabas; Carolyn, waiter, Joe, Mrs. Johnson.

Barnabas Collins

Josette Du Prés

Sarah Collins

Jeremiah Collins

1790: Angélique (Lysette Anthony).

1790: Barnabas Collins (Ben Cross) and Josette Du Prés (Joanna Going).

1790: Joshua Collins (Stefan Gierasch).

1790: Naomi Collins (Jean Simmons).

1790: Jeremiah Collins (Adrian Paul).

1790: Abigail Collins (Julianna McCarthy).

1790: Daniel Collins (Joseph Gordon-Levitt).

1790: Sarah Collins (Veronica Lauren).

1790: Peter Bradford (Michael T. Weiss).

1790: Millicent Collins (Barbara Blackburn).

1790: Natalie Du Prés (Barbara Steele).

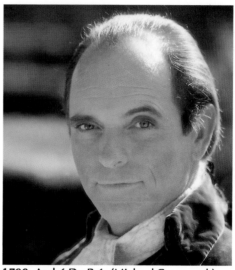
1790: André Du Prés (Michael Cavanaugh).

1790: Ben Loomis (Jim Fyfe).

1790: Reverend Trask (Roy Thinnes).

1790: Barnabas and Naomi; Angélique; Reverend Trask.

The Collinwood Miniature.

1790: Victoria and Josette (Joanna Going); Victoria and Bailiff Henry Evans (Eddie Jones).

1790: Victoria (Joanna Going).

1790: Abigail (Julianna McCarthy).

1790: Crone (Courtenay McWhinney).

1790: Judge Braithwaite (Brendan T. Dillon).

1790: Natalie (Barbara Steele).

1790: Angélique (Lysette Anthony).

1790: Peter (Michael T. Weiss).

1790: Angélique (Lysette Anthony).

1790: Natalie (Barbara Steele).

1790: Ben (Jim Fyfe).

1991: Phyllis Wicke (Ellen Wheeler).

1991: Maggie (Ely Pouget).

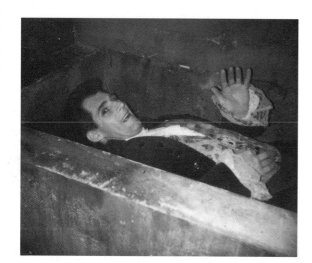 

1790: Barnabas; Ben and Barnabas; Jeremiah; Joshua; (opposite) Jean Simmons and Armand Mastroianni; Sam H[...]
Barbara Steele, Matthew Hall; Margaret Hussey, William Gray, Lisa Magdaleno, Linda Campanelli, M.M. Shelly Moo[...]
Matthew Hall, DeAnn Heline, Dolores Pleviak; Ruth Kennedy and Barbara Steele; Rosalie Wallace; Dan Curtis, Ly[...]
Loring, David Gerber.

NBC Press Conference with Ben Cross, Jean Simmons, Dan Curtis.

NBC Press Party at Greystone: Dan Curtis, Veronica Lauren, Joanna Going, Joseph Gordon-Levitt; Rebecca Staab and Michael T. Weiss; Costumed hostess, Ely Pouget, Roy Thinnes, Barbara Steele, Julianna McCarthy, Rebecca Staab.

Victoria's return from 1790.

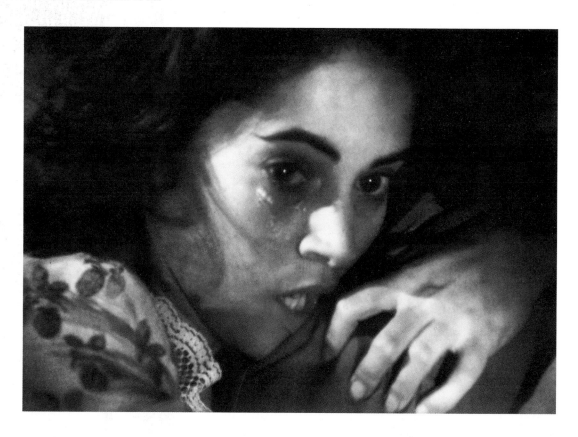

hadows Rally at NBC-TV in Burbank, California: The actors join the fans' support efforts.

Episode Guide

Episode 1 (Pilot).
Original Airdate: January 13, 1991.

Written by Dan Curtis, Steve Feke, Hall Powell, Bill Taub.
Directed by Dan Curtis.

Character List: Barnabas Collins, Elizabeth Collins Stoddard, Victoria Winters, Roger Collins, Dr. Julia Hoffman, Carolyn Stoddard, Willie Loomis, Joe Haskell, David Collins, Maggie Evans, Sarah Collins, Sheriff George Patterson, Professor Michael Woodard, Mrs. Sarah Johnson, Daphne Collins, Sam Evans, Dr. Hyram Fisher, Deputy Jonathan Harker (a.k.a. Paramedic #2), Paramedic #1, Local Tough (a.k.a. Muscles), Gloria, Gardener (a.k.a. Boy #1), Blue Whale Customers, Roadhouse Customers & Band, Villagers, Nurse.

(Portions in italics were not included in the original telecast, but were subsequently added to the extended home video version.)

My name is Victoria Winters. My journey is just beginning. A journey that I am hoping will somehow begin to reveal the mysteries of my past. It is a journey that will bring me to a strange and dark place...to a house high atop a stormy cliff at the edge of the sea...to a house called Collinwood. *To a world I've never known, with people I've never met...people who tonight are still only vague shadows in my mind, but who will soon fill all the days and nights of my tomorrows."*

On a cold autumn day, a train winds around the New England coastline as beautiful twenty-five-year-old Victoria Winters gazes out at the ocean. She ponders her uncertain future as she heads towards Collinsport, Maine, a small and isolated fishing village. She is to be employed as a governess by the wealthy and powerful Collins family who reside in the mysterious old mansion on Widows' Hill called Collinwood.

At Collinwood, Mrs. Sarah Johnson, the family housekeeper for forty years, assists matriarch Elizabeth Collins Stoddard in preparing Victoria's room. Mrs. Johnson assures Elizabeth that she has made the right decision in bringing Victoria to Collinwood. Elizabeth's attractive eighteen-year-old daughter Carolyn Stoddard enters, remarking that Victoria will have her hands full in dealing with nine-year-old David Collins, Carolyn's cousin and son of Roger Collins, Elizabeth's younger brother.

Elizabeth's niece, Daphne Collins, informs her aunt that she has completed the household taxes and is leaving for the Blue Whale Bar to help owner-bartender Sam Evans with his bookkeeping. While smoothing out the comforter on Victoria's bed, Mrs. Johnson discovers a shoebox hidden under a pillow. When Elizabeth opens the container, she is horrified to find a dead rat inside. After Elizabeth drops the box, Carolyn sarcastically suggests that the rodent is David's welcoming gift for Victoria.

In the drawing room, after being informed of David's prank, Roger remarks to Elizabeth that his son needs a psychiatrist instead of a governess. He mentions that they've not even met Victoria, who was hired by their lawyer. He's also frustrated that he hasn't been able to convince his sister to send David to boarding school. She reminds him that the local school will never take the boy back. *Elizabeth tells Roger that David needs a family. An emotional Roger reveals that he talked David into taking a walk with him the previous night along the beach. He confides that his son asked if Roger liked him. With tears in his eyes, Roger tells Elizabeth that, kneeling, he told David that he loved him more than anything in the world. Roger sadly recounts how David immediately pulled away from him and ran off. Elizabeth assures her brother that in time he and his son will get to know each other. But Roger isn't certain. He admits painfully that he resents David's being alive. Asking God's forgiveness, he says he would have left David in a burning room if it would have saved Roger's wife's sanity.*

Victoria's train arrives at the Collinsport station. In the darkness, she steps onto the platform with her suitcase and discovers no one is there to meet her. Soon after, Victoria has walked to the Blue Whale. There she has met Daphne, who phones Collinwood and informs Mrs. Johnson that Victoria has arrived. Mrs. Johnson halfheartedly assures Elizabeth and Roger that her nephew, servant Willie Loomis, must be on his way to retrieve the governess, but Roger storms out to find him. Mrs. Johnson remarks to Elizabeth that Willie can't seem to get anything right.

In his room above the Collinwood stables, Willie, age thirty, looks over antique books and maps and takes a drink from a bottle of bourbon. Roger rushes inside, screaming at Willie for not meeting Victoria's train. Roger empties Willie's liquor bottle, warning him to straighten up immediately or he'll be fired. After Roger comments on the research materials, Willie insists they're examples of his attempts to become better educated. Roger impatiently pushes him out the door to retrieve Victoria.

Outside the Blue Whale, Willie pulls up in his old truck. Inside at the bar, Sam advises Willie that he doesn't want any trouble after refusing Willie's request for a drink. Sam's twenty-seven-year-old daughter, waitress Maggie Evans, expresses her contempt for Willie. Daphne and Victoria watch from their table, where they are seated with Daphne's boyfriend, Joe Haskell, a rugged fisherman in his late twenties. An obnoxious Willie doesn't want to taxi Victoria until he's received a drink. As Sam's anger grows, Joe grabs Willie and prepares to throw him out. When Victoria intervenes, Joe offers her a ride to Collinwood, but she insists she can ride with Willie, who smirks with glee as they leave together.

Willie escorts Victoria to his truck outside and snickers as Joe watches from the Blue Whale entrance. Willie chauffeurs Victoria away. Joe marches back inside to the bar, complaining that Willie should learn proper manners. He becomes playful and grabs Daphne, lifting her over his shoulder. Sam and Maggie watch with amusement as Joe carries Daphne outside. He takes Daphne to his car and places her in the back seat. He climbs in with her. Willie's truck winds up the long driveway to Collinwood and into the courtyard.

Victoria is in awe of the great mansion. Entering the front door leading to the great hall, she is greeted by Elizabeth and Carolyn. As Willie proceeds upstairs with Victoria's luggage, Carolyn advises Victoria that Willie is strange but harmless. The three women head for tea in the drawing room. In the kitchen Mrs. Johnson prepares sandwiches as Willie enters and stuffs himself with food. She asks her nephew why he makes things so difficult, and Willie responds that things were fine before Roger came to live at Collinwood. He grins as he tells his aunt that they'll be rich after he finds the jewels in a secret room in the Collins family tomb. He informs her that they were buried during the Revolutionary War by an ancestor named Barnabas and his father. Believing Willie's comments to be nonsense, Mrs. Johnson advises him to do what he's supposed to do and to avoid foolish schemes that will only get him into trouble.

In the drawing room, Victoria is finishing tea with Elizabeth and Carolyn. She asks Elizabeth how long David has been without his father. Elizabeth reveals that David had been apart from Roger for six years until she brought David back from England when his mother became ill. Elizabeth confesses that David has been through difficult times but insists the boy is intelligent and creative. Carolyn makes a snide reference to David's pranks. Roger enters and introduces himself to Victoria. She admires an impressionistic landscape painting and asks if it is a Seurat. Elizabeth responds that it is a copy, Roger interrupts sharply, stating the painting was done by another artist. Victoria admits that art is one of her favorite subjects to teach. Roger warns her that David will be a challenge for her. He bids goodnight and leaves the room.

In the darkness of the Collins family cemetery, Willie approaches the mausoleum, flashlight in hand, carrying a bag of tools over his shoulder. After consulting cryptic notes on a crumpled sheet of paper, he descends the stairs to the dark and cobwebbed crypt. The flashlight beam illuminates a carved stone lion's head with a rusted iron ring hanging from its mouth. Willie excitedly discovers a stone dove on the opposite wall as detailed in his notes. He then twists the iron ring and watches gleefully as a section of the wall creaks open to reveal a secret room. He enters the chamber and ducks when a flock of bats come winging out. Inside, he discovers a huge stone sarcophagus bound with heavy chains. Certain that the jewels are inside, he lights a wall torch and begins to chisel the chains with a crowbar.

At Collinwood, as the women leave the drawing room and enter the great hall, Elizabeth tells Victoria that she'll meet David at breakfast the next morning. Carolyn escorts Victoria upstairs, informing her that most of the rooms in the mansion are closed off. In the secret room, Willie eagerly removes the last set of chains and slides open the sarcophagus lid. Suddenly a hand shoots out and grabs him by the throat, pulling Willie down as he screams.

In her bedroom at Collinwood, Victoria unpacks her bag. *Carolyn enters with extra blankets. Victoria expresses her enthusiasm for meeting David. The sound of distant howling is heard. Carolyn teasingly tells Victoria that the sound is from strange creatures in the woods. Victoria looks out the window and sees the dark silhouette of a man among the fog-laden trees. She summons Carolyn to look, but Carolyn does not see the figure. She advises Victoria to get some rest, then departs.* In the bathroom she looks around and pulls back the shower curtain. She is frightened as David leaps out screaming. Pleased with himself, David tells Victoria that he doesn't want her at Collinwood. He attempts to rush out of the room, but Victoria slams the door shut, insisting that she has no intention of hurting him. He warns her she must open the door, and after she does they walk to his room. Shrugging off Victoria's assistance, David climbs into bed and declares that he'll continue to scare her. She responds that she wants to be David's friend and leaves the room as David stares wide-eyed into the darkness.

Daphne finishes reviewing Sam's account books at the Blue Whale while Maggie teases her about Joe. Daphne leaves to retrieve her car from Rotolo's gas station. While walking down the street, Daphne senses she's being followed as dogs howl in the distance. She frantically rushes to her car and jumps inside. Suddenly a figure dashes in from the passenger side and grabs her by the throat as she screams.

Later, an ambulance and police cars have arrived with lights flashing. Paramedics tend to an unconscious Daphne as a horrified crowd, including Maggie and Sam, stand by. Deputy Jonathan Harker informs Sheriff George Patterson that it looks as if a wild animal has tried to tear out Daphne's throat. Harker applies a dressing to the bloody wound. Patterson wonders where Daphne's lost blood has gone. Later at the Collinsport Mercy Hospital, a deathly pale, unconscious Daphne has been attached to life-support equipment. *Dr. Hyram Fisher finishes examining her. Sitting next to the bed, Joe keeps vigil. Fisher urges him to take a break, but Joe insists he will stay.* In the corridor Elizabeth and Carolyn rush to meet Fisher, who reports Daphne has been stabilized and is receiving infusions of blood. However, she remembers nothing of her attack. Carolyn consoles Elizabeth as they enter Daphne's room. *Carolyn gives Joe a comforting kiss as Elizabeth tearfully stares at Daphne.*

In the cemetery a caped figure hurries among the tombstones and into the mausoleum. In the secret room, Willie lies on the floor, blood oozing from an open wound on his neck. The figure's hand is seen opening a hidden panel and scooping into an old mariner's chest full of gemstones, coins, and jewelry. The next morning in the hospital laboratory, Dr. Fisher examines Daphne's blood samples as Patterson arrives for an update. The doctor informs him that Daphne's wound couldn't have been caused by an animal since human saliva has been found in the wound.

At Collinwood, on a rainy morning, Roger sits in the dining room eating breakfast while Mrs. Johnson tends to the buffet. Victoria enters and inquires about Daphne's condition. Roger reports there has been no change. He asks Victoria if she's met David. She admits that David succeeded in scaring her but insists that Roger not administer discipline to the boy. Roger warns that Victoria will find David to be a difficult child. She replies that things have been hard for David and feels the boy needs time to adjust. Later that morning, Elizabeth answers a knock at the front door and welcomes Sheriff Patterson. Roger joins them in the great hall. Noticing Victoria on the other side of the spacious room, Elizabeth calls her over and introduces her to the sheriff. Patterson asks Elizabeth if he can speak to Willie, reporting that he's heard Willie was acting strangely at the Blue Whale. Victoria admits Willie nearly hit Joe, but that nothing really happened. The sheriff reveals that an animal was not responsible for the attacks. Elizabeth is aghast, wondering what kind of person could have committed the deeds. Patterson conveys he doesn't necessarily think Willie was the culprit. Roger offers to go with the sheriff to see Willie. Roger and Patterson drive up to the stables and rush inside. Upstairs in Willie's room, Roger finds empty liquor bottles and suggests that Willie is somewhere sleeping off a hangover. Patterson instructs Roger to notify Willie to come to the sheriff's office for questioning.

Patterson visits the seaside cottage home of Professor Michael Woodard, an eccentric expert on archaeology and parapsychology. When the sheriff mentions Daphne's severe loss of blood, Woodard refers to documented cases of unbalanced people who believe themselves to be vampires and actually drink human blood.

Patterson gives him a full report on Daphne, thanking Woodard in advance for any help he can provide. That night at Collinwood, the wind blows fiercely as a dark figure holding a cane walks across the courtyard to the main entrance and knocks on the door. After Mrs. Johnson opens the door, the visitor identifies himself as Barnabas Collins, a cousin from England. Mrs. Johnson escorts him into the foyer and leaves to inform the family in the dining room. Grasping his wolf's-head cane, Barnabas glances across the massive great hall and moves toward his portrait above the lower stairway landing. Elizabeth enters and welcomes him, clearly transfixed by his resemblance to the portrait. Later, in the drawing room, Barnabas has been introduced to Roger and Carolyn, who expresses her amazement at their visitor's appearance, identical to the stairway portrait of their ancestor. Barnabas comments that the Collins blood has a persistent strength. He points out that his cane and black onyx ring are his most treasured possessions since they are the same ones featured in the portrait which he claims is of his ancestor and namesake.

Barnabas announces that he recently arrived in Boston, where he's investing in a shipbuilding firm, and may stay on. When Roger questions him about his London background, Barnabas changes the subject, exclaiming that he's heard many vivid stories of Collinwood's past. He elaborates on the history and building components of the mansion and promptly requests permission to reside in and restore the Old House, the family's original mansion nearby that has long been abandoned. He reminds them that the "original" Barnabas was born there. An intrigued Elizabeth gives her permission as does Roger. Suddenly, David comes running in the room, followed by Victoria, who apologizes for interrupting the gathering. Barnabas is clearly startled by Victoria's appearance. Elizabeth introduces Victoria and David, who exclaims that Barnabas must be a ghost. Elizabeth laughs and informs the boy that Barnabas will be restoring the Old House, where David often plays. David does not like the idea and yells out that Sarah lives there.

Roger tries to quiet the boy, but a curious Barnabas asks for an explanation. Carolyn reveals that David claims to have a friend named Sarah who lives at the Old House. David warns Barnabas that he won't let him take away the Old House. Barnabas asks him who Sarah is, and David shows him a small portrait that pictures a nine-year-old girl. Barnabas attempts to conceal his shock at the picture. Roger intervenes, assuring Barnabas that David has an overactive imagination. Victoria excuses herself to take David to bed, and she and Barnabas express their mutual pleasure in meeting. Later that night, Barnabas enters the Old House, cluttered with overgrown vines and branches. Inside the foyer he painfully speaks out, announcing to his father that he has returned home.

The next afternoon in the Collinwood schoolroom, Victoria is teaching United States geography to a distracted David, who is constantly peeking inside his desk. Losing patience with the boy's indifference, Victoria demands to see what David has inside his desk. She's stunned when she sees a large tarantula moving inside and demands that David return the creature to the outdoors. Before he leaves, David menacingly remarks how awful it would be if a tarantula showed up in Victoria's bed. Carolyn enters to give Victoria moral support and offers to take her to the stables to go horseback riding.

While driving Victoria to the stables, Carolyn reveals that she recently returned to Collinsport at her mother's request after pursuing a career in photography. She drops Victoria off at the stables and leaves. Victoria gives sugar cubes to a chestnut mare named Carolyn. She's startled by the sudden appearance of a lethargic Willie, who's noticeably changed since their previous encounter. Victoria exclaims that everyone's been looking for him and that he's a possible suspect in Daphne's attack. A surprised Willie asks what has happened to Daphne and nervously insists he had nothing to do with it. Victoria notices that Willie is wounded in the neck. A moment later Roger arrives on horseback and drags Willie off to see the sheriff, despite Victoria's pleas that Willie isn't well. In the Collinwood kitchen, Sheriff Patterson interrogates Willie as to his whereabouts during the time of Daphne's attack. Willie insists he was in his room over the stables getting drunk and that for the last three days he's been working elsewhere. A disbelieving Roger grows impatient as Victoria suggests Willie may be telling the truth. Suddenly Barnabas enters and claims that Willie has been working for him. He apologizes for not telling the family sooner. Willie says he took the job since he knew Roger would be firing him. Barnabas insists that Willie wants to make a new start. Patterson gives Willie permission to leave with Barnabas, and Mrs. Johnson expresses her admiration for Barnabas' efforts to rehabilitate her nephew.

That evening, Victoria walks through the corridor outside David's room and hears the whispered voices of David and a little girl. When the voices stop, Victoria knocks on the door and enters. She sees only David lying in bed and asks him who he was talking to. He admits he was speaking with Sarah. Although doubtful, Victoria pretends that everything is normal and suggests they visit the Old House the next day. But David replies that Sarah told him Barnabas is evil. Victoria asks David to introduce her to Sarah, but David doubts Victoria believes in Sarah's existence. Victoria tries to kiss David goodnight, but he turns away. She insists that he and she will become good friends.

The next day, Victoria and David approach the Old House as workmen clear away vegetation. They enter the foyer and find Willie in the drawing room. When Victoria asks for Barnabas, Willie replies that he has gone to Portland. David slips unnoticed into the hallway and heads down the stairs to the basement. But Willie stops him, grabbing the boy, who insists he can go where he wants. Victoria appears and facilitates David's cooperation. As the boy runs back upstairs, Victoria apologizes for David's behavior, unaware of the secluded coffin that lies in the basement room below.

At the Three Gables, a roadhouse just outside of town, Carolyn dances with a local boy on the crowded dance floor as a rock band plays. At the bar, a mini-skirted party girl named Gloria drapes herself over her tough punk boyfriend Muscles, who has his eyes fixed on a flirtatious Carolyn. After Carolyn takes a drink from his beer, Muscles makes a move on her as Gloria watches angrily. He sends away Carolyn's dancing partner and tries to take over, but Carolyn teasingly rejects his advances and walks off in the crowd. Muscles returns to the bar as Gloria storms outside. In the parking lot she's momentarily startled when she encounters Barnabas, who apologizes for frightening her. Gloria becomes flirtatious and asks for a ride home. Barnabas responds by grabbing her and sinking his fangs into her neck while his red eyes glow with blood lust. As Gloria screams out in horror, Muscles comes running. Barnabas raises his head with blood dripping from his mouth, slams Muscles against a van, and bites him in the neck.

Later that night, patrol cars with lights flashing arrive in the parking lot. Sheriff Patterson and Deputy Harker join the crowd as paramedics examine the dead and bloodied bodies of Gloria and Muscles. A horrified Carolyn is among the onlookers. At the hospital lab Dr. Fisher reveals to Patterson and Woodard that in addition to finding human saliva once again, he has discovered a strange cell in Gloria's and Muscles' blood that is also present in Daphne's blood sample. Fisher confesses he's dumfounded, and Woodard suggests calling in a blood expert he knows from New York University named Dr. Julia Hoffman.

During a downpour, Woodard greets Julia when she arrives by train. The next day at the hospital, Dr. Fisher reports to Joe, Carolyn, and Elizabeth that Daphne is inexplicably much better, but she still has no memory of what happened to her. Julia and Woodard emerge from Daphne's room, and Elizabeth and Joe express their eagerness for Daphne to go home. Elizabeth suggests that Julia stay at Collinwood while Daphne recuperates. Fisher responds that Daphne can be discharged in another day if she continues to do well. Julia cooly remarks that may be possible and excuses herself to run some tests.

Julia visits Daphne's room at Collinwood. Daphne kisses Joe, who's sitting next to her in bed. Daphne convinces Julia to postpone an injection until later. As Julia leaves, Joe and Daphne resume their kissing. At dusk, Victoria comes out of the woods bordering the Old House and knocks on the front door. After waiting and knocking again, she enters the house and calls out for Barnabas and Willie, who comes scrambling up from the basement. Victoria apologizes for entering, explaining that she's looking for David. Willie nervously follows her to the drawing room. She offers compliments on the restoration work. Noticing that nightfall is approaching, Willie encourages Victoria to return home, suggesting that it is dangerous for her to be out because of recent happenings. In the basement, the coffin opens as a hand pushes the lid from inside.

Upstairs, Victoria tells Willie to call her Vicki, instead of Miss Winters, and he thanks her for believing him when no one else did. She asks again for Barnabas. Willie tries to hurry her out, assuring her Barnabas is busy and he'll tell him she came to visit. But Barnabas appears in the doorway before Victoria can depart. He welcomes her to the Old House and tells her that although Willie's concern is admirable, there is nothing for her to worry about. Barnabas takes Victoria's hand and kisses it lightly while giving Willie a piercing look. He sends his jittery servant from the room. Victoria mentions that she should be leaving, but Barnabas insists she spare a few moments. He escorts Victoria upstairs to the third-floor bedroom of Josette Du Prés, Barnabas' eighteenth century fiancé. Staring at Josette's portrait over the fireplace, Victoria is astonished to notice her physical resemblance to Josette. Barnabas comments that she and Josette are very much alike.

As his mind focuses on the past, Barnabas gives Victoria a selective, but emotional, history of Josette, revealing that she came from the West Indian island of Martinique where the "original" Barnabas met her on a family business trip involving shipping. He mentions that the two were engaged but never married because Josette died from a fall off Widows' Hill. After Victoria is gone, Barnabas angrily yells up the stairs to Willie, who comes running down tensely. Barnabas hurls him down the stairs onto the floor and demands to know why he was trying to warn Victoria. He repeatedly beats Willie with his cane as the terrified servant cries out in pain. Moments later Barnabas rushes back into Josette's room. Staring at the portrait, Barnabas exclaims that Josette is back and vows not to lose her again.

During the day, Sheriff Patterson and a group of frightened townspeople watch as deputies discover the body of a dead woman floating near the shore below Widows' Hill. Patterson's patrol car moves up the winding driveway at Collinwood. In a mansion room converted to a lab, Julia tells Patterson and Woodard that there may be a way to bring back Daphne's memory. In Daphne's room, Patterson and Woodard watch as Julia hypnotizes Daphne with a crystal medallion. In a trance, Daphne becomes hysterical as Julia questions her. She recalls the attack and screams out about the teeth and red eyes of her attacker. Julia quickly calms her by putting her to sleep. In the hallway, Patterson remarks how close they are to learning the attacker's identity, but Julia says that Daphne must rest. Woodard suggests that a deputy be assigned to keep watch over Daphne since she's the only one still alive who can identify the attacker.

In the daytime, Victoria and David are greeted by Willie in the Collinwood courtyard. Victoria is shocked by the bruises on Willie's face, which he claims are from a fall while working. He hands her a dinner invitation from Barnabas written in old-fashioned handwriting on parchment. Victoria tells Willie to convey her acceptance to Barnabas. As Willie shuffles off, David tells Victoria he thinks Willie is strange. That night in the great hall at Collinwood, Joe helps Willie move an antique dresser out of the house, while Elizabeth and Barnabas examine other pieces to be removed. He informs her that a clock was a wedding present from André Du Prés, whose daughter Josette was to marry Barnabas in 1790. Julia descends the stairs and Elizabeth introduces her to Barnabas, explaining that Julia is staying at Collinwood to help Daphne recover.

An intrigued Barnabas inquires about Daphne's status and remains calm although startled when Julia mentions that they nearly broke through Daphne's amnesia. Upstairs, Daphne awakens, staring blankly in the distance. She gets out of bed slowly and walks trance-like into the hall and down the upper stairs. Barnabas thanks Elizabeth for the furnishings as Joe reenters and spies Daphne at the top of the stairs. As Daphne stares at Barnabas, he attempts to mask his emotions while gazing back at her. She collapses and Joe bounds up the stairs and kneels by her, cradling her in his arms. Julia and Elizabeth rush up beside them. As Daphne revives, Julia takes her pulse and follows Daphne's stare through the railing to Barnabas standing below. Julia declares they should move Daphne to a downstairs bedroom. Elizabeth apologizes to Barnabas as she, Joe, and Julia lead Daphne back to her room.

In the candlelight of the Old House drawing room, Barnabas presents Victoria with a music box that was purchased by Barnabas for Josette in 1790 on the day of their wedding announcement. As the tinkling melody plays, Victoria is enchanted and confesses that she's been thinking about Josette ever since she saw the portrait. She says it feels as if they're connected in some strange way through the centuries. Barnabas responds by stating his belief that souls from the past can have eternal rebirth, that the true nature of life is never-ending, and that time can never defeat life. Victoria is overwhelmed by Barnabas' romanticism. As Barnabas prepares to walk her home, Willie comes down and unsuccessfully offers to escort her. As they walk through the woods, Barnabas reiterates how they both resemble the portraits of Collins ancestors and how romantic it would be if they were the reincarnations of Barnabas and Josette. The ghostly figure of Sarah Collins watches them from the woods. At the Collinwood entrance, Victoria thanks Barnabas for a lovely evening, and he kisses her hand goodnight. They express their hope of being together again soon.

In her bathroom, Victoria, dressed in her robe, brushes her hair, then crosses into her bedroom. Outside Barnabas stands among the trees staring up towards her windows. She looks out, unaware of his presence. As his vampire urges take control, Barnabas' eyes glaze with redness and he hisses as he bares his fangs. Suddenly the sound of a little girl's voice is heard echoing his name from the distance. Barnabas freezes as he spies the ghost of his nine-year-old sister Sarah dressed in white. He calls out to her in disbelief. She replies that he must stop. Overjoyed at the appearance of his dead sister, he walks towards her, but she runs away into the dark woods. Frantically he cries out for her to return, but she has disappeared. He begs her to come back and asks her not to hate him, insisting that he cannot help himself.

Episode 2
Original Airdate: January 14, 1991.

Written by Dan Curtis, Steve Feke, Hall Powell, Bill Taub.
Directed by Dan Curtis.

Character List: Barnabas Collins, Victoria Winters, Elizabeth Collins Stoddard, Roger Collins, Dr. Julia Hoffman, Carolyn Stoddard, Willie Loomis, Joe Haskell, David Collins, Dr. Michael Woodard, Mrs. Sarah Johnson, Sheriff George Patterson, Maggie Evans, Sam Evans, Daphne Collins, Deputy Jonathan Harker, Reverend, Deputies, Mourners.

My name is Victoria Winters. I am a stranger in the great house of Collinwood, but there are other strangers here too... a man with riveting eyes, new to the land, but not to its past. But fate has also sent a third uninvited guest, one who has swept through the once quiet village, and come to Widows' Hill, where they say cries of sorrow have been heard for centuries. Tonight they will be heard again, for the third visitor... is death."

In Daphne's room at Collinwood, Julia administers a hypodermic in Daphne's arm while Joe and Carolyn watch. Professor Woodard enters the room, which is guarded by Deputy Harker in the hallway. Daphne reports that she's feeling fine, but Woodard wants to know about her fall down the stairs. Joe responds that Daphne had been sleepwalking, but she recalls nothing of the incident. Woodard presents her with a small silver cross on a chain and asks her to wear it during the coming night. Julia expresses her astonishment at the request, but Woodard urges her to indulge him. Daphne agrees and Joe assures the professor that both he and the deputy will be guarding Daphne through the night. The group leaves Daphne alone with Joe, who comments on the strangeness of Woodard's request. Daphne asks Joe to promise her that once her ordeal is over the two of them will always be together. Joe agrees and kisses her.

In the great hall, Julia and Woodard privately discuss matters. The professor wants an explanation of Daphne's sleepwalking. Julia remarks that something unknown must have frightened Daphne. Woodard thinks whoever's responsible for Daphne's attack will return and that Daphne will eventually remember what's been happening to her. Later that night, Daphne lies sleeping. On the sofa, Joe has also fallen asleep. In an armchair, Deputy Harker reads a magazine. He rises and awakens Joe for guard duty. After the two men switch places, Harker quickly falls asleep. Unnoticed by Joe, Daphne begins to turn her head restlessly. Barnabas stands in the misty darkness staring at Daphne's windows, his eyes ablaze. He bares his fangs. As Joe unintentionally falls asleep, Daphne continues to toss and turn.

Her eyes snap open and she sits up and rips the cross from her neck. In a trance, she rises, crosses to the French doors and steps out into the night.

In the Collinwood formal gardens, Daphne appears in her billowing white nightgown as Barnabas beckons her. A look of anticipation appears on her face as she is drawn inexorably to him. As they embrace, Barnabas begins to passionately kiss Daphne. After caressing her, he bares his fangs and buries his face in her neck. Daphne writhes in ecstasy. In Daphne's bedroom the following morning, Joe awakens to discover that Daphne is gone. He awakens the deputy, and the two men run out to search. Scouring the grounds, they find Daphne in the garden by the fountain, where she lies bloody and lifeless.

A cold rain pours down as the family and friends of Daphne gather in the Collins family cemetery for her funeral. As the minister delivers the eulogy, the mourners stare sadly at Daphne's casket, which is carried to the family mausoleum. In her lab at Collinwood, Julia analyzes Daphne's last blood sample in a microscope as Woodard enters. He's wondering if she's learned anything new. Julia admits that she was testing a new vaccine on Daphne, one that was developed from the aberrant cells discovered in the attack victims. She claims that the vaccine was working to eliminate the cells from Daphne's blood. After a pause, Woodard asks Julia if she believes in vampires. Julia expresses surprise, but Woodard refers to the attack victims' bodies being drained of blood, human saliva in the wounds, and of Daphne's reports of teeth and red eyes. Woodard confesses that if he conveyed his thoughts to the sheriff, his sanity would be questioned. Julia mentions that if Woodard's suspicions are correct, then the success she was having with Daphne might indicate that the creature responsible could possibly be cured. However, Woodard insists that vampirism isn't a disease, telling Julia that vampires are the living dead. Julia replies that his theory will be very difficult to prove, but Woodard expects the proof he needs will be immediately forthcoming.

At dusk, a melancholy David is playing in the gardens. As he bounces a ball against the steps, he chants that if he catches it Daphne isn't dead. When he notices it's getting dark, he heads for the house. He runs along the path to the abandoned swimming pool and hears the echoing sound of someone calling his name. Frightened and confused, David calls out for the voice to identify itself. He's astonished to see Daphne emerging from the dark pool house. She assures the boy that it's really she, and he responds that he knew she wasn't dead. As she gets closer to David, her deathly pale face is revealed along with glowing eyes. He begins to back away. Daphne insists she isn't going to hurt him. When Daphne opens her mouth and bares her vampire fangs, a horrified David screams and runs for Collinwood.

In the Collinwood dining room, the family sits solemnly at the dinner table as David comes running in, shouting of his encounter with Daphne. Roger scolds him for being outside when he was supposed to be taking a nap. He tells his son that it is not time for pranks. The boy runs to Victoria and pleads with her to believe him, insisting he's not lying. When Woodard inquires as to where David spotted Daphne, Joe berates the professor for adding to the child's fear. Julia watches intently as David tells Woodard where he saw Daphne. Joe erupts again, walking over to David and assuring him that he didn't really see Daphne, but David insists otherwise. Joe hugs the boy and tries to convince him it was just his imagination. Woodard warns a tearful Joe not to go outside and suggests that Victoria take David to his room. After the two depart, Woodard declares that they can verify whether or not David is telling the truth by opening Daphne's grave. As everyone stares with astonishment, Elizabeth angrily puts down her napkin and announces she'll not listen to any more of Woodard's talk. But Julia convinces her to listen. Woodard says he believes Daphne was destroyed by a vampire and that she nows walks as one of the living dead. Roger jumps to his feet, saying that he's heard enough. He bids everyone a good night as he strides out of the room. Woodard apologizes to Elizabeth for the bluntness of his talk but insists that he truly believes what he's said. Elizabeth quietly leaves; Joe, Carolyn, and Julia remain with the professor. Woodard again urges Joe not to take his warning lightly, especially because of his relationship with Daphne. Joe angrily leaves.

Later that night in the family cemetery, Joe walks among the gravestones carrying a flashlight. He enters the mausoleum and walks towards Daphne's tomb, touching her name plate. He prepares to open the tomb when he hears his name called out. He turns around in shock to see Daphne standing in the stairway of the crypt with her death-white face and burning eyes. With her fangs bared, she moves slowly toward Joe. Terrified, he backs up against the wall. As she kisses him, she tells him not to be afraid and that they're going to be together in a world without end. She sinks her fangs into Joe's neck. He screams out in horror.

The next day, Joe lies in a bed at Collinwood with a bandage on his neck as he receives a blood transfusion. He makes unintelligible sounds while he tosses and turns. Julia fills a hypodermic as Roger and Carolyn watch. Woodard enters and Julia informs him that Joe was found that morning barely conscious wandering near the cemetery. Roger adds that they opened Daphne's coffin. Woodard interrupts, saying that he knows, reporting that Sheriff Patterson has placed a curfew on the town. Julia injects the hypodermic needle in Joe's arm, and he screeches out Daphne's name. At the Blue Whale, Maggie lays a pattern of tarot cards on a table while Sam works on a model of a boat. Maggie reacts fearfully when she draws the death card. She shows the card to her skeptical father, warning that someone else is going to die. Roger arrives, claiming he's come to town to pick up a few things. He reports that Joe's in pretty bad shape and admits no one knows what's happening. Roger tells Maggie that he stopped by because Carolyn would like her to come to Collinwood. He offers Maggie a ride. As they prepare to leave, Sam tells Maggie to call when she's ready to come back to town, but Roger insists he'll bring Maggie back. Sam looks displeased as they leave.

Outside the Blue Whale, Roger sarcastically comments to Maggie on the pleasure of seeing her father first thing in the morning. Maggie asks him what Carolyn wants, and Roger responds that it's not what Carolyn wants, it's what *he* wants. Maggie gives him a knowing look as she gets into Roger's car. Later at her studio apartment, Roger and Maggie make love in her bed. Roger tells Maggie that he doesn't know what he would do without her, commenting that she's the only one who keeps him sane. Roger wishes he had the same passion for his work that Maggie has for hers. But Maggie insists that no artist ever completely loses the need to create. She assures him that he'll recover his creative abilities. She gets up to pour some coffee, and Roger joins her. He tells her he's never witnessed anything as strange as what's been happening at Collinwood. Maggie hesitantly reveals that she believes a vampire is responsible and warns that it is only the beginning.

At Collinwood, Mrs. Johnson welcomes a visiting Barnabas and comments to him about the recent frightening events. Barnabas assures her that her nephew Willie is fine. In the drawing room, Barnabas greets Elizabeth, Roger, and Julia. Barnabas apologizes for being away during the family's crisis, claiming he's been in Boston on business and that Willie has informed him of the terrible things that have happened. Elizabeth expresses her gratitude to Barnabas, telling him that his presence is always a comfort. Barnabas mentions that he saw several deputies on the estate and asks why they are present. Roger responds that no one knows where Daphne is but the consensus is that she'll be returning for Joe. He reveals that Joe is recuperating at Collinwood. Barnabas says he finds the whole situation extraordinary and asks Julia if she or Woodard have an explanation. Julia says they have no sound medical answers, just theories based on legend. When Barnabas inquires where Victoria is, Elizabeth tells him she's with David. Roger mentions how frightened the boy is.

While setting her cup of tea on the mantel, Julia inadvertently glances in the mirror above the fireplace and is startled to see reflections of Roger and Elizabeth but none of Barnabas. As she reacts, Roger extends an offer for Barnabas to stay at Collinwood as a safety precaution, but Barnabas declines. Julia looks back at the group and then stares back into the mirror. She stands frozen when she again sees no reflection of Barnabas. Barnabas asks what the sheriff plans to do, and Roger responds that Daphne will have to be stopped. Julia reminds Barnabas that they're still left with one major unanswered question: who is responsible for Daphne's condition? Barnabas coolly acknowledges Julia's comment and turns to Elizabeth, telling her to let him know if there's anything he can do to help. Barnabas bids everyone goodnight as Roger leads him out of the room. Julia stares intensely.

Later, a police car drives slowly outside Collinwood, flashing its searchlight. Inside, Joe lies asleep as Julia takes his pulse. She tells Carolyn that he'll probably sleep through the morning. She says she'll check again on him later and advises Carolyn to get some rest. They leave the room as a deputy stands guard at the door. In David's bedroom, Victoria sits guard while the boy sleeps. She writes the name of Josette repeatedly on a pad of paper. Roger enters and checks on his son. He summons Victoria into the hall and questions her about David's reaction to everything that's been happening. She says the boy is confused and still frightened that Daphne might hurt him. Roger expresses his frustration, and Victoria returns to David's room. The patrol car continues to keep watch. In his room, Joe opens his eyes. When the deputy's back is turned, Joe knocks him out and slips out of the room, unseen by Roger, Woodard and Patterson, who have set up a command post in a room down the hall.

Outside, Joe stumbles up to the stables. Through an open loft door he spies Daphne staring down at him and raising her arms. Joe runs up the stairs towards her. Inside the dark and cluttered loft, he pulls the bandage off his neck as he approaches Daphne. He enters her arms and they fall into a deep embrace. Daphne kisses Joe passionately. Outside, two police cars arrive. A group of deputies with flashlights and large silver crosses begin to search. Joe and Daphne are lying on a mattress with her face buried in his neck, draining him of blood. A deputy enters the loft. Daphne raises her head, but the deputy sees nothing. He descends the stairs, preparing to leave. When Daphne again penetrates Joe's neck with her fangs, Joe's arm flops sideways, knocking over a stack of old pots. The deputy comes running back up the stairs and shines his flashlight on Daphne. A startled Daphne rises. Her eyes are glowing; she hisses like a wild animal. The deputy yells for help as she prepares to attack him. He deflects her with the cross and chases her into a corner. The other deputies enter with crosses, and Daphne backs off, raising her arms to shield her eyes from the crosses. Suddenly, Joe lunges forward to protect her, screaming for the deputies to leave Daphne alone.

Outside, the sheriff arrives in his car with Roger and Woodard. They run inside the loft, and Patterson yells for his deputies to get Joe out. Roger and two deputies pull away a struggling Joe as Patterson and the other deputies corner Daphne with their crosses. She snarls with rage while baring her bloody fangs, but the deputies pin her down. At Patterson's prompting, Woodard opens his black bag to reveal a large mallet and a sharp wooden stake. He places the stake over Daphne's heart and pounds it through her chest. Her eyes open wide as she shrieks in pain. Joe screams out in agony as the professor slams the stake again. Joe breaks away from Roger and stumbles over to Daphne's bloodied body. Her eyes stare at him as she faintly speaks Joe's name. She gasps and dies in his arms. Her face is serene, indicating that she is finally at rest. Joe sobs wildly.

In her lab at Collinwood the next day, Julia reflects in her journal that it will be a long time, perhaps never, before the recent horrors will be forgotten. She adds that a new and important discovery may be at hand as she prepares for a confrontation with the one she believes has perpetrated the terror. At dusk, Julia rushes up to the Old House and peeks inside the drawing room window. She opens an unlocked side door and enters nervously. She's startled when Willie's hand grabs her shoulder. He wants to know what she's doing, exclaiming that she shouldn't be there. Julia inquires if Barnabas is at home. Willie says that Barnabas is away, but Julia comments that he'll soon be present since Barnabas comes to life when the sun sets. A terrified Willie pretends not to know her meaning. Julia insists he tell her where Barnabas is. When Willie throws a nervous glance at the cellar door, Julia heads towards it. Begging her not to go down the stairs, Willie desperately follows Julia as she descends to the basement. She discovers a closed door and enters to find Barnabas' coffin in the room lit only by candelabra.

Julia walks up to the coffin as Willie follows nervously, still begging her to stop. Julia gathers her courage and opens the lid to see Barnabas lying inside in a trance-like state. Suddenly his eyes pop open. Julia thrusts a cross towards Barnabas. He puts his hand over his face and firmly tells her to put it away. She refuses until he gives his word that he will not harm her. Upstairs a few minutes later, Willie tosses logs on the fire as Barnabas enters the drawing room. Julia sits in front of the blazing fireplace. Barely able to control his anger at Willie, Barnabas sends him out of the room. Julia explains her desire to help Barnabas. At first believing that Julia is either extremely naive or insane, Barnabas eventually becomes fascinated by her suggestion that she may be able to give him back a normal life. She tells him how, through analyzing the blood of his victims, she's discovered a destructive cell in Barnabas' blood. If she can eliminate the cell or make it dormant, she believes Barnabas can live a normal human life. Barnabas informs Julia that the curse of his existence is beyond the realm of science. He reveals that he hasn't seen the light of day or felt the warmth of the sun for two hundred years. He admits he has been compelled by desires he cannot control and has committed acts which sadden and repulse him. He expresses his longing for a return to a normal life. But Julia persists, and Barnabas becomes further engrossed. She convinces him to give her a chance to help him, and an expression of hope comes over his face. Julia is clearly exhilarated over the task she faces.

Episode 3.
Original Airdate: January 14, 1991.

Written by Jon Boorstin.
Directed by Dan Curtis.

Character List: Barnabas Collins, Victoria Winters, Elizabeth Collins Stoddard, Roger Collins, Dr. Julia Hoffman, Carolyn Stoddard, Willie Loomis, Joe Haskell, David Collins, Professor Michael Woodard, Mrs. Sarah Johnson, Sheriff George Patterson, Sarah Collins, Daphne Collins.

(The opening voice-over was not included in the original broadcast since episodes 2 & 3 were aired together in a two-hour format.)

My name is Victoria Winters. I am a newcomer to the great house of Collinwood. There is another recent arrival, a being older than the great house itself... trapped outside of time by an ancient curse... a tortured creature who may soon free himself of his torment, if only he can conquer the evil powers that drive him."

At the Old House, Barnabas sits trembling in his bedroom. He sweats fiercely as he fights the urge to prowl for a victim in the night. Willie ushers in Julia, who's carrying her medical bag. Barnabas informs her that she is late, and she responds that she was unable to leave Collinwood until everyone was asleep. His eyes burn as he stares at her. The strain and torment of his violent urges nearly overwhelm him. Julia warns him that the serum may be toxic, but Barnabas assures her that nothing could be worse than his present condition. She fills the syringe with a sample of Barnabas' blood and then injects another syringe of serum into Barnabas' vein, warning him that it will burn. As the fluid spreads through his body, Barnabas is struck with massive pain. He describes the feeling as that of a cutting knife and says his blood feels as if it is boiling inside him. Twisted in pain, he falls back in his chair with his eyes shut. An alarmed Julia hastily examines him. He regains consciousness and announces the pain has gone. As Julia watches cautiously, Barnabas cracks the hint of a smile and turns gratefully to her. For the first time, a glimmer of hope enters his voice. He announces that one day they will see the dawn together. A pleased Julia stares into his eyes.

Just before dawn in her lab, Julia places Barnabas' blood sample into a collection of test tubes. She writes in her journal that she plans to divide the blood into twelve separate control units. After each inoculation a new sample will be drawn so that the change in Barnabas' blood chemistry can be accurately charted over the course of the experiment. The sun begins to rise as she writes that the first test will be to establish the effect of the sun's rays on the original sample. She places a test tube of blood in the window. As the sun shines on the tube, the blood inside begins to bubble and hiss. Fascinated, Julia watches as the tube explodes and the spilt blood evaporates into a powdery residue.

After sundown, Barnabas and Victoria walk through a meadow, both exhilarated by the breezy evening. They recite poetry and Victoria playfully kisses Barnabas on the cheek and runs towards the cliff overlooking the ocean at Widows'

Hill. Barnabas yells for her not to go there and chases after her. He looks ahead and envisions the image of a young woman in a white lace dress. He calls out Josette's name and imagines that she is jumping off the cliff to the jagged rocks below. Barnabas kneels in agony, staring at the crashing waves. Victoria suddenly appears behind him, insisting that she's fine. The wind howls as Barnabas gathers his composure and tells Victoria the legend of Widows' Hill. He recounts that on stormy nights the wives of fishermen would come there to search for their husbands' ships. He mentions that many wives became widows and joined their dead husbands by jumping off the cliff. Victoria asks if Josette died there, and Barnabas confirms she did.

At dusk, David enters the Collinwood foyer. Looking around, he calls out to see if anyone is home but receives no reply. He heads up the stairs but stops when he hears a sound. Carolyn appears but does not speak. She walks slowly toward him with a strange, vacant look on her face. Her eyes appear angry and glow red. David nervously moves back from her. She suddenly opens her mouth, reveals two fangs, and hisses. David screams in terror and runs up the stairs. Along the upstairs corridor David races to his room but jumps back when he sees Daphne inside. She comes at him with her fangs bared and eyes glowing. David sprints to Victoria's room as Daphne and Carolyn stalk him. He finds Victoria at her desk and screams to her for help. But when she turns to him, her eyes are burning and fangs protrude from her mouth. The other two women enter, and David finds he is surrounded by terror. He opens his eyes to discover that his whole ordeal has been a nightmare. David is lying in bed as Victoria attempts to comfort him. She gives him a drink of water, and he tells her about his horrifying dream. He's convinced that Daphne is coming back. Victoria offers to stay with him for awhile. For the first time, David accepts her offer of friendship. She turns off the light and keeps watch over the boy as he stares wide-eyed into the darkness.

During the daytime, David is playing in the woods on the Collinwood grounds and enters the family cemetery. Clutching a stick like a sword, he enters the mausoleum and examines the urn at Daphne's resting place. Suddenly a voice calls out his name, and David discovers Sarah's ghost has appeared. She calms his fears and assures him that Daphne will never come back. She tells him there is someone else in pain who needs his help but says she can't tell him who because it's someone very close to him. David is desperate to know who it is, but Sarah ignores his plea and starts singing London Bridge. She walks up the stairs and disappears.

In her lab at Collinwood, Julia enters in her journal that progress continues after ten weeks of experimentation. She writes that Barnabas' blood is still vulnerable to the sun's rays but that its resistance grows. In the window she has placed two test tubes of blood. Upon pulling the drapes apart, the sunlight causes one vial to explode instantly. The other bubbles but does not erupt. Continuing in her journal, Julia mentions that Barnabas has not fed on blood for over two months and that she is convinced it is only a matter of time until he will be ready to face the dawn. She smiles at the thought that she will be the cause of his new-found freedom.

At night in his bedroom, Barnabas receives another injection from Julia as Willie observes. Barnabas remarks that the injections are becoming easier to endure. Julia explains that his blood chemistry is almost normal and that he should begin to feel warm. She points out he now has a gray hair, a positive sign that he's aging as a human. Willie chimes in with his enthusiasm over the discovery. An eager Barnabas expresses his impatience, but Julia insists they cannot endanger success by rushing the experiments. However, she does prompt Willie to unveil a surprise, a full-length mirror which Barnabas reluctantly approaches. He's overjoyed to discover that for the first time in two centuries he can see his own reflection. He excitedly grabs Willie and proclaims that they shall hang mirrors in every room. Willie beams with pleasure as Julia controls her emotions. She again urges Barnabas to be patient, assuring him that if he is, everything he wants will come true. Barnabas places his hands on her face, admitting that he owes everything to Julia, vowing to give her his gratitude. Julia is overwhelmed with happiness. Later in Josette's room, a solitary Barnabas stares at Josette's portrait, declaring to her that soon the two of them will be together again.

At the Collinwood lily pond, Joe lies asleep on a lounge chair in the afternoon sun. Carolyn awakens him, serving lunch. He's been shaken by a bad dream and tells Carolyn he's got to get out of town to escape all the memories that haunt him. He suggests he might move to Bimini. Carolyn tells him she'd miss him if he did and runs her fingers down his arm. He stares ahead with concern. At Woodard's cottage, Julia and the professor have finished dinner. Julia compliments him on his culinary abilities. The old friends sit in front of the fireplace as Woodard inquires about Julia's progress with her work. He wonders why Julia is still at Collinwood. Julia mentions she's still treating Joe, but Woodard tells her he knows that she's still in town because she thinks a vampire was responsible for the attacks and that it will strike again. Julia pretends the suggestion is absurd. Woodard plays along but concedes they both know the real threat still exists. He reports that he and the sheriff suspect Barnabas might be involved since he's new in town and hasn't been seen during the day. An expression of concern crosses Julia's face.

In Josette's room at the Old House, Barnabas recites a love sonnet to an entranced Victoria. He tells her it was written by his namesake for Josette but that it might have been written for her. He stands close to her as they stare at each other intensely. They kiss and Victoria puts her arms around Barnabas. They embrace as their passion grows. Barnabas' animalistic urges begin to overwhelm him, and his eyes start to burn. He gazes at Victoria's vulnerable neck and starts sweating. He breaks away and turns from her. Hurt and confused, Victoria asks what is wrong. He asks her to leave, telling her that Willie will escort her home. He tells her he doesn't feel well and requests no more questions. A confused Victoria complies and departs as Barnabas remains with his back toward her, masking his pain as his fangs glisten in the candlelight.

Later, Julia rushes with Willie through the woods to aid Barnabas. She asks Willie why Victoria was with Barnabas. Willie tells her they were just talking when Barnabas began to revert to his vampire status. Willie hesitantly confesses that he's afraid Barnabas might attack Victoria. They enter Barnabas' bedroom to find Barnabas staring out at the moon. Julia rushes to his side. Barnabas tells her they can wait no longer; he is losing control. Julia fears the experiments could fail if things are hurried, but Barnabas is adamant that she complete the process before morning. Julia takes a new blood sample and then injects vaccine into Barnabas' arm. Barnabas' face contorts with pain.

Just before sunrise, Barnabas sits tensely in an armchair staring outside. He remarks to Julia that he'd forgotten how the sky could be so many colors. Barnabas cups the sunlight in his hands and exclaims that after two hundred years his cold hands are warm once again. He's elated to see the sun. Watching closely, Julia smiles and Willie stands by in awe. Suddenly Julia notices the test tube sample of blood beginning to bubble rapidly as the sun's rays pass through it. Julia orders Willie to block the sun by drawing the drapes, but Barnabas defiantly tells Willie to leave the curtains open. The test tube is bubbling more strongly and starts to whistle. Barnabas is overcome by pain and sinks to his knees. Willie pulls the drapes closed as Julia examines a trembling Barnabas. The sound of knocking is heard coming from the front door. Julia and Willie carry the weakened Barnabas to his bed. Julia dispatches Willie to send away whoever is visiting.

At the front door, Willie is terrified to find Roger, Woodard, and Sheriff Patterson waiting outside. Roger announces that they have come to see Barnabas. Willie says he is still asleep. Patterson insists it's important. Woodard sarcastically adds that they'd like to see Barnabas before he leaves for Boston or Portland since he's always away when someone wants to see him, particularly during the daytime. Much to the surprise of the visitors, Julia comes down. She tells them Willie summoned her to examine Barnabas, who she reports is quite ill. Woodard remarks it's odd Willie didn't mention that Barnabas was sick. Julia tells them he has a raging fever that kept him awake all night. She insists it isn't advisable to see Barnabas under the circumstances, but the sheriff asserts they must talk to him about Daphne and the other attack victims. Julia wants to know if they are suggesting Barnabas is a suspect, but Patterson responds they're not making any accusations. Saying they want to see Barnabas in the daylight, Woodard prompts the sheriff to produce a search warrant.

The group enters the house, and Patterson requests that Willie take them to Barnabas. Woodard starts for the stairs, but suddenly Barnabas' voice is heard. He shakily stands on the upper stairway. Woodard can't believe his eyes. Gripping the banister, Barnabas stands in the shadows away from the sunlight beaming through the window below him. Roger apologizes for the intrusion, placing the blame on Woodard. The sheriff agrees with Roger that they should leave and let Barnabas rest, but Woodard is determined to delve further. He suggests that Barnabas needs more sunlight. Barnabas forces a smile, commenting that the professor may be right. Defiantly, Barnabas moves into the sun's rays and stands shaking. Unable to watch Barnabas' agony any longer, Julia tells the visitors they must leave immediately. Willie leads a fragile Barnabas back up the stairs. Patterson again expresses his apologies and gives Woodard an annoyed look. Julia warns Woodard that if anything should happen to Barnabas, she will hold him personally responsible. Before Woodard reluctantly departs with Roger and Patterson, he tells Julia privately that he doesn't know what has just happened, but he intends to find out. She pretends ignorance, but he urges her not to throw her life away, warning her that Barnabas destroys everything he touches. Julia says only goodbye.

Outside the Old House, Patterson and Roger berate Woodard for making them all look like fools, but Woodard insists the facts haven't changed and that all the evidence still points to Barnabas. He declares that Barnabas has merely tricked them. Patterson orders Woodard to leave Barnabas alone until he finds hard evidence. Woodard hesitantly agrees although he's clearly lost in his own thoughts. Back in his room, Barnabas is being examined by a cautious Julia. Willie watches nervously as she injects Barnabas with more serum. Overwhelmed with relief, Barnabas' pain subsides and he falls asleep. Julia tells Willie that Barnabas should sleep until sundown and commands him to keep the room totally dark and to notify her should there be any change. She also warns Willie to keep an eye out for Woodard and to call the sheriff if he does show up again.

Later, Willie sits alone with Barnabas as he sleeps. He watches over him and talks about going fishing and water rafting with Barnabas when he's better. Upon hearing knocks from the front door, Willie is instantly panicked. He hurries out of the room. At the front door, he's relieved to find his aunt. Entering the foyer, Mrs. Johnson congratulates Willie on the refurbishing of the house. Willie notices she is holding a foil-wrapped package in her hands. He's thoroughly elated when she tells him she's brought him his favorite snack, nutloaf. Willie eagerly tears open the wrapping and takes a bite out of the loaf. Mrs. Johnson tells him how proud she is of him and that his late father would be too. She notices Willie's nervous behavior, but he insists nothing is wrong. He tells her he's very busy and thanks her for the nutloaf. As he leads her to the door, his aunt insists he must come by for dinner soon. Before she leaves she gives him a warm maternal kiss on the cheek.

In the Collinwood courtyard, Woodard arrives in his car and is greeted by Elizabeth at the front door. After being invited inside, Woodard confesses to Elizabeth that he, not the sheriff, was the one responsible for the confrontation with Barnabas at the Old House. Elizabeth tells the professor that he could have saved himself from embarrassment by bringing his suspicions to her first. Woodard nods in a conciliatory manner and asks if Julia is in. Elizabeth informs him that she's out by the lily pond. He walks through the drawing room and looks out the French doors to see Julia reading. Woodard sneaks up the stairs and into Julia's lab. He discovers a test tube of blood in her refrigerator and jumps back in shock after it explodes in his hand when he holds it up to the sunlight. He discovers a locked desk drawer and breaks it open with a lab tool. He finds Julia's private journal and scans through it while taking photos of the pages with a miniature camera. A few moments later he scurries back downstairs and encounters Elizabeth in the great hall. She asks if he found Julia, and he nervously replies that he did. He apologizes again. Elizabeth insists he's forgiven and says she'd like everyone to forget the entire unpleasant affair. Woodard expresses his gratitude and departs.

Later, Julia enters the drawing room from the terrace. Elizabeth stops her in the great hall and comments on how gracious it was for Woodard to drop by to apologize. But Julia tells a confused Elizabeth that Woodard didn't speak to her during his visit, adding that the professor has been acting a bit strange lately. Julia worriedly starts up the stairs. In her lab she discovers the broken test tube glass on the floor along with the powdery residue. She then notices that the lock on her desk has been broken. She's relieved to see her journal is still there, but upon opening it she realizes Michael has tampered with it. Fearfully talking to herself, she calls Michael a fool.

That night a storm rages while Julia visits Barnabas in the Old House drawing room. Barnabas has been told that Woodard knows everything. Julia defends her need to keep a medical journal. Barnabas rushes out to the foyer, exclaiming that he has business to tend to. Julia urges him to let her try to reason with Woodard, but Barnabas wants to deal with the professor himself. He summons Willie to escort Julia back to Collinwood. Willie is hesitant to go out in the downpour, but Barnabas is adamant. Julia offers a final plea but to no avail. At Woodard's cottage later, the fireplace roars as the storm continues outside. Having unsuccessfully tried to phone the sheriff, Woodard leaves another urgent message for Patterson to call. The phone and power lines go dead as the crack of thunder is heard and lightning flashes across the room. In the kitchen, Woodard retrieves a flashlight to examine the circuits in the breaker box. Suddenly a screech is heard as Woodard's frightened cat jumps from the top of the refrigerator. Then the wind begins blowing through the house. Woodard discovers the French doors in his upstairs bedroom are open. He quickly closes them. Hearing a sound, he descends the stairs to the living room and looks around nervously. Suddenly a hand shoots out, grabbing him by the throat.

Woodard finds himself staring at Barnabas, who tells Woodard that he's made a serious mistake and that the professor's curiosity will now bring him into Barnabas' bleak universe.

Episode 4.

Original Airdate: January 18, 1991.
(Aired January 25, 1991 in Pacific Time Zone)

Written by Dan Curtis, Steve Feke, Sam Hall.
Directed by Dan Curtis.

Character List: Barnabas Collins, Victoria Winters, Elizabeth Collins Stoddard, Roger Collins, Dr. Julia Hoffman, Willie Loomis, David Collins, Maggie Evans, Sarah Collins, Sheriff George Patterson, Professor Michael Woodard, Mrs. Sarah Johnson, Deputy Jonathan Harker, Angélique, Cafe Waiters & Customers, Villagers.

My name is Victoria Winters. Storm winds lash the great house of Collinwood and all within it. For a secret has been uncovered...a secret as ancient as the house itself, a secret that on this night will turn friend against friend, and death will claim one of them."

In her lab at Collinwood, Julia speaks on the telephone with Sheriff Patterson, who has called to inquire where Professor Woodard is. A concerned Julia confirms that Woodard was at Collinwood earlier in the day, but she doesn't know where he is at present. The sheriff agrees to pick her up to go searching. At Woodard's cottage, the sheriff's patrol car pulls up in the stormy darkness. At the front door, Julia and Patterson are surprised to be greeted by Woodard, who invites them inside. Patterson tells him he became worried since he'd been trying to reach him for several hours. The professor responds that the phone is out of service because of the storm. The sheriff wants to know what Woodard has to tell him, considering Woodard was trying to reach him all night before the phone went dead. Woodard tells Patterson that he's sorry, claiming he stumbled down another dead end. The sheriff wants an explanation. Julia notices that Woodard is avoiding eye contact with her. Woodard confirms he found a personal diary with information he thought would lead to the killer. Julia's face shows fear, but Woodard won't reveal anything further. Patterson mentions how Woodard had phoned Deputy Harker and told him that he photographed vital information that could identify the killer. Woodard confirms this but says it was all a mistake.

Upon learning that the film hasn't been developed yet, Patterson requests that Woodard give him the film. Woodard retrieves his camera from the desk and gives it to the sheriff, who removes the film, puts it in his pocket, and suggests he and Julia leave to get it developed. A nervous Julia glances at Woodard as they head for the door. From the rear, Woodard calls out to Patterson. When Julia and the sheriff turn around, they are shocked to see that Woodard's eyes have turned red. He snarls and lunges at Patterson after revealing two fangs. He hurls Patterson across the room, but Patterson manages to reach his revolver. After pulling the trigger repeatedly, he realizes the bullets are useless. Julia watches, frozen with horror. Suddenly she notices an African hunting spear on the wall. As the professor gains control over Patterson, he prepares to sink his teeth into the sheriff's neck. But Woodard lets out an agonizing scream as Julia rams the spear through his back.

Woodard struggles to his feet with the spear protruding from his back. Howling like a wild animal, he advances on Julia with his fangs bared. He grabs her and is about to bite her throat when Patterson jumps at Woodard's back. He jams the spear in deeper, forcing it to burst through the professor's heart, causing the vampire to drop to the floor, dead. Julia and Patterson look down in complete horror.

Later at the Collinsport police station, Patterson and Julia enter as Harker hangs up the phone. He reports to the sheriff that Dr. Fisher and the coroner have just taken Woodard's body to the hospital. Patterson gives him the roll of film, saying he wants it developed immediately. He also gives the deputy his bloodied coat, asking him to get rid of it. Harker leaves to carry out the requests. Patterson offers Julia a drink of coffee, and they go into his office. Later, Harker returns and tells the sheriff that Wally the deputy would like Patterson to come to the darkroom. Julia remains, nervously watching Patterson as he leaves the room. Moments later, the sheriff returns with a large folder. Patterson tells Julia to look at the contents. She hesitates, then slowly opens the folder to find a stack of blank photographic prints. Patterson informs her that the negative was exposed and that there was an image, but when the negative was put in the printer the image disappeared from the negative. Julia hides her feeling of enormous relief.

At Collinwood, Elizabeth sits alone in the drawing room by the fireplace. Roger enters and places a comforting hand on her shoulder, asking if she's all right. She says she's not sure. She feels as if a dark cloud has descended over their lives and fears their happy moments are gone. Roger concurs and kisses her cheek after Elizabeth mentions her pleasure over his being at Collinwood along with Carolyn and David.

In the Old House drawing room that night, Julia meets Barnabas, who informs her that he would have killed Woodard, but the professor chose otherwise. Julia prepares a syringe of serum. Barnabas rolls up his sleeve in anticipation. He tells her that Woodard's demise is for the best since it protects them both. Julia is appalled by Barnabas' insensitivity. Julia coldly administers the serum into Barnabas' arm. Softening his mood, Barnabas assures Julia that he's not without sympathy for her feelings. He says he knows Woodard was her friend but insists he wasn't the one who actually killed him. He informs her that the shot has had a calming effect with little pain. She points out that unless there are any more killings, he should now be safe from suspicion. Barnabas wonders if there has been a setback in the cure. Julia says there may have been, but she feels he can still spend limited amounts of time in the daylight. Barnabas tells Julia that he shares her guilt over Woodard's death. He holds her hands as he excitedly remarks that they must now share hope for the future and finish what they've started together. He crosses the room and retrieves Josette's music box. As its melody plays, he tells Julia that it was a gift he gave to someone he loved very dearly two hundred years ago. He smiles meaningfully at Julia when he says he looks forward to the day when he can give it to the woman who will take her place. Julia is clearly affected by his words.

In his room at Collinwood, David plays with Revolutionary War toy soldiers. As he maneuvers the figures on the play battlefield, several of the soldiers begin to move on their own. David grins and plays along, eventually calling out for the ghost of Sarah, who he knows is responsible. She appears and asks him what battle he's playing this time. He responds it's the battle of Bunker Hill on June 17, 1775. Sarah tells him it was called Breed's Hill then. David asks her which is better, now or then. She responds that now is different and that then was happier, at least for awhile. David says that he too can remember when it was happy at Collinwood, but that it was a long time ago. In the hallway, Victoria approaches, overhears the children's voices, and knocks on David's door. As she enters the room she sees only David sitting on the floor with his soldiers. She picks up one and asks where he got them. He tells her they're two hundred years old and that Sarah gave them to him. Victoria plays along with David's claim and asks if he gives Sarah things in return. He acknowledges that he's given several items to Sarah, including marbles and baseball cards, but he's uncertain what she does with them. Victoria suggests that someday she and David might exchange gifts. Flashing a devilish smile, David agrees. As she leaves the room, Victoria suggests David might write an essay about the soldiers.

In the hallway, Victoria starts toward the stairs but suddenly senses something and turns to see the figure of Sarah at the end of the corridor. Victoria heads toward the girl, who disappears through a closed door down another hallway. Victoria runs to the door and is stunned to find it locked. But she finds the key lying on the floor, inserts it in the lock, and opens the door which leads to the abandoned west wing. At the end of the dusty hall, Victoria spies Sarah waiting in an open room. Victoria enters and discovers she is in the west wing library, where Sarah sits at a desk looking through an old book. Victoria approaches the girl and identifies herself, but Sarah already knows who she is. Victoria asks Sarah what she is looking at. Sarah responds that she's reading about her brother Barnabas. Victoria stares in amazement as her curiosity grows. Sarah hands her the book, which Victoria discovers is the diary of Sarah Collins, from 1787. Looking up, Victoria realizes that Sarah has vanished. The sound of David's voice comes from the doorway. He smiles as he asks Victoria if she now believes that Sarah is real. He wants to know what Sarah gave her, and she tells him it's Sarah's diary. David responds that Sarah is trying to tell her that someone at Collinwood is going to get hurt, but he doesn't know who. Victoria and David make an agreement to tell each other whenever they see Sarah in the future. David thinks that no one else should know, especially Barnabas, who he still insists is evil. He runs from the room.

In the family cemetery, Victoria locates Sarah's small, weathered tombstone, listing her date of birth as 1781 and date of death as 1790. Later, Victoria walks along the beach with Barnabas on a sunny afternoon. She remarks that over two centuries of Collins children must have splashed in the waves. She suggests that perhaps some of their ghosts still come there to play. She and Barnabas express their hope that children's spirits have time to play. Reaching into her coat pocket, Victoria pulls out Sarah's diary and tells Barnabas she has a gift for him. He frowns when he recognizes it and sharply asks where she got it. He grabs her arm tightly, and Victoria pulls away. Gathering his composure, Barnabas apologizes for frightening her and informs her that he knows the book is the diary of his ancestor's little sister. Victoria explains that she found the diary in the library in the closed-off wing at Collinwood but refrains from revealing further details. Barnabas thanks her for giving it to him.

As they continue walking along the shore, Victoria mentions to Barnabas that he's told her about Josette and Barnabas, but he's never mentioned that Josette married someone else. Barnabas confirms that Josette married Jeremiah Collins, Barnabas' younger brother, a fact which Victoria learned from the Collins Family

History. Victoria mentions her curiosity over the marriage, and Barnabas assures her that although history may not report it as so, Josette really loved Barnabas. As they continue their walk, Sarah watches from the cliff above.

At dusk, a heavy rainstorm falls as Barnabas reads Sarah's diary in the Old House drawing room. Willie sits nearby, listening to an emotional Barnabas read a passage detailing a trip that he and Sarah took to the fair two hundred years ago. Barnabas admits that words cannot express how much he loved his sister. Willie tells him that Sarah sounds like a nice sister and asks how she died. Tears well in Barnabas' eyes as he responds that Sarah became very ill. Willie wonders if Barnabas believes David's stories about seeing Sarah. Barnabas corroborates David's claims, admitting to Willie that he too has seen Sarah's ghost. He also mentions that he believes that, although Victoria may have been unaware of it, Sarah must have led her to the diary. Barnabas is convinced that Sarah is trying to tell him something. He then discovers a piece of paper sticking out of a slit in the lining of the back cover. Barnabas frowns as he examines it. A curious Willie looks over his shoulder to see a miniature painting of a beautiful blond woman. Willie comments on the woman's attractiveness, but Barnabas doesn't respond. Suddenly he viciously crumples the painting in his hand and hurls it into the fireplace. Willie is puzzled by Barnabas' actions. As the flames consume the painting, the fire suddenly bursts forward. The face of the beautiful blond woman gradually materializes in the flames. Willie hides behind Barnabas, who watches defiantly as the woman's evil apparition emits a mocking laughter. The image begins to fade, and the fire settles down. Barnabas informs a trembling Willie that the woman's name is Angélique and that she is the true curse of his existence. Barnabas fearfully remarks that she is a force so evil and powerful that she is able to reach across the centuries to destroy him.

During the day, Victoria is teaching arithmetic to David in the Collinwood school room. As she goes over a multiplication problem, David is peeking into his desk. She orders him to reveal what he's concealing. He opens the desk and a small unframed painting of a sailboat lies inside. David reluctantly hands it to Victoria. She wants to know where he found it, and he replies that there are many paintings in a room where he's not supposed to go. After she promises not to tell his father, Victoria insists they should return the artwork. David leads her to the secret location. They go up the winding stairway to the third floor, where David takes Victoria to a locked room. Using a ring of old keys, he unlocks the door to an abandoned art studio. The cobwebbed room is filled with stacks of paintings and art supplies. Victoria flips through some of the canvases and is impressed with the beauty of the artwork. She's certain David knows who painted them, but he won't reveal anything. She discovers a draped, unfinished drawing of a nude blond-haired woman holding a baby in her arms. Victoria asks David if he has any idea who the subject of the painting is, but he shakes his head no. Suddenly, Roger bursts into the room and angrily asks how they got inside the studio. Victoria covers for David by telling Roger that the room wasn't locked. She claims it was her idea for David to show her around the upper floors. Roger retorts that she has no business doing that. David bolts out of the room. Victoria apologizes but insists they haven't disturbed anything. She mentions her admiration of the artwork. Roger irritably replies that her job is not to admire anything but to teach David. He chastises her for entering areas of the house and of the family's lives that don't concern her. As his anger subsides, he tells her that the room and everything in it no longer exist. After Victoria leaves, Roger stares at the draped portrait. At her studio, Maggie concentrates while sculpting the clay figure of a man's face. Abruptly, Roger enters, a look of torture on his face. The two embrace passionately.

At Collinwood, David slips quietly along the main upstairs corridor and into Roger's room. From the dresser he retrieves a handkerchief. He then removes several pipe cleaners from the desk and places them in a plastic bag. He adds strands of Roger's hair from a brush. At her studio, Maggie smokes a cigarette as she lies in bed with Roger, who asks her how long she's going to put up with him. She assures him she's with him indefinitely. Roger reminds her that she's the most important person in his life. Maggie asks what he'd do if Laura, his wife, ever came back. Roger doesn't want to talk about her, but Maggie points out that Laura is not like other people. In his bedroom, David has constructed a voodoo-type doll made from the items he collected from Roger's room. As if in a trance, David sets the doll on fire. At the same moment in Maggie's studio, Roger gasps in pain as he clutches his stomach. A terrified Maggie cries out as Roger says he's burning. In David's room, the boy watches the doll burn. Roger rolls onto the floor, and Maggie holds him. She sees a supernatural vision of the burning doll with David's face in the background. In David's room, Victoria suddenly enters and yells out to David as she extinguishes the fire. David comes out of his trance and looks around in confusion. At Maggie's studio, Roger's pain has gone away. As he stares at Maggie, he expresses his wonder at what has just happened.

In the Collinwood drawing room, Victoria tells Elizabeth about the fire and how David didn't appear to know what he was doing. She shows Elizabeth one of Roger's buttons which was on the burning doll. Elizabeth is visibly shaken trying to figure out David's behavior. She reveals to Victoria that David was expelled from the local school after he nearly burned it down. Mrs. Johnson enters to inform Victoria that Maggie is on the phone. Later that day, Victoria and Maggie meet at a restaurant at the Collinsport pier. Victoria is curious why Maggie felt it was urgent for them to get together. Maggie warns her she must be very careful with David. She claims the boy tried to kill his father. Victoria is incredulous as Maggie tells her about her own psychic abilities, which Victoria admits Carolyn has mentioned. Maggie tells how she saw a vision of David burning the doll and Victoria putting out the fire. Victoria is dumfounded. Maggie confesses she was with Roger during the incident and reveals that it almost killed him. She admits that they are having an affair and that Victoria is the only person she can turn to. She tells Victoria that David is being controlled by his mother. Victoria mentions that the boy's mother is in an institution in England, but Maggie replies that it doesn't matter. She believes Laura knows about her relationship with Roger and that she's trying to kill him because of it. Maggie insists that Laura is a witch with evil powers and warns Vicki to watch David very carefully whether she believes it or not.

At night in the Old House drawing room, Willie cheerfully carries in a large vase of flowers. An upbeat Barnabas has ordered a small dinner table for two in front of the fireplace. Barnabas enters and instructs Willie to place the flowers on the mantel. Barnabas' mood sours when he notices Sarah's diary on the table. Willie insists he doesn't know how it got there. Barnabas replies that he had put it away in his desk and gives Willie an irritated stare. After straightening a candelabrum and noting the time, Barnabas announces that Victoria will be arriving soon, and Willie assures him that the wine is chilled.

Suddenly, the windows blow open, and a large gust of wind blasts into the room. Lying on the table, Sarah's diary opens by itself, and the pages begin to flap in the wind. Willie reacts with fright as the fireplace starts to flare wildly. He closes the windows and summons Barnabas to observe the open diary. Sarah's writing begins to appear on a blank page. She spells out words of warning, telling her brother that he must stop his plans for the young girl with the dark hair. Otherwise, the writing states, the girl and Barnabas are in terrible danger. Barnabas picks up the diary as Willie asks what it all means. Barnabas angrily denies it means anything and storms across the room. But Willie isn't convinced. He realizes it is a warning from Sarah telling Barnabas to stay away from Victoria. Barnabas angrily pushes Willie against the door and tells him never to mention Sarah's name. Willie insists that he intends no harm; he's simply scared for Victoria and Barnabas.

Softening his mood, Barnabas lets Willie go and apologizes for his heated behavior. He assures Willie that he won't let anything happen to himself or Victoria. Willie wonders if Angélique is the one trying to hurt them. Barnabas says he doesn't know but declares that nothing is going to stop him from being like other men. He says that when Josette comes to him this time, things will be different. He takes Willie by the arm and tells him what a loyal friend he is, promising Willie that he won't forget it. Willie warmly responds that there's nothing he wouldn't do for Barnabas. Barnabas smiles and hands Willie the diary to return to the desk. Barnabas leaves to change clothes. Moments later in the study, Willie places the diary on Barnabas' desk. After he leaves the room, the book flips open to reveal the small painting of Angélique that was destroyed in the fire.

Episode 5.
Original Airdate: January 25, 1991.

Written by Matthew Hall.
Directed by Armand Mastrioanni.

Character List: Barnabas Collins, Victoria Winters, Dr. Julia Hoffman, Carolyn Stoddard, Willie Loomis, Joe Haskell, Maggie Evans, Sam Evans, Mrs. Sarah Johnson, Villagers.

My name is Victoria Winters. Evening has descended at Collinwood, and for one man it is an evening filled with the promise of hope. But tonight, betrayal awaits. The treachery of a confidante will shatter that hope. And his own true evil will be revealed."

It is nighttime at the Old House. In the drawing room, Barnabas and Victoria are seated at a table in front of the fireplace, having just finished dinner. Willie pours coffee. Victoria compliments him on the tasty dinner, but he confesses that his aunt prepared the squab. Barnabas dispatches him from the room, telling Willie that he and Victoria no longer require his services for the remainder of the evening. Victoria bids Willie goodnight as he leaves the room. She congratulates Barnabas on the tremendous improvement he's brought about in Willie. Barnabas presents her with a ribbon-wrapped gift box. Victoria is overwhelmed to find Josette's music box inside. She insists that it is an item too important to Barnabas for her to accept. But he insists that is why he wants her to have it. As the melody plays, Victoria stares dreamily at the box. After she mentions that she believes the song is a minuet, Barnabas convinces her to dance the minuet with him. They move slowly across the candlelit room and end the dance in an embrace.

The next day at Collinwood, Victoria plays the music box in her room. In the corridor outside, Julia hears the melody, and a curious look comes across her face. She enters Victoria's open room and is shocked to see the music box playing. She walks over to the table, closes the box, and picks it up. In her adjoining bathroom, Victoria notices the music has stopped and reenters her bedroom, surprised to find Julia holding the music box. Startled, Julia claims that she was curious when she heard the music playing. Pretending not to know its origin, she asks Victoria where the box came from. Victoria reveals that it was a gift from Barnabas. A tense Julia conceals her shock. Victoria comments that Barnabas has an old-world charm and admits the two of them are becoming close. Trying to gain her confidence, Julia prompts Victoria to confess that she's uncertain if she and Barnabas are in love. The tension grows as Julia agrees not to disclose the relationship of Victoria and Barnabas to anyone and encourages Victoria to confide in her in the future.

Outside the front of the Old House, Willie is chopping wood when Julia arrives looking for Barnabas. Willie tells her that he's walking in the woods, enjoying the daylight. Julia warns that too much sunlight could be dangerous, and Willie agrees. He remarks that he likes his aunt's blueberry hotcakes as much as Barnabas loves the sun. Julia asks Willie if he knows how much she cares for Barnabas. He replies that he does. Julia wants to know about Barnabas' relationship with Victoria, warning Willie that Barnabas' life may be at risk. A nervous Willie admits that he's been concerned about Barnabas' infatuation with Victoria. He takes Julia to Josette's room to show her the portrait of Josette, pointing out Victoria's strong resemblance to it. Julia is astonished at the portrait's resemblance to Victoria. Willie tells her who Josette was and how Barnabas believes that Victoria is her reincarnation. Willie discloses that Barnabas plans to marry Victoria. Astounded, Julia insists that it is impossible, claiming that emotional attachments can set back Barnabas permanently. But Willie explains that is why Barnabas is so eager to finish the experiments; he wants to be normal when he weds Victoria.

A door is heard slamming downstairs. Willie panics when he realizes it is Barnabas. He tells Julia he's afraid Barnabas will kill them if he finds them there. Willie grabs Julia and hustles her into the adjoining dressing room. Seconds later, Barnabas enters Josette's room, unaware that Willie and Julia are hiding a few feet away. He approaches the portrait and speaks to Josette, telling her how sweet it would have been if she were with him during his walk in the sunshine. He tells her that he read some of their favorite poetry and declares that he will soon be able to come to her again. Pausing a moment, he then leaves the room. A relieved Willie slips out of the dressing room and makes certain that Barnabas has gone. He tells Julia that he'll go downstairs and distract Barnabas so that she can leave the house unnoticed. Julia agrees; she stares at Josette's portrait as Willie cautiously departs.

In her lab at Collinwood, Julia writes in her journal that she has recently come to understand the true nature of the relationship between Barnabas and Victoria. She adds that unfortunately it has proven harmful to the successful completion of the experiment. Later, Julia mixes fluids from test tubes into a beaker. She has written additional comments in her diary. She feels that she must now put the experiment on hold, maintaining the subject at his current level. She has decided that she will never fully cure Barnabas until his relationship with Victoria is ended.

At the Collinsport pier, Carolyn drives into the parking lot next to Joe's fishing boat. Joe untangles his nets. She playfully asks permission to board. She salutes and steps on board with Joe's assistance. She congratulates him on his restoration efforts and convinces Joe to take her out on a cruise. Later that afternoon, the boat, named Daphne, floats at sea as Joe suns himself on the deck. Carolyn appears from the cabin, offering to prepare a lunch of potato chips and canned meat. Upon learning there's no can opener on board, she tosses the meat on the floor. She sits on top of Joe, planting a kiss on his face. Joe resists, commenting that she never changes. Carolyn insists he should relax and stop being so brave, trying to persuade him to start enjoying himself again. Joe starts to succumb to Carolyn's wishes but suddenly pulls away and declares that the cruise is over. He goes to the bridge to restart the engine as Carolyn maintains a determined expression on her face.

That night in Barnabas' room, Julia administers serum to Barnabas. Julia inquires how he feels. Barnabas replies that he possesses the joy of knowing that the old Barnabas Collins will soon fade into oblivion with a new one taking his place. While looking optimistically into the mirror, he's eager to know how much longer he must wait until he's a normal human again. Julia insists they must continue to practice moderation and not rush things. Barnabas puts his hands on her shoulders and looks at her with sincerity, telling her how he feels a sense of renewed life and rekindled emotions. He wants to feel alive, grow old, and die when the time comes.

At the Blue Whale, Carolyn and Joe sit in the near-empty establishment eating hamburgers. At the bar, Maggie is working on a crossword puzzle while Sam polishes glasses. Joe teases Sam about the hamburgers. Maggie suddenly stares at Carolyn and sees a vision of a hideously aged man and Carolyn screaming in horror. Maggie blinks and then sees a normal Carolyn still sitting with Joe. But again Maggie sees supernatural visions, including Barnabas' sarcophagus in the secret room of the mausoleum and Carolyn again screaming as the old man with fangs attacks her. Maggie is brought out of the trance by the voice of Sam telling her it's closing time. After Joe pays for the meal, a shaken Maggie tells him and Carolyn to be careful on their way home. Carolyn looks at her curiously and smiles as she grabs Joe, touting him as her protector. After they leave, Sam asks Maggie if something is wrong, but she shakes her head no.

At the front entrance of the Old House, Barnabas and Victoria hurry up the stairs as rain falls. They rush inside, and moments later they sit in front of the drawing room fireplace. Victoria remarks how much she loves the Old House. She marvels at its absence of electricity and telephones. Barnabas proudly responds that the house is just as it was during the eighteenth century. Barnabas' comment reminds Victoria to ask him if he will be attending Elizabeth's costume party. He confirms he'll be there. Victoria reports Elizabeth has told her that the Collins family always dress as their ancestors for the party. Both Victoria and Barnabas joke about who Barnabas will portray. He informs her that he and Willie have uncovered some old trunks in the attic which contain family clothing from the past. Victoria becomes excited when Barnabas says the collection probably includes some clothes she can wear.

In Josette's room, Victoria holds up a beautiful gown that once belonged to Josette. Victoria expresses her appreciation for the Collins family's deep sense of ancestry. She reveals to Barnabas that she is an orphan and doesn't know anything about her true family. She says she's always wondered what it would be like to know where she came from. She then looks at Josette's portrait, admitting that after Barnabas showed her the painting she felt a connection to someone for the first time because of her resemblance to Josette. Barnabas lovingly supports her feelings and assures her that Josette's dress will fit her. They return to the drawing room as the storm continues to rage outside. Looking out the windows, Victoria wonders how she will get back to Collinwood. Barnabas suggests that she spend the night at the Old House to avoid the storm. At first she is hesitant, but Barnabas convinces her that she should stay. He tells her that Willie will prepare the bed for her to sleep in Josette's room. He assures her that they'll get her back to Collinwood in the morning before anyone is awake.

Later in Josette's room, Victoria is dressed in an old-fashioned dressing gown. An emotional Barnabas bids her goodnight and departs, closing the door behind him. Victoria walks over to the fireplace and speaks to Josette's portrait. She says that since she's in Josette's room, wearing Josette's nightgown and sleeping in Josette's bed, she almost feels as if she really is Josette. In the drawing room, Willie anxiously asks Barnabas if he can do anything for him, but Barnabas declines and tells him to go to bed. He assures Willie that Victoria will be fine. Willie tries to pretend that he is not worried and reluctantly heads up the stairs.

In the drawing room, Barnabas sits by the fire reading an old book as thunder and lightning rage outside. He restlessly stares into the flames. In Josette's room, Victoria is sleeping soundly despite the howling storm. Still staring into the fireplace, Barnabas envisions the sight he saw earlier of Victoria wearing Josette's gown. Growing more restless, he walks to the windows and looks out at the storm. Turmoil builds in his face. He begins to pace about, clenching his hands. Unable to resist further, he departs, walks up the stairs, and enters Josette's room. He stands looking at the sleeping Victoria, torn by his raging emotions. He moves quietly to the side of the bed as his eyes flame with redness. He moves down towards Victoria with his mouth open and his fangs protruding from his mouth. About to sink his fangs into her neck, he resists with tremendous strain. Trembling, he stands upright and forces himself out of the room. Victoria, sleeping, remains unaware.

At the family cemetery minutes later, Barnabas and Willie battle the storm as they head to the mausoleum. They enter the secret room, and Barnabas commands a terrified Willie to chain him in his coffin. Willie dislikes the idea, but Barnabas insists it is necessary for Victoria's safety. He tells Willie to return with Julia, and the two men struggle to remove the coffin lid.

At Collinwood, Willie slips quietly up the stairs and into Julia's bedroom. He startles her by placing a hand on her shoulder and informs her that she must come with him immediately. At the cemetery, Willie leads Julia through the pouring rain into the mausoleum. In the secret room, Willie panics when he discovers Barnabas' coffin is empty. Suddenly, Barnabas emerges from the shadows. He wants to know what Julia has done to him. With fangs bared and eyes burning, he growls and hisses, pushing Willie away. Julia is terrified, but Barnabas demands an answer.

Julia declares she was only trying to help protect Barnabas from himself. Appearing as if he is going to attack, Barnabas' anger is explosive. Julia replies that his relationship with Victoria is dangerous and self-destructive. Barnabas grabs her face as Willie cowers in the corner. Barnabas is incensed that Julia has meddled with his affairs. Willie rushes over, trying to pull Barnabas off Julia, but a fierce Barnabas pushes him aside and orders Julia to explain further. She admits that she diluted the potency of the serum because she knew he would marry Victoria after he no longer required the treatments. She tells Barnabas that Victoria is wrong for him and that his romance with her would ruin the experiment. An enraged Barnabas declares that the experiments are over and demands a final injection of serum to end his affliction immediately. He admits he's willing to risk everything for Victoria. Tears fill Julia's eyes. Barnabas commands her to retrieve the necessary materials from her bag. She reluctantly obliges and injects a syringe of fluid into his arm.

The next morning the sun shines brightly as Barnabas sits over breakfast in the drawing room. Victoria enters and joins him, replying that she slept soundly. Willie pours a cup of coffee for Victoria. He offers to prepare eggs for her, but she declines, even though Barnabas comments on what a good cook Willie has become. Victoria says that she must get back to Collinwood, but Willie insists that she take time for toast and quickly leaves the room. As Barnabas reaches for his coffee cup, he notices that his hand appears to be shriveling. He abruptly pulls back his hand, spilling the coffee. As Victoria watches, he tells her he's being clumsy and assures her that he hasn't burned himself. He quickly hides his hand below the table.

Willie reenters with cinnamon toast for Victoria and suggests she should try it with strawberry jam. Barnabas worriedly glances at his concealed hands again and is stunned to see that both hands have become old and wrinkled. He thanks Willie for his hospitality and suggests Victoria should be getting back to Collinwood. He insists that Willie escort her. Victoria leaves the room to retrieve Josette's dress. Barnabas informs Willie to bring back Julia immediately. He shows Willie his deteriorating hands. Willie assures Barnabas that his face hasn't aged. Victoria returns, thanks Barnabas for her visit, and expresses her anticipation of wearing Josette's dress at the costume party. She is confused by Barnabas' aloofness. Willie leads her out of the room as Barnabas says goodbye, keeping his back to her. Alone, he stares in horror at his hideous hands.

Willie and Victoria quietly enter the great hall at Collinwood. Victoria thanks Willie and goes up the stairs. He waits for her to disappear before going upstairs for Julia. But he's interrupted by Mrs. Johnson, who is curious as to why Willie is visiting so early. She's pleased when he claims that he's come to see her. He makes up a story about wanting her advice for planting roses. She invites him to the kitchen for his favorite blueberry pancakes. He's severely tempted but overcomes the urge. His aunt tells him she'll come visit him in a few days and heads for the kitchen. Willie prepares to go upstairs, but Julia is already walking down. He hurriedly informs her of Barnabas' condition and insists she must treat him. Julia apologetically informs Willie she can no longer help Barnabas. Willie desperately pleads with her, trying to convince her that Barnabas didn't mean what he told her, but Julia won't change her mind. In extreme panic, Willie runs out of the house as a tormented Julia watches.

In the Old House foyer, knocks are heard coming from the front door, but no one answers. The door opens to reveal Carolyn stepping inside. She calls out for Barnabas and Willie. Looking around, she walks down the hall and into the drawing room. From behind, she sees Barnabas slumped in a high-backed chair facing the window. She calls out to him but receives no reply. As she approaches him, she apologizes for disturbing him, telling him that her mother wanted her to remind Barnabas about the costume party. There is still no response. Carolyn steps beside the chair and begins screaming hysterically when she sees Barnabas. His face has now taken on the appearance of a grotesque old man. He grabs Carolyn and pulls her down as he opens his mouth and sinks his fangs into her neck. Willie enters the foyer. He dashes to the drawing room at the sound of Carolyn's shrieking. He's horrified to see the ancient-looking Barnabas hunched over Carolyn's limp body, draining blood from her neck. Willie screams out to Barnabas, who immediately raises his blood-soaked face. Barnabas looks down at Carolyn, realizes what he's done, and lets out a wail of torment. He staggers to his feet and sits in the chair. He commands Willie to close the drapes in order to block the sunshine.

Suddenly his appearance begins to revert to normal. Willie watches in amazement, then rushes to the unconscious Carolyn. As he weeps, he futilely tries to clean the blood off her. He cannot believe Barnabas attacked her, but a dazed Barnabas insists he had no choice. Barnabas is distraught to discover he is once again not casting a reflection in the mirror. Willie is equally heartbroken. Barnabas slams a fireplace poker against the mirror, breaking it. He walks slowly over to Carolyn, raising his hand to her while calling out her name. Suddenly she opens her eyes and rises, with Willie's help. She walks to Barnabas as if in a trance. Barnabas places his hand on her arm and looks deep into her eyes. He tells Carolyn that she will soon walk with him as his partner in the night. He caresses her face and informs her that she will follow his commands, then places a soft kiss on her lips. Barnabas orders Willie to stay with Carolyn until she regains her strength. He is then to take her back to Collinwood. Barnabas instructs an obedient Carolyn that she is to tell no one what has occurred. With extreme fury, he tells Willie that Julia is responsible for the ordeal and insists that he will take revenge on her.

Episode 6.
Original Airdate: February 1, 1991.

Written by Jon Boorstin, Dan Curtis, Steve Feke.
Directed by Armand Mastrioanni.

Character List: Barnabas Collins, Victoria Winters, Elizabeth Collins Stoddard, Roger Collins, Dr. Julia Hoffman, Carolyn Stoddard, Willie Loomis, Joe Haskell, David Collins, Maggie Evans, Sarah Collins, Sheriff George Patterson, Mrs. Sarah Johnson, Angélique, Proprietor, Party Guests, Villagers.

My name is Victoria Winters. Tonight death will again come calling to the great house of Collinwood. And a young woman will embark upon a terrifying journey through the mists of time... a journey to unlock secrets buried for centuries deep within the high stone walls of the great house... secrets which unveil the truth behind the evil, the treachery, and the curse which haunts the Collins family."

The afternoon sun shines through the trees as Willie leads Carolyn down the path to Collinwood. Willie asks Carolyn if she is all right, but she doesn't answer. She stares blankly ahead. A silk scarf hides the fang wounds on her neck. Willie nervously sends her on her way. Inside the great hall she is greeted by Julia and Elizabeth, who wonders where Carolyn has been. She tells her mother that she had things to do and assures her that Barnabas will be at the costume party that evening. Elizabeth walks away. Julia watches Carolyn closely, telling her that she understood Barnabas wasn't feeling well. Carolyn coyly responds that he's feeling fine. She heads up the stairs, leaving Julia curious. In the second floor corridor, David leaps out from a stack of linen to scare Carolyn, but she walks straight on as if he weren't there. David watches in disbelief.

That night at the Old House, Barnabas sits in the drawing room, dressed in his eighteenth-century clothes. As he stares deeply into the fire, Willie enters. He's brought Barnabas his freshly ironed cape. After helping Barnabas put it on, Willie commends him on his appearance and remarks that it's a shame Barnabas cannot see himself in the mirror. Realizing he's said something he shouldn't, Willie apologizes. Barnabas suggests Willie leave for Collinwood but notices something is bothering him. Willie tells him that he's afraid Barnabas might harm Victoria now that he's reverted to his full-fledged vampire state. Barnabas assures him that he'll do everything in his power not to hurt Victoria. He says he'll find a way not to see her again. Willie departs to assist his aunt with preparations for the party.

At Collinwood, the festivities are in full force. In the great hall a crowd of costumed guests mingle and dance as a string quartet plays in the background. A long dining table has been positioned down the middle of the hall. Roger comments to Sheriff Patterson that nothing keeps the citizens of Collinsport away from an evening of free food and drink. Joe offers Carolyn a glass of champagne. Trance-like, she declines. With an emotionless stare, she tells a confused Joe that she is fine and walks away. The small ghost of Sarah watches unnoticed from the upstairs balcony. Willie offers Maggie hors d'oeuvres from a silver tray. As Joe walks up, Willie recommends the caviar. Julia approaches and greets a nervous Willie, who quickly walks off after offering her a canapé.

Julia catches up to Willie and asks how Barnabas is doing, wondering if he'll be at the party. Willie insists he can't talk at the moment and rushes off after seeing Barnabas enter. Worried, Julia suddenly notices Barnabas being greeted by Elizabeth and the sheriff. After Patterson escorts Elizabeth away, Carolyn walks up to Barnabas, and the two whisper to each other as Julia watches from the distance. Julia works up her nerve and walks over to them. She wishes them a good evening. Carolyn stares, says nothing, and walks off. Julia awkwardly tells Barnabas that she's relieved to see him. She says that she had wanted to come to his aid when Willie told her he was ill, but that she couldn't because she was angry and hurt. Barnabas sarcastically replies that he understands. Unsuccessfully she tries to convince him her concern is sincere. He assures her that her worries are unnecessary. She remarks that if the experiments are to continue, he must tell her what happened. But he reminds her of their last conversation in which he told her that he no longer required her services. Making certain that no one can hear them, Julia urges him to let her help him. Barnabas spurns her, claiming that she has made him once again what he was. He warns her that he will have his revenge on her. Julia, terrified, stares at him.

Barnabas walks toward the stairway as Victoria descends, escorted by David. She is wearing Josette's eighteenth-century dress. Barnabas is transfixed by her stunningly beautiful appearance. Julia observes the attraction between Barnabas and Victoria. After Victoria crosses over to Barnabas, she asks him if she looks like Josette. Barnabas takes her hand and replies that she *is* Josette. After a pause, Barnabas abruptly lets go of her hand, excuses himself, and walks away. Victoria is confused at his behavior.

Later in the evening, the guests dine at the massive table. Julia looks nervously at Barnabas, who stares back intently. Roger and Maggie give each other a private, affectionate glance. At the head of the table, Elizabeth taps a crystal glass with silverware and rises. She thanks everyone for being part of the annual Collinwood costume dinner party and offers a toast to the group. All raise their drinking glasses in return. Later on the terrace, Barnabas stands alone in the moonlight, staring into the misty fog. He is joined by Victoria. She compliments Barnabas on his costume, then asks him if there is something wrong. A pained Barnabas announces that he has something difficult to tell Victoria. She wonders why Barnabas has been avoiding her. He tries to continue speaking, but Elizabeth interrupts them. She asks Victoria if she'll put David to bed, commenting that he's running wild in the house. Victoria quickly walks inside. Elizabeth apologizes to Barnabas and asks if everything is all right. He assures her he's fine and tells her that his mind has been far away all evening. When she suggests he come inside to get warm, Barnabas tells Elizabeth that she reminds him of his mother. He recites a favorite childhood poem which Elizabeth happily recognizes and joins in. She mentions how grand it would be to be a child again. Barnabas wistfully remarks that he would give anything to be young again. After Elizabeth heads inside, Barnabas' face grows sad as he looks off into the dark night.

Later in the drawing room, most of the party guests have departed. Maggie sits in front of an Ouija board on the table as Elizabeth watches. Maggie describes how the mystical game works. She says that she and Roger will keep their eyes closed. She explains that anybody can ask anything they want, and if the board can't answer with a yes or no then it will answer using the alphabet. Roger jokingly asks if the state of Maine will ever secede from the Union and name Collinsport as its new capital. Elizabeth urges him to be serious and Maggie laughs. Barnabas enters from the terrace. Maggie instructs Roger to close his eyes, and the two place their fingers on the Ouija board indicator. With their fingers touching it, the piece moves gradually over the board and stops on the word "no." Roger laughs after he and Maggie open their eyes. She asks if someone has a real question. The sheriff says he does. He wants to know if the person who caused all the recent troubles in Collinsport is still around. The relaxed atmosphere in the room becomes tense, and Barnabas shows concern. Elizabeth tries to dissuade George from pursuing his query, but Roger interjects that the question is legitimate. Carolyn rises and walks over to the table as Elizabeth bemoans bringing up unpleasant memories.

Again Roger and Maggie close their eyes as Patterson repeats his question. This time the piece stops on the word "yes," drawing attention from Joe. Barnabas shoots a quick look at Carolyn. Roger denies Elizabeth's accusation that he purposely moved the indicator. Elizabeth finds the game ridiculous, but Roger responds that he's beginning to find it interesting. Patterson continues his Ouija questioning. He asks if the person who caused the trouble is someone they know. Elizabeth announces that the indicator is not moving and that it's time for the game to end. A persistent Roger suggests it may not be moving because the answer is yes. He encourages Paterson to ask for a name. Julia glances nervously at Barnabas. The sheriff asks what letter the killer's name begins with. Barnabas stares intently at the board. The indicator drags Maggie's and Roger's hands across the top of the Ouija board. It circles wildly. Everyone watches in fascination. Carolyn glances nervously at Barnabas. Suddenly the indicator settles on the letter "C." Roger asks if the letter represents a first or last name, commenting that there are a lot of C's in the room.

Barnabas' concern grows as he fixes his eyes upon Carolyn. Patterson asks if the letter "C" belongs to the attacker's last name. The indicator confirms that it does. Roger jokes that he has an alibi. He and Maggie urge Patterson to continue. Elizabeth states she doesn't see the humor in the activity and wants it stopped. Roger asks the board which letter the first name of the attacker begins with. The indicator starts moving back and forth on the bottom of the board while the spectators watch, mesmerized. Barnabas concentrates his powers on Carolyn. Before the indicator settles on a revealing letter, she steps forward and shoves the Ouija board to the floor. She proclaims that the whole thing is stupid. Elizabeth chides her for behaving like a wild animal. Carolyn replies that she cannot believe everyone is taking the game seriously. She storms out of the room. Roger sarcastically apologizes to Patterson, commenting that they almost had the killer's identity. Roger concedes that the party is over, bids everyone goodnight and leaves. Barnabas directs a private, deadly stare at a concerned Julia.

Later that night, Barnabas approaches Collinwood from the woods. In her bedroom, Carolyn sleeps as the wind blows through her open windows, billowing the curtains. Suddenly her eyes snap open. Outside, Barnabas hisses, showing his fangs. Carolyn slowly sits up, gets out of bed, and walks trance-like out of the room. Outside, Carolyn walks through the moonlit formal gardens towards a waiting Barnabas. As she goes into his arms, he caresses her face. She unbuttons his shirt and massages his chest. As she leans ecstatically against him, he opens his mouth and sinks his fangs into her neck. Carolyn writhes in ecstasy as blood runs down her neck.

During the following day, Carolyn and Joe leave Collinwood and walk toward his car in the courtyard. An almost listless Carolyn wears a scarf around her neck. Joe asks her if their trip is necessary. He wonders if she is feeling all right and comments that she's been acting strangely. Carolyn replies that she is fine, but Joe isn't convinced. He wants them to go to his boat, but Carolyn declines and gets into Joe's car.

In Collinsport, Carolyn and Joe walk along the waterfront. Carolyn looks in the window of an antique store and goes inside with Joe following. The elderly proprietor greets them. Carolyn informs the old man that she's interested in the apothecary case displayed in the window. The proprietor retrieves the case and brings it to the counter, telling Carolyn it's a rare eighteenth-century artifact. Joe is skeptical, wondering why Carolyn would want such an item. Without an explanation, she orders Joe to buy it. He bargains for the price, finally offering thirty-five dollars. The proprietor warns them that some of the old bottles contain poison that is still deadly.

In the great hall at Collinwood, Mrs. Johnson is carrying a tray of tea. Carolyn intercepts and offers to take the tray. Mrs. Johnson gives it to her, requesting her to tell Elizabeth that she'll be in momentarily with sandwiches. Carolyn carries the tea into the drawing room where Elizabeth and Julia are visiting. After Carolyn pours Julia's tea, she secretly adds a packet of arsenic to the cup. As Julia is about to drink it, David comes racing into the room, screaming at Julia not to drink her tea. He insists that it is poisoned. Carolyn watches silently as Elizabeth scolds David for his behavior. But he persists in saying that Julia's tea is poisoned, revealing that Sarah told him. Elizabeth apologetically tells Julia that David is acting out another of his pranks. Julia raises the cup to her lips. David suddenly knocks it out of her hands. Elizabeth is shocked and angered by David's actions and orders Carolyn to take him to his room. David insists he couldn't let Julia drink her tea. He then apologizes to Julia before Carolyn escorts him out.

Julia assures Elizabeth that no harm has been done. Upstairs in the corridor, Carolyn is clutching David. He breaks away from her, declaring he can get to his room by himself. He tells Carolyn that she's been behaving spooky lately. She stares at him. In his room David finds Sarah He tells her that he hopes she is correct, because he's in trouble over what he did.

Carolyn gazes into the mirror in her room, adjusting the scarf around her neck. Julia knocks on the door and enters. She comments on David's odd behavior, but Carolyn implies that David always behaves strangely. Julia notices an agitated expression on Carolyn's face as she adjusts her scarf. She asks how Carolyn is feeling. Clearly annoyed, Carolyn retorts that she's fine but is tired and would rather not discuss David or her health at the moment. Julia responds that she'd like to speak to her about Barnabas. She wants to know what is happening between Carolyn and him. Carolyn turns on her stereo, and loud music fills the room. She denies anything is going on between her and Barnabas. Julia turns off the stereo. Carolyn discards the pretense when Julia asks her why she broke up the Ouija session. Carolyn angrily counters by asking Julia why she tried to hurt Barnabas. Julia feigns ignorance. The tone of Carolyn's voice becomes threatening as she lights a match and warns the doctor that she will be sorry for what she's done. She orders Julia out of the room.

After dark, Barnabas stands at the edge of the woods. He bares his fangs as he stares toward Carolyn's room. Carolyn lies asleep. She acknowledges Barnabas' summons and rises. In a trance-like state, she walks to the door. Moments later in the kitchen, Carolyn enters as if sleepwalking. She crosses to a knife rack and withdraws a large, sharp butcher knife. She walks up the stairway as Barnabas remains outside, forcing his will upon her. Carolyn enters Julia's room, approaches the bed, and plunges the knife repeatedly into the figure under the covers. As she heads for the door, she's startled by the appearance of Julia, who rips the scarf from Carolyn's neck to reveal Barnabas' fang marks. Carolyn screams in agony and rushes out of the room.

Minutes later at the Old House, knocks are heard coming from the front door. In his sleeping attire, Willie comes running down the stairwell and opens the door. Julia forces her way into the foyer and demands to see Barnabas. Willie is terrified; he doesn't know what to do. He tells Julia's that she's making a big mistake and warns her to leave immediately. But she's determined to see Barnabas. Barnabas appears at the top of the stairs. Julia moves up the stairs, demanding an explanation from him. She wants to know why he is trying to kill her. She declares that she has never betrayed him. Barnabas walks slowly down the stairs, replying that she was responsible for turning him into a loathsome two-hundred-year-old man. He remarks that Carolyn was in the wrong place at the wrong time, adding that attacking Carolyn was the only way he could reverse the aging process. He insists the entire series of events is Julia's fault and refuses to listen to her rebuttal. He grabs her, twists her head viciously to the side, and opens his mouth with fangs bared.

As he is about to sink his teeth into Julia's neck, Willie comes running up, but Barnabas hurls him to the floor. Before Barnabas can attack Julia, Sarah appears at the top of the stairs, imploring Barnabas to not harm Julia. He releases Julia. Barnabas, overcome by emotion, kneels down in front of Sarah as tears fill his eyes. He's overwhelmed that she has come back to him. Sarah says he must understand that some people want to help and that he must not hurt them. Tears stream down Barnabas' face. He promises he will never again do anything to make her run from him. Sarah takes his head in her hands and strokes his hair. Julia and Willie watch with astonishment. Tears run down Willie's face.

Sarah warns that unless all that has happened can be changed, then Barnabas and everyone at Collinwood will be lost forever. Barnabas doesn't understand. Sarah replies that someone must go back. Suddenly she is interrupted by the sound of maniacal laughter filling the room. Floating above them, the ghostly apparition of Angélique appears. A howling wind roars through the house as the laughter grows louder. Moments later the turmoil dies down, and Angélique's spirit disappears. A badly shaken Barnabas notices that Sarah has disappeared. He looks at the empty stairs, calling for his sister to return. Julia asks Barnabas for an explanation of what they just experienced. Barnabas' anger turns to resignation. He reminds Julia that he once told her there are forces in the world that are evil beyond comprehension. He informs Julia that they've just seen Angélique, remarking that even time cannot destroy her.

Julia insists they must attempt to learn why Sarah was trying to warn them. Barnabas reveals that Sarah is frightened of him because of something that happened long ago. Julia suggests she knows someone who can help them contact Sarah's spirit. The next day at the Collinwood lily pond, Julia speaks with Maggie about the possibility of conducting a séance. She informs Maggie that she has told Roger and Elizabeth the truth and that they have reluctantly agreed with Julia's plan to contact Sarah, adding that Victoria's corroboration of seeing Sarah helped convince them. Upon prompting from Maggie, Julia also confirms that Barnabas is willing to be part of the séance. Maggie announces that the ceremony will be held after dark.

That night, a fierce storm rages over Collinwood. In the middle of the great hall, a round table has been set up in front of the fireplace. Sarah's portrait sits on the table. Victoria enters from the drawing room carrying the Collins Family History. Maggie, Elizabeth, Roger, Julia, Carolyn, and Barnabas are seated around the table. Maggie mentions that familiar objects can be helpful in making contact during the séance. Victoria sits and places the book in front of herself on the table. Maggie urges everyone to concentrate on Sarah. Roger remarks that he finds it very difficult to believe they are conducting a ceremony to contact a little girl who died two hundred years ago. He sarcastically suggests they try to reach Abraham Lincoln instead. Elizabeth gives him a stern look, reminding him that they all agreed to the séance. Maggie instructs everyone to place their hands on the table so that everyone touches in an unbroken circle. Everyone responds except Carolyn, who is sitting next to Barnabas. He prompts Carolyn to complete the circle. Roger asks Maggie how they will know when Sarah makes contact. He's curious if they will see her. Maggie replies that actual physical appearances are rare. She feels the most they can hope for is a voice or some other signal. Elizabeth wonders if there's anything else they should be aware of before they begin. Maggie informs her that should Sarah's spirit come to them, they must be careful not to scare her away with negative thoughts.

Maggie begins the ceremony, saying that they have gathered to contact another world. Maggie asks Sarah to speak out and send a message to those who are in danger. She begs Sarah to help everyone understand the forces that are trying to destroy the inhabitants of Collinwood. Maggie reiterates her plea as thunder and lightning penetrate the dark, candlelit room. Suddenly a moaning wind gusts through the great hall. Victoria's eyes shut as Sarah begins to speak through her. As everyone stares at Victoria, Maggie urgently instructs the others to keep their hands touching. Maggie speaks to Sarah, again asking for her help. Still communicating through Victoria, Sarah confirms that there is evil at Collinwood and warns that everyone will die unless someone changes things. Victoria's body trembles. Suddenly a deafening clap of thunder drowns the room, and a powerful gust of wind blows out the candles. In the darkness, Victoria clutches the history book and screams wildly. Roger jumps up to turn on the lights, and everyone turns to stare at Victoria. They are stunned to see that in her place is a strange young woman dressed in eighteenth-century clothing. Disheveled and bewildered, she collapses on the floor. The group gathers around the unconscious stranger. Elizabeth cries out, wondering where Victoria has gone. Barnabas fearfully stares at the unknown woman.

Later, the unknown woman lies resting in a Collinwood bedroom as Julia examines her. Maggie and Barnabas stand watching while Carolyn, Elizabeth and Roger sit on a sofa. Julia announces that the stranger's vital signs are normal. She speculates that the girl was in some kind of accident and reports that she's still in deep shock. Elizabeth asks Maggie if she has an explanation for what's happened. Maggie believes that a transference of entities has taken place. She thinks that Victoria is now where the stranger came from. Barnabas worries. Maggie further comments that if anything should happen to the unknown woman, they probably won't be able to get Victoria back. After looking through the stranger's traveling satchel, Roger finds a letter, which he reads aloud. The document is a letter of recommendation for a governess named Phyllis Wicke. Dating from the year 1790, the parchment letter is addressed to Joshua A. Collins. Everyone is stunned when they realize Victoria has traveled back in time to take Phyllis Wicke's place in 1790. David enters the room and confirms their suspicions, announcing that Sarah has told him about Victoria. Barnabas' face registers an alarming concern.

Episode 7.
Original Airdate: February 8, 1991.

Written by Jon Boorstin.
Directed by Paul Lynch.

Character List, 1790 Scenes: Barnabas Collins, Naomi Collins, Josette Du Prés, Victoria Winters, Reverend Trask, Natalie Du Prés, Millicent Collins, Ben Loomis, Peter Bradford, Daniel Collins, Sarah Collins, André Du Prés, Abigail Collins, Angélique, Joshua Collins, Jeremiah Collins, Crone, Girl, Workmen.
1991 Scenes: Barnabas Collins, Elizabeth Collins Stoddard, Roger Collins, Dr. Julia Hoffman, Carolyn Stoddard, Willie Loomis, Joe Haskell, Maggie Evans, David Collins, Phyllis Wicke.

My name is Victoria Winters. A séance in the great house at Collinwood has torn a hole in the fabric of time, merging past and present... drawing one woman down through the centuries, offering up another in her place. Now those left behind strive desperately to unlock the mystery of those crossed destinies and the terrible threat they contain."

A violent storm rages in the darkness outside the Old House. In the drawing room Barnabas stares out the windows as Julia and Willie enter. At Julia's prompting, Barnabas admits he knew Phyllis Wicke two hundred years earlier when she was engaged as tutor to the Collins children. He reveals that when she first arrived she had had an accident on the road and appeared just as she did when she showed up at the séance. He says that although Phyllis survived the accident, she died soon after from a fever. Willie begins to panic, fearing that the same thing will happen to Victoria. Barnabas is speechless as he resumes staring out at the storm.

In the year 1790, Victoria walks up the stairs in front of the Old House on a sunny afternoon. The house appears new, with a lush, manicured lawn and planter boxes full of blooming flowers. Clutching the Collins Family History, Victoria stares in amazement. Two young children, a boy and a girl, suddenly rush out from the side of the house. The girl accidentally runs into Victoria, who recognizes her as Sarah. Victoria believes the boy is David, but he tells her that his name is Daniel. He declares that Victoria must be the new tutor and asks if the volume she's holding is a new lesson book. Victoria is totally perplexed.

A man's voice calls out to the children, and Victoria is pleased to see Barnabas come from the house. She confuses Barnabas when she calls out his name. He does not know who she is but asks if he can be of any assistance. She wonders why he, like the children, is dressed in eighteenth-century clothes. Looking at her a bit oddly, Barnabas apologizes for staring. He explains that she resembles his fiancé, for whose arrival he is awaiting. Victoria mentions Josette's name and remarks that if she is having a dream, it is an incredibly real one. Daniel tells Barnabas that she is the new tutor, which Victoria confirms and gives her name. Barnabas comments that her style of dress is rather unusual. He welcomes her into the house. The children accompany them. Walking through the foyer, Victoria is fascinated to see that the interior looks almost the same as it did when she last saw it. Barnabas escorts her to the drawing room. A hand is seen holding a tarot card on the table. The wicked woman card has been drawn. Barnabas introduces Victoria to his mother Naomi as the new tutor. Victoria is startled to see that Naomi bears a striking resemblance to Elizabeth. She's equally amazed when Barnabas introduces her to the other two women in the room, his aunt Abigail Collins and the countess Natalie Du Prés. Abigail looks exactly like Mrs. Johnson, and Natalie is identical to Julia. Victoria calls the women by the names of their twentieth-century counterparts. Everyone stares at her with bewilderment.

Naomi is alarmed by Victoria's strange behavior, and Barnabas reiterates that she claims to be the new tutor. Observing Natalie's fascination with Victoria, Barnabas realizes she too has noticed Victoria's resemblance to Josette. Natalie walks over to Victoria to get a closer look. She admits that Victoria resembles Josette but insists that Josette has noticeably more delicate features. An intrigued Barnabas assures his mother, who's never met Josette, of their close similarity in appearance. Abigail, who has been watching Victoria with a suspicious eye, requests Victoria to repeat her name. Naomi asks what has happened to the tutor they hired named Phyllis Wicke. Victoria doesn't know what to say. Barnabas has been studying Victoria very closely and intervenes on her behalf. He suggests to his mother that it is not an appropriate time to ask questions of Victoria since she has apparently had a long and difficult journey. Natalie agrees that Victoria should rest and offers to help her find a more suitable dress, suggesting that one of Angélique's may suffice. She leaves the room with Victoria, whom Barnabas is watching with eyes transfixed.

Upstairs in Natalie's bedroom, the Du Prés' maidservant, Angélique, buttons up a simple maid's dress on Victoria. Angélique stares curiously at her as Natalie and Abigail stand by. Natalie asks Angélique if she notices Victoria's resemblance to Josette. Angélique readily confirms she does, but Natalie attempts to downplay the resemblance. Victoria asks her when Josette is to arrive. Natalie replies that

Josette will be in town soon since Josette's marriage to Barnabas is less than two weeks away. An excited Victoria expresses her enthusiasm for meeting Josette. While Natalie decides that the maid's dress will suffice for Victoria, Abigail picks up Victoria's twentieth-century dress and examines it. She discovers the washing instructions label inside and is puzzled by the symbols on it. Surprised by Abigail's confusion, Victoria explains that the instructions suggests the garment should be machine washed, tumble dried, and pressed with a cool iron. Abigail has no idea what Victoria is talking about. She's further dumfounded to see a zipper, which she refers to as metal stitchery. She wants to know where Victoria has come from.

Uncertain of how she should respond, Victoria says she can tell them where she is from if they tell her where she is. Convinced that Victoria is afflicted with a mental disorder, Abigail informs her that she is at the Collins estate near the village of Collinsport. Victoria accepts the information but is puzzled by the news that the town is part of the Territory of Massachusetts. Natalie sarcastically comments that the area is overrun by bears, snakes, and savages. Angélique watches silently. Her concern growing, Victoria inquires as to what year it is. Abigail is astonished at Victoria's question. Natalie informs her that it is the year 1790. Victoria cannot believe what she has heard. She smiles and makes a reference to the children's fantasy story *Alice In Wonderland*, asking where the Mad Hatter and Queen of Hearts are. Natalie and Abigail look at each other in amazement. The countess suggests Victoria should get some rest. Natalie instructs Angélique to prepare Victoria's bed. Victoria doesn't want to rest, but Abigail advises her to do so, assuring her they'll see that she ends up where she belongs. The women depart from the room and close the door, leaving Victoria alone. She hears Abigail in the hallway remarking that Victoria is insane and that she will have Joshua summon the bailiff. In shock, Victoria crosses the room. Looking out the window, she decides she must get back to Collinwood.

On the Collinwood grounds, Victoria rushes along a dirt path up to the house. She is unnerved to see that the mansion is under construction. She enters the house through the main doorway. She walks into the great hall where workmen are busy painting and chiseling. Becoming thoroughly demoralized, she approaches the massive fireplace and speaks out to God begging for help. She suddenly realizes that she may be able to get back where she belongs the same way she arrived, through a séance. Looking around, she finds a barrel and moves it to the exact spot where she was sitting during the séance in 1991. She takes a deep breath and closes her eyes tightly.

Upon opening her eyes, she is distraught to see that nothing has changed. She shuts her eyes and calls out to Sarah, pleading for her help. She hears a man's voice tell her that she can find Sarah in the nursery. Frightened, Victoria turns around to discover a young man who strongly resembles Joe from 1991. He introduces himself as Peter Bradford. He appears intrigued by Victoria's uneasiness. He informs her that Joshua Collins will be moving the Collins family into the mansion in a few days. Victoria recalls that Joshua is Barnabas' father. Peter tells her that Barnabas and Barnabas' brother Jeremiah are his closest friends. Beginning to realize the impact of her predicament, Victoria bursts into tears. Peter apologizes, thinking he's said something to upset her. Victoria assures him that he's done nothing wrong. She reveals her name. Peter asks if she has been accidentally hit on the head. She tells him she's the tutor but mixes up David's name with Daniel's. She reports that those she met upon her arrival were kind to her but think she is mad. A concerned Peter assures Victoria that she is not insane and asks if there was talk of the bailiff. Victoria nods that there was. Peter replies that under the circumstances she must not go back to the manor house. He warns that if the family thinks she is mentally unsound they will ship her off to a madhouse.

Victoria replies that she must stay at Collinwood, insisting it may be her only chance to get back. A mystified Peter tells her that he will not try to understand what she has said but stresses that she must convince the Collins family she is sane if she expects to stay. Since Daniel already thinks Victoria is his new tutor, Peter instructs Victoria that she will be the new tutor. Peter leads a confused Victoria into the unfinished drawing room. From a work desk, he locates a quill pen, a bottle of ink, and paper. He begins to write a letter of introduction for Victoria to present to Joshua. The letter is written as if it were penned by Victoria's previous employer. Peter warns Victoria that Joshua is quite stern and suggests that if she has any trouble she should enlist Barnabas' assistance. Peter vows that Barnabas can be a staunch and loyal friend and promises to speak to him on Victoria's behalf. He again stresses that should Joshua decide she is mad then nothing will change Joshua's mind. Victoria's face registers an expression of alarm.

Later in the Old House drawing room, Joshua finishes reading Victoria's letter of recommendation, describing it as impressive. Barnabas, Naomi, Abigail and Natalie are also present. Abigail staunchly asks Victoria what has become of Phyllis Wicke. Victoria claims she doesn't know, saying she heard only that Phyllis wasn't able to come so she took the liberty of traveling to Collinsport to see if she could serve in Phyllis' place. Joshua continues to peruse the letter, commenting that the handwriting looks familiar. Barnabas speculates that perhaps Joshua has seen the writing before on a bill of sale. A young man in his early thirties enters the room, inquiring if Victoria is the pretty young lady who has been causing a commotion. Barnabas smiles and introduces Victoria to his younger brother, Jeremiah, whom he deems irrepressible. Jeremiah takes Victoria's hand, and with a grand eighteenth-century flourish, brings it to his lips. Joshua grumpily intervenes, informing Jeremiah there is business being conducted. Jeremiah humorously apologizes to his father for his lack of restraint.

Turning her suspicious eyes on Victoria, Abigail blurts out that earlier in the day Victoria didn't even know what year it was. In her defense, Victoria claims that she was dazed after falling from a horse. But Abigail continues to assert that Victoria didn't fall because she has no cuts or bruises. She tries to convince her brother, Joshua, that Victoria is insane and insists Barnabas can verify Victoria's mental instability. However, Barnabas refuses to support his aunt's allegations. Joshua begins to interrogate Victoria. She assures him that she is well educated in grammar, penmanship and mathematics. She is perplexed when Joshua orders her to open her mouth. After a repeated command, she complies.

Joshua peers inside and comments that Victoria's teeth appear to be sound. An appalled Naomi reprimands Joshua for his tactics. He reciprocates that it is important to examine Victoria. He informs Victoria that she is hired, contingent on the children's approval. Barnabas objects to his father's offer to pay Victoria thirty dollars a year along with room and board. But Victoria, relieved at being accepted, insists that Joshua's terms are fine. He retorts by telling her not to gloat, warning that she will be watched. Victoria glares at Abigail, who is watching her with mean-eyed scrutiny.

Later, Victoria is organizing the Old House schoolroom when Barnabas enters. She thanks him for his support. He notes that Peter has taken a liking to her. He then proceeds to warn Victoria of his aunt Abigail. He explains that although she might appear eccentric, she can actually be quite dangerous. Victoria assures him that she'll be careful. Barnabas asks if there's anything she'd like to tell him. Victoria doesn't know where to begin. Barnabas wants to know how she knew his and Josette's names before they met. Victoria doesn't answer. Barnabas reveals that there is something about Victoria that makes him feel they have met before, possibly in another place and another time. She replies that he must feel that way simply because of her resemblance to Josette. Barnabas acknowledges she may be correct. He bows and leaves the room.

That night, Victoria is in her bedroom, a small room in the servant's quarters. She hurriedly hides her twentieth-century dress and the Collins Family History in the dresser as Angélique knocks on the door. She enters carrying newly altered dresses for Victoria, who apologizes to Angélique for taking her dresses. Angélique informs her that the situation will be remedied when her mistress arrives. Victoria is surprised to learn that Natalie is not Angélique's mistress. Angélique reveals that she serves Josette, which has been intended ever since they were children together in Martinique. She reveals that her mother was servant to the Du Prés family for many years. Victoria is eager to learn more about Josette. Angélique admits Josette is lovely and assures Victoria that she'll like her because everyone else does. Victoria thanks Angélique for her help and asks if she's staying in the room next door. Angélique affirms her location and invites Victoria to notify her should she need anything. However, she requests not to be interrupted tonight. She implies a romantic liaison is planned.

Later, Barnabas sits in his bedroom, reading by the fire. A seductive Angélique appears, closing the doors behind her. Displeased to see her, Barnabas tells Angélique she should not be in his room. Angélique answers that she is tired of waiting for an invitation. She lets her dress fall, revealing her underwear. She walks over to Barnabas and sits beside him, insisting that he has been waiting for her visit ever since she came to the house. Denying such thoughts, Barnabas asks why Angélique persists in pursuing him, emphasizing that she knows he loves Josette. Angélique slyly remarks that he said that once before. She moves closer to him, asking if he remembers how it feels when they touch. Barnabas takes her by the arm and pushes her away, demanding to know why she ignores his refusals.

Looking defiantly into his eyes, Angélique mentions that she remembers Martinique and insists that Barnabas also remembers. He counters that things were different then, claiming their affair would never have happened if Josette hadn't gone to France. Angélique accuses Barnabas of lying. But Barnabas persists in his defense, declaring he thought at the time he would never see Josette again. Angélique places a smoldering kiss on his lips. She tells Barnabas she can take him places where Josette has never been. They kiss again. She begins to loosen the lacings of her underwear. Barnabas succumbs to her sensuality, and the two passionately embrace.

The next day, Victoria runs up the steps leading to the entrance of the Old House, along with Daniel and Sarah. At the top of the stairs on the terrace, Peter is talking with Barnabas and Jeremiah. Peter is the first to greet Victoria. After she follows the children into the house, Peter comments that Victoria should sit next to him at the wedding. A teasing Jeremiah interjects that he has other ideas. Smiling, Peter asks Jeremiah when his fiancé is to arrive. Jeremiah replies that he hopes she does not. Peter continues to needle Jeremiah, reminding him of Joshua's plans to have his two sons participate in a double wedding. Barnabas mockingly asks Jeremiah how he can be so certain that Millicent Collins is an unacceptable bride since Jeremiah hasn't seen her since she was twelve years old. Jeremiah recalls her having pimples on her face and gaps between her teeth. Barnabas suggests that even if Millicent is ugly, in time Jeremiah may learn to love her. Peter adds that at least Jeremiah might love Millicent's wealth, jokingly suggesting Joshua would approve of that. The three men laugh heartily.

At the Old House stables, Jeremiah and Barnabas witness the arrival of Millicent's stagecoach, driven by Collins family servant Ben Loomis. The coach, covered with trunks, comes to a halt. Barnabas hastily hands Jeremiah a bouquet of wildflowers he has gathered for Jeremiah to present to Millicent. Jeremiah watches as a young woman looks out and her hat falls off. She steps out as Jeremiah hastily retrieves her hat and welcomes her. He introduces her to Barnabas, who reminds Jeremiah to give Millicent the flowers. Upon presenting her with the bouquet, she promptly informs Jeremiah that in the future he should remember that her favorite flower is a red rose. Barnabas laughs. Jeremiah acknowledges her request. Throwing a bemused look at Barnabas, Jeremiah takes Millicent's hand to kiss, but she pulls away. She announces that she needs to rest. She complains about Ben, saying that during their journey he hit every hole in the road just to cause her grief. Ben retorts that he's never claimed to be a coachman. An indignant Millicent declares that Ben should be beaten for his improper behavior. She does suggest, however, that he should first unload her luggage. Jeremiah is amazed at the number of bags Millicent has brought. She remarks that Ben will have to return to Collinsport for the remainder of her things. Jeremiah follows her to the house.

In the Old House drawing room, Jeremiah tells his father that he would rather die and go to hell than to marry Millicent. Joshua replies that his son should be grateful, and that Jeremiah will do as he dictates. Naomi attempts to calm her husband, but Joshua orders her to be quiet. Accepting his apparent fate, Jeremiah informs his father that he has given him fair warning. As Jeremiah starts for the door, Joshua declares that he is also giving Jeremiah warning, advising him to act like a Collins. Abigail sneaks into Victoria's bedroom. She searches through the dresser drawers. She overlooks the family history book but locates Victoria's twentieth-century dress. Abigail grabs the dress, examines it, and leaves the room.

In a dark, candlelit chamber, screaming is heard as the Reverend Trask performs an exorcism on a young girl strapped to a table. Abigail, carrying Victoria's dress, descends into the alcove. She is led by an ugly crone, who tells her that Trask is doing the Lord's work. Abigail is instructed to wait across the room while Trask completes the exorcism. Violently crying out against Satan, he dips a ladle into a boiling cauldron and pours a hot liquid on the girl. The girl's screams subside to a whimper. Trask tells the crone that time will reveal whether or not he has saved the girl from the devil. He unstraps the girl and instructs the crone to return her to her mother. He says that the girl must be kept in bed and may have to be tied down. He insists she must be fed only white foods and should be brought back to him in four days. He also declares she must be prayed for and that she is only a small portion of Satan's broader infestation. The crone blesses Trask and ushers out the devastated girl. A dumbstruck Abigail gathers her composure and introduces herself to Trask, who knows of the Collins family. She informs him that she has found strange signs on Victoria's dress. Trask is fascinated by the zipper. He insists it is not the product of mortal hands. A vindicated Abigail points out the washing label symbols, explaining that Victoria easily translated their meaning. Trask's curiosity grows as Abigail discloses that Joshua has hired Victoria as the new tutor. She claims she fears for the children's safety. The crone returns. Abigail mentions

132

they had been expecting Phyllis Wicke, but that she never appeared. The crone interrupts, reporting that she heard the mail coach had overturned the previous morning with Phyllis on board. She adds that when the coach was rescued, Phyllis had inexplicably disappeared. Trask warns Abigail that if Victoria is truly a representative of the devil, then everyone at Collinwood is in danger. Abigail responds with a look of determined righteousness.

At night in the Old House drawing room, Abigail unleashes her allegations regarding Victoria as Joshua, Barnabas, Jeremiah, Naomi, and Natalie listen. She stresses the strange disappearance of Phyllis Wicke and the mysterious appearance of Victoria in her place. Barnabas replies that if an accident occurred and if a woman actually disappeared, then it must have been Victoria, not Phyllis. He remarks that they do not have to look to God or Satan for an explanation. Abigail resumes her oratory, warning that if Victoria is a disciple of the devil then she can turn them all into goats or strangle everyone in their own blood. Barnabas again objects, calling his aunt's behavior foolish.

Victoria enters the room, having been summoned by Joshua. Joshua asks Victoria how she arrived at Collinwood. She is uncertain how to respond, but Barnabas assists her by specifically inquiring if she came by mail coach. Joshua insists that he will ask all the questions. Victoria confirms that she travelled by mail coach. Abigail interrupts, making reference to Victoria's original claim that she fell from a horse. Ignoring his sister, Joshua asks Victoria if anything unusual happened on her journey. She says that she does not remember. Barnabas again comes to her defense, pointing out to his father than when Victoria arrived she was in a daze after being hit on the head when the coach overturned.

After a studious pause, Joshua informs Victoria she may leave the room. When she is gone, Naomi comments that Victoria seems to be a nice girl and she wishes everyone would leave her alone. Abigail asserts that Victoria is a witch. Natalie adds her evaluation of the situation by speaking a French motto that says evil will come to those who think evil. Joshua demands to know where Abigail heard about the incident involving Phyllis Wicke. She reluctantly admits she learned about it while visiting Reverend Trask. Jeremiah and Barnabas laugh at the revelation, but Joshua is not amused. He makes it known that he considers Trask a charlatan, but Abigail believes he does God's work. Joshua further states that Trask is a lying, treacherous conniver. He proclaims that if Trask is involved with Abigail's claims then he will not investigate the matter further. Abigail pleads with her brother to reconsider, but he is unrelenting in his decision. He orders an insulted Abigail to leave the room.

In 1991, Phyllis Wicke lies asleep in a Collinwood bedroom. She remains attached to an infusion machine. Elizabeth sits watching as Julia enters to examine the girl. Elizabeth reports that Phyllis has been restless. Julia offers to watch the girl to give Elizabeth a break, but Elizabeth insists she'll stay. Julia replies that she'll return in an hour and departs. Elizabeth picks up a novel and begins to read as Phyllis turns restlessly. Later, Elizabeth has fallen asleep. Phyllis abruptly sits up, terrified and disoriented. Upon seeing the infusion machine attached to her arm, she panics and pulls the needle out of her arm. Later in the corridor, Julia approaches Phyllis' room and notices the door is open. She enters the room, where Elizabeth is still asleep. Julia is stunned to discover that Phyllis is missing.

In 1790, Barnabas enters his dark bedroom carrying a candle. As he closes the door, he encounters Angélique, who has been waiting for him. He wants to know what she is doing. She replies by asking him if he really believes he can resist her. Barnabas admits that he cannot undo what he has done in the past, but he assures

Angélique he will never again succumb to her advances. He pushes her away. Angélique taunts him, declaring that Barnabas cannot make himself a virgin for Josette. Barnabas grabs her by the arms and forces her roughly to go to the doorway. He reiterates that they will never again be alone together. Angélique glares at him with raging eyes. She hatefully insists that Barnabas is wrong, stating that their relationship is not over. Angélique stalks out of the room, leaving Barnabas shaken.

In the morning at the Old House stables, Ben works at a hot forge, hammering a horseshoe. Angélique interrupts him. She walks toward him and seductively says that she wants him. She holds up a doll made of straw and asks if he recognizes it. An impatient Ben looks at her as if she is out of her mind when she tells him that the doll is him. Angélique tells Ben that he now works for her. Ben impatiently responds that he hasn't got time for her and tells Angélique to go to the house.

Suddenly, Angélique slams the doll into her open hand. Ben instantly doubles over in pain. She throws the doll to the ground, causing Ben to fall violently on his back. She stamps her foot on it. Ben screams in agony. She picks up the doll and commands Ben to stand. Ben staggers up, staring fearfully at Angélique. He wants to know what she is. Angélique replies that she is his mistress. He blurts out that she is a witch and tells her to stay away from him. He backs up against the stable wall in fright. Angélique informs him that she will borrow his soul and his will. Ben tries to escape, but she again debilitates him by pinning the arms of the doll together. Ben struggles furiously and pleads with her to stop. She lifts the right arm of the doll, causing Ben's right arm to also rise. As Ben stares numbly, she notifies him that he will do everything she commands as long as she needs him. She tells him that he will remember nothing of their encounter. She will summon him when Josette arrives. She snaps her fingers, and he comes out of the spell. She walks away as Ben stares in disbelief.

That night, Victoria sits at a desk in her room, writing in a journal. She writes that she is keeping a diary so that no matter what happens to her there will at least be a record of the extraordinary events that have surrounded her. She notes that she has been mysteriously thrust backward in time. She stops writing when she hears the sound of a coach arriving. She crosses to her window and looks outside to see Ben driving a coach. After the coach stops, Ben helps an unknown man get out of the coach, followed by a woman Victoria cannot see. Victoria puts away her journal and rushes into the corridor. Standing on the second floor balcony, she stares down to the foyer as Joshua extends a welcome to Josette, telling her they've been awaiting her eagerly. Unnoticed, Angélique walks up behind Victoria to see what is happening. Victoria unsuccessfully tries to catch a glimpse of Josette's face. Josette is accompanied by her father, André Du Prés. She compliments Joshua on the beauty of the house. She walks to the foot of the stairway, pulls back her hood, and looks around. As if she has sensed Victoria's presence, she looks up to the second floor balcony. Victoria catches a clear view of Josette and is stunned beyond belief to see that Josette's appearance is virtually identical to her own. For a brief moment it appears the two women have locked eyes. Victoria whispers that Josette is herself. As Victoria continues to stare at Josette, Angélique observes Victoria's mesmerized reaction.

𝕰𝖕𝖎𝖘𝖔𝖉𝖊 8.
Original Airdate: February 15, 1991.

Written by Linda Campanelli, William Gray, M.M. Shelly Moore.
Directed by Paul Lynch.

Character Lis, 1790 Scenes: Barnabas Collins, Josette Du Prés, Victoria Winters, Naomi Collins, Reverend Trask, Natalie Du Prés, Millicent Collins, Ben Loomis, Peter Bradford, Daniel Collins, Sarah Collins, André Du Prés, Abigail Collins, Angélique, Joshua Collins, Jeremiah Collins, Referee.
1991 Scenes: Barnabas Collins, Elizabeth Collins Stoddard, Roger Collins, Dr. Julia Hoffman, Carolyn Stoddard, Willie Loomis, Joe Haskell, Maggie Evans, Sheriff George Patterson, Mrs. Sarah Johnson, Deputy Jonathan Harker, Phyllis Wicke.

My name is Victoria Winters. A séance in the great house of Collinwood has opened a bridge through time. Across a span of centuries, two women have traded places. One has been thrust into an unimaginable future... the other hurled into the past, where she comes face to face with herself."

Standing on the second floor balcony overlooking the Old House foyer, Victoria remains transfixed by the appearance of Josette. Angélique continues to hover behind Victoria. Barnabas and Naomi greet Josette as Joshua and André stand by. Josette's face lights up as Barnabas approaches and takes her in his arms. He thanks God that she has arrived at last. A fascinated Victoria continues to watch from upstairs. Angélique walks up to her and makes her presence known. Joshua asks André if he and Josette had a difficult journey across the ocean. André replies that the eleven-day trip was marred by constant wind and rain. Angélique tells Victoria she must go to her mistress. Angélique heads down the stairs. Josette tells Barnabas that she has never forgotten the dark fire of his eyes. Natalie excitedly rushes down the stairs with her arms outstretched as Josette calls out her name. The two women hug. Natalie tells Josette how wonderful she looks.

Josette spies Angélique approaching, calls out her name, and runs toward her. Exclaiming that she has missed her, Josette embraces Angélique, who stares arrogantly at an uncomfortable Barnabas. Joshua directs Ben to carry the Du Prés' luggage upstairs. Angélique offers to fetch Josette's traveling case, but Josette declares she will retrieve it herself. Barnabas interrupts, insisting that Angélique take care of the matter. He invites Josette upstairs so he may take her to her room. Angélique jealously watches them as Barnabas hesitates on the stairs and kisses Josette. Victoria ducks out of view as Barnabas and Josette continue up the stairs. A rebuffed Angélique heads for the bags, bumping into Ben. She tries to pass him, but he purposely blocks her passage. She hurls an accusatory warning in French to him and pushes the smirking servant aside.

In Josette's room, Barnabas enters with his fiancé, who is enthralled with the beauty of the room. Barnabas reminds her that the house will be theirs after the wedding. Suddenly she is surprised to notice her portrait hanging above the mantel. Barnabas divulges that he had the countess bring it. As their romantic attraction overwhelms them, Barnabas tenderly touches Josette's face. He refers to her striking beauty, and she returns the compliment. Barnabas reaches to the mantel for a small velvet bag tied with a cord. He hands it to Josette, telling her it was especially made for her in Boston as a wedding gift. He discloses that he cannot wait until their marriage to give it to her.

A touched Josette blushes as she removes a gold music box from the bag. She calls it exquisite and opens the box, which begins to play a familiar melody. She recognizes the music from the first dance they shared. Barnabas reveals that he had the music created in a box just for her. As they are about to kiss, Angélique enters the doorway carrying Josette's traveling case. She apologizes for interrupting the lovers as they pull apart. Barnabas curtly orders Angélique to put the case down, notifying Angélique that Josette will call her if she is needed. Angélique sweetly acknowledges the command, curtsies and departs. Josette closes the door, then tells Barnabas there was no reason to speak so bluntly to Angélique. Barnabas apologizes, saying that he only wants to be alone with Josette. He invites her to meet him outside in the gardens. She agrees. He seizes her and kisses her passionately. He tells her he'll be waiting and leaves.

As Barnabas walks out of Josette's room, Angélique watches from another room. She enters Josette's room as Josette freshens up her makeup. Angélique again pardons herself for intruding, but Josette informs her there is no reason to apologize. She tells Angélique to refrain from calling her mademoiselle, but Angélique refuses, insisting that she is Josette's servant. She offers to prepare Josette's bath, but a smiling Josette reveals she must go now. Angélique assures her that when she returns a bath will be waiting for her along with her favorite rosewater. Josette hugs Angélique warmly, expressing her pleasure at her presence. She kisses Angélique on the cheek and hurries out the door. Speaking to herself, Angélique declares that her rosewater is exactly what Josette needs.

In the formal gardens under the moonlight, Josette finds Barnabas waiting for her. Josette rushes into his arms, and they embrace passionately. At the Old House, Angélique mixes her magical rosewater as her supernatural vision watches over Barnabas and Josette embracing on the grass in the garden. Later in Josette's bathroom, Angélique pours her rosewater into the tub where Josette is dreamily soaking in warm water. Josette tells Angélique that she promised Barnabas she would make him forget every woman he has ever known. She adds that he mentioned he's already forgotten them. Angélique instructs her to relax. Josette calls Angélique a treasure. Angélique stares with cold, devious eyes.

In Jeremiah's dark bedroom, Angélique pours droplets of rosewater and herb oil onto the pillow. The liquid evaporates into steam. She speaks a hushed incantation, exclaiming that the fire of a new love will burn in the hearts of Josette and Jeremiah. Thunder begins to rumble in the skies. In the middle of the night, a shaft of lightning cuts through the sky, and thunder roars. In his room, Jeremiah sleeps restlessly. In her room, Josette is also tossing in her sleep. Angélique sits in her room as the storm lights up the sky. She molds together two soft clay figurines. She recites an incantation, stating that two souls, two hearts, and two lives shall be as one. She crushes the clay figures together, bewitching Josette and Jeremiah to have identical dreams about a forbidden rendezvous. The dream meeting takes place in Jeremiah's bedroom. The door swings open suddenly. Josette stands in the doorway with her nightgown billowing. Jeremiah is mesmerized as she walks toward him. The room appears to be engulfed by beams of light. Jeremiah reaches out to Josette. They romantically embrace and fall into bed together.

In her room, Angélique has positioned the clay figures together on a table. She stares at them, telling the sweet lovers to dream on, claiming they will soon be helpless and lost. Josette and Jeremiah continue to dream of their shared passion. In his room, Jeremiah suddenly awakens as the windows fly open.

The next morning in the dining room, the family and guests are gathered around the table eating breakfast. Josette arrives late. Barnabas hastily rises to greet her and kiss her hand. He wishes her a good morning and inquires if she is feeling well. Josette admits she did not sleep well. Jeremiah quickly glances at Josette. Millicent mentions that she too barely slept, commenting it must be something about the house. Barnabas escorts Josette to a chair beside his. Josette directs a quick look at Jeremiah. Barnabas invites Josette to visit the shipyards with him later. Josette declines Barnabas' offer, saying she thinks it would be best if she stayed at the house today. Josette again glances at Jeremiah. He's also staring at her. Feeling tormented, Jeremiah excuses himself from the table. He announces that he told Peter he would meet him at the new house. Naomi suggests he finish his breakfast, but Jeremiah replies he isn't hungry. He hurries out. Joshua wonders why his son is behaving so peculiarly. Millicent exclaims that it's starting to seem as if Jeremiah is avoiding her.

In 1991, Sheriff Patterson's police car drives up to Collinwood. When the car stops, the sheriff and Deputy Harker get out. The deputy reaches into the back to take the arm of a frightened Phyllis Wicke. She pulls away from Harker as her body trembles, crying out not to be touched. Patterson opens the other back door, telling her everything will be all right. He gets inside to pull her out. The bedraggled Phyllis says that the mistress mustn't see her in her condition. The sheriff assures her that Elizabeth is a very understanding woman. Phyllis nervously gets out of the car. She stares in amazement at the car, but Patterson promises her it won't harm her.

Joe, Roger, and Maggie sit in the kitchen, exhausted and dirty from their all-night search for Phyllis in the rainy woods. Roger declines Elizabeth's offer of more coffee, suggesting that they resume searching. Joe agrees, stating that he's going to pick up Barnabas and Willie at the Old House to help. Mrs. Johnson enters with the news that Phyllis has been found. Elizabeth informs everyone to stay in the kitchen while she deals with the sheriff. Mrs. Johnson follows her into the great hall. Patterson informs her that some hunters found Phyllis wandering in the woods. Wrapped in a blanket, Phyllis sits in front of the fireplace with the deputy standing next to her. Patterson informs Elizabeth that Phyllis claims she is the new tutor at Collinwood. Elizabeth looks at her nervously. Phyllis introduces herself. She tells Elizabeth that she should have received word of her arrival by the post mail. She reveals that her carriage was overturned and starts to express concern that she may have lost her sanity. Patterson interrupts, telling Elizabeth that the girl is running a strong fever.

Elizabeth crosses to the girl, looking at her closely. Patterson points out that he told Phyllis that Victoria has been doing a fine job of tutoring. But he confesses he thought he should check out her claim anyway, considering the strange things that have been going on. He indicates they will take her to the sanitarium at Meadeville. Elizabeth expresses her gratitude to the sheriff, telling him that they have indeed employed Phyllis. Patterson is thoroughly confused. Elizabeth remarks how good it is to see Phyllis and how worried everyone was about her. Mrs. Johnson takes Phyllis' arm to escort her upstairs. Phyllis turns to Patterson and informs him that his services are no longer required. She tells him he may roll away in his car, referring to it as a metal contraption. She then advises Elizabeth that things are quite different in Connecticut. Mrs. Johnson leads Phyllis up the stairs.

Patterson asks about Victoria. Elizabeth answers that she is taking a brief vacation. The sheriff remarks that Phyllis is a rather strange person and an odd choice for a tutor. Elizabeth retorts that Phyllis is the product of a very formal education. Patterson accepts Elizabeth's explanation but does ask if she knows why Phyllis has never seen a car before. Mrs. Johnson calls out from the upper stairway where Phyllis has collapsed. Elizabeth hurries to assist, telling Patterson that they'll speak later. He responds that she can count on that and suggests that the girl belongs in a hospital.

Later, Julia examines a delirious Phyllis, who is back in bed, attached to monitors. Elizabeth, Roger, and Maggie attempt to enter the bedroom, but Julia instructs them to wait outside. Moments later she joins them in the corridor, reporting that Phyllis has diphtheria. Julia announces that everyone will have to be re-immunized immediately. Elizabeth wonders if they should move Phyllis to a hospital, but Roger reminds her that that would not be a good idea under the circumstances. Maggie begins to warn them of the risk that Victoria might never return, but stops midsentence and offers to stay and help keep an eye on things. Elizabeth expresses her gratitude. Julia confirms that Phyllis could die.

At the Old House, a raging Barnabas paces back and forth in the drawing room. He exclaims to Julia and Willie that a fever is what killed Phyllis in 1790. Julia assures him that everything possible is being done to save Phyllis but acknowledges there is a strong chance she will die. Barnabas implies that Julia might approve of that outcome. She responds with a look of outrage. A stammering Willie wants to know what will happen to Victoria. Out of control, Barnabas grabs Willie by the shirt and begins snarling. Julia cries out for Barnabas to leave Willie alone. Barnabas turns toward her with his eyes glowing red. Julia shrinks back in fear as his fangs appear. Barnabas orders Willie and Julia out of the room. They depart as a troubled Barnabas stares after them with his eyes radiating and fangs revealed.

At Collinwood, the moon shines down on the great mansion. With burning eyes and bared fangs, Barnabas stares at Carolyn's windows. In her bedroom, Carolyn lies asleep. Barnabas appears inside and approaches her bed. Suddenly, Carolyn's eyes open and she turns to welcome Barnabas. He lowers himself towards her and starts to caress her. As their passion builds, he sinks his fangs into Carolyn's neck.

In 1790, Josette hears singing as she walks along the upstairs corridor in the Old House. In the school room, she finds Victoria playing a guitar and singing *Somewhere Over the Rainbow* to Sarah and Daniel. Sarah informs Josette that Victoria is going to teach them the song. Josette tells Victoria that she's never heard it before. Victoria explains that the song is about a girl named Dorothy who loses her way and wants to go home. Josette introduces herself to Victoria. Struck by their physical resemblance, Josette asks Victoria to walk over to the mirror. As the reflections of the two women are seen side by side, both Josette and Victoria stare in amazement. The children watch with playful fascination. Victoria suggests that Daniel and Sarah return the guitar to Jeremiah's room, and they depart. Josette asks Victoria about her family and where she originates. She replies that she doesn't know and that she's an orphan.

Josette discloses that she feels there is more than a resemblance between herself and Victoria. Although she cannot explain it, she believes they somehow know each other. Victoria looks at her without responding. Josette suddenly turns away, agitated. She exclaims that she can't explain or understand anything. Surprised by Josette's apparent anxiety, Victoria assures her that Barnabas loves Josette. Josette agrees and adds that she loves him. Victoria says she knows that is true. Again they look at each other with disturbed fascination. Josette wonders why she feels that Victoria does know about her love for Barnabas. Victoria is speechless. Josette takes her hand and tells her that she likes her and knows Victoria will be her friend. Josette hurries out of the room as a troubled Victoria stands watching after her. Josette rushes into her bedroom, closes the door, and slumps back against it. Speaking as if to Barnabas, she pledges her love for him.

Inside the stables, Jeremiah sits on a bale of hay, reflecting on his obsessive dream about Josette. He repeats the vision in his mind until he is interrupted by Josette. He jumps to his feet. Their eyes reflect turmoil, excitement, and fear. Josette declares that she had to see Jeremiah. He admits that he was thinking of her and reveals his dream of the previous night. Josette divulges that she too had the dream. Jeremiah asks what is happening to them. He reaches out for her, grasping her by the shoulders. Josette begs him to refrain. She tries to break away, but she can no longer resist Jeremiah's advances. He kisses her and they cling to each other feverishly. Suddenly Josette draws back, terrified. Jeremiah grabs her as she screams, demanding to be released. Outside, Victoria wanders past the stables lost in thought with wildflowers in her hand. Upon hearing Josette's cries, she hurries to the stable door and spies Josette and Jeremiah embracing inside. She watches in shock, then runs off.

In the Old House drawing room, Natalie is reading the tarot cards. Victoria enters the room. The countess comments that Victoria looks as if she's just had a fright. Victoria hesitates, then discloses that she's just seen Josette and Jeremiah embracing as lovers in the stables. Natalie holds up her hand of cards, declaring that the cards have anticipated Victoria. She informs Victoria that she has been keeping watch on her, remarking that Victoria always seems to know more than she is willing to tell. Victoria insists that she doesn't know anything about what is happening but merely wants to avert a tragedy. She turns and runs out as Natalie requests an explanation. The countess turns over another tarot card; it is the wicked woman. With piercing eyes, Natalie stares at the cards.

Josette is standing at the window of her room when she hears Natalie knocking on her door. Natalie enters and asks Josette if she has gone completely mad. Josette does not face her. Outside in the corridor, Abigail passes by and hears Natalie speaking. Noticing that Josette's door is partially open, Abigail eavesdrops on the conversation. Natalie exclaims that she knows of Josette's rendezvous at the stables with Jeremiah. The countess asks her niece if she and Jeremiah are lovers. Josette quietly insists they are not. An impatient Natalie demands to know what the two were doing, then grabs her and turns her around. Josette replies that she does not know. Tears are rolling down Josette's face. She falls into Natalie's arms and reveals that her encounter with Jeremiah seemed as if they were bewitched by magic. In the corridor, Abigail listens in awe.

In her room that night, Victoria pens a new entry in her journal. She writes that she feels as if the walls are shrinking around her. She's afraid that she may have revealed too much but feels it was necessary. She wishes the family history could be wrong and that Josette and Jeremiah could be stopped. She speculates that she may have been brought back in time to alter the family history. She fears if she changes one moment of history then other events might be changed as a result. She wonders if those changes would permanently trap her in 1790. A powerful storm breaks outside.

In his room, a troubled Jeremiah sits in the darkness with his head in his hands, staring hypnotically at the flame of a candle. The door quietly opens and a disoriented Josette appears. Jeremiah quickly crosses to her. They embrace fiercely as thunder and lightning penetrate the room. Angélique sits in her room before a burning candle performing an incantation. She chants, ordering the fire to burn deep and to fill their hearts. The bewitched Jeremiah and Josette fall to the floor in a passionate embrace. Angélique continues to stare into her candles as she envisions the couple's sorcerous liaison.

In her room, Victoria suddenly sits up in bed, frightened by the raging storm. Her window has blown open, and rain is pouring in. She jumps out of bed to fasten the shutters. Looking outside, she sees a bolt of lightning illuminating everything in sight. She's stunned to see Jeremiah and Josette running from the house towards the stables. She realizes that the history book is coming true. The next morning, Victoria rushes into Josette's room and finds Natalie inside. The countess informs Victoria that it is too late. Josette's dresses are scattered over the furniture. Victoria reveals that she saw the two lovers running away last night in the darkness. Natalie declares that Victoria knew it would happen, reiterating that Victoria had warned her about a tragedy.

Barnabas enters and asks where Josette is as he looks around the disheveled room, puzzled. Natalie warns him that he must be strong. Becoming increasingly agitated, Barnabas demands to know what has happened to his fiancé. Natalie reveals that Josette has run off with Jeremiah and that Victoria witnessed the incident. Victoria confirms the countess' story. A disbelieving Barnabas laughs and asks the two women if they are out of their minds. Realizing they are serious, he races out of the room as Victoria and Natalie follow.

Barnabas rushes into Jeremiah's room. Natalie and Victoria appear behind him as he looks across the empty room. As reality sinks in, Barnabas is perplexed and horrified. He exclaims that it makes no sense. He wonders when Jeremiah and Josette could have been together. He insists that his and Josette's relationship is a lie. In a rampage, he slams a glass into Josette's portrait. Trembling with rage and despair, he vows that he will find Josette and Jeremiah. He lurches to the door and runs out as Natalie and Victoria watch in fear.

Inside the stables, Barnabas calls out for Ben, who admits he saw Josette and Jeremiah during the night and didn't know what to do. He divulges that Jeremiah mentioned Boston and suggests to Barnabas that the couple is likely to travel on the Post Road. Ben offers to ride with Barnabas, but Barnabas declares that the matter is between him and his brother.

At their room in a Boston roadside inn, Josette tells Jeremiah she wishes they could inform their families that they are safe, but Jeremiah replies that it is not yet time. As he is kissing her, the door to their room suddenly bursts open, and Barnabas storms inside. Josette and Jeremiah stare at him in shock. Jeremiah steps toward Barnabas, informing him that neither he nor Josette intended to do what they did, and they didn't want to hurt Barnabas. Barnabas yells out, calling Jeremiah a bastard. He lashes out with his riding crop and slashes Jeremiah across the face. Barnabas grabs Jeremiah and throws him against the wall. Tears fall down Josette's face as she watches, screaming in terror. She begs Barnabas to stop hurting Jeremiah.

The two men scuffle and fight. In desperation, Josette exclaims that she and Jeremiah have been married and tells Barnabas there is nothing he can do. A devastated Barnabas slowly turns to her, releasing his grip on Jeremiah. Barnabas contemptuously calls Josette a whore and tells her that she and his brother deserve each other. As Barnabas turns to leave, Jeremiah pulls himself up and tells Barnabas that he wants satisfaction. Barnabas replies that he shall have it. They set a duel for the following dawn. Barnabas departs and Josette falls into Jeremiah's arms, clinging desperately. She cries out to God and asks Jeremiah what they have done.

At the Old House, Joshua and André pace the floor while Natalie watches. Naomi sits silently on the sofa while Millicent weeps into a handkerchief. Joshua refers to the crisis at hand as confounded insanity. He tells André that he holds Josette responsible. André retorts that Joshua is practicing Yankee justice by blaming the victim of the crime. A disgusted Natalie intervenes, exclaiming that blame is irrelevant. She demands that the duel must be prevented. Alluding to the duel as an execution, Joshua replies that Jeremiah is no match for Barnabas. He insists that Barnabas must listen to reason. Peter enters the room and announces that Barnabas will see no one; he will speak only of the arrangements for the duel. Peter will stand as second to Jeremiah, and Ben will assist Barnabas. Joshua asserts that his son is mad and proclaims he'll hear no more talk of the duel. He fumes out of the room, and André follows. Naomi rouses from her deep thoughts. In denial, she states that her sons love each other and that they would never hurt one another. Peter and Natalie look at her, speechless. Millicent whines that she is being neglected, mentioning how she was to marry Jeremiah. She feels no one has shown proper sympathy for her. Peter asks God to have mercy on everyone.

In her dark room, Victoria retrieves the Collins Family History from the dresser. She sits on the bed and reads by the light of an oil lamp. She finds the chapter that discusses the unexpected elopement of Jeremiah and Josette. She is alarmed to read that Jeremiah is to die in the duel, described as a firearms accident.

At dawn, Barnabas descends the Old House staircase. As he reaches the main floor, Sarah races down after him, crying out his name. Victoria follows as Barnabas lifts Sarah into his arms. Sarah begs Barnabas not to go. She does not want him or Jeremiah to die. Barnabas holds her. He promises his sister that no harm will come to Jeremiah. Sarah asks if Barnabas will be hurt. Barnabas looks at Sarah, kisses her, then asks Victoria to take her back to bed. Sarah doesn't want to go, but Barnabas insists that she not make matters more difficult than they already are. A sad Sarah runs up the stairs past Victoria. Gathering his composure, Barnabas prepares to depart. Victoria urges him not to fight, warning that despite his intentions, Jeremiah will die. Barnabas is intrigued. She reveals that she has a certain insight, which Barnabas himself has noticed. But Barnabas is adamant that Jeremiah will not die. He leaves the house. Victoria watches in fright, unaware that Abigail has heard everything as she stands quietly above.

Barnabas and Ben walk grimly along a path in the woods. On the roof of the Old House, Angélique stands next to a stone gargoyle as she reaches out to the sky. She proclaims that she will be with Barnabas. She sends a supernatural command to Ben, telling him that it's time. In the woods, Ben hears Angélique's voice in his ears as he continues to roam the path with Barnabas. Angélique reminds Ben that he will be her eyes and ears. On the rooftop, Angélique continues staring at the sky. In the formal gardens, Peter paces nervously and checks the time on his pocket watch.

Several yards away, Jeremiah and Josette stand silently embracing as Barnabas watches them. Jeremiah informs Josette she must leave. Her eyes well with tears. Barnabas and Ben walk toward them. Jeremiah kisses Josette. Clinging to Jeremiah, Josette insists she wants to stay. He replies that she is with him always. Josette tears herself away and runs into the woods. Barnabas and Ben approach Peter, who urges Barnabas and Jeremiah to reconsider their decision for the sake of their family. Peter looks at the two brothers. He prompts Jeremiah, who responds that they shall proceed as planned. Peter informs Barnabas that the choice of weapons is his. Ben brings forward the pistol case. Barnabas reaches for a pistol from the open box, hands it to Ben and walks off. Jeremiah selects his weapon and strides away. Ben and Peter follow with the weapons. In a hushed voice, Barnabas instructs Ben to refrain from placing a bullet in his gun. Ben is aghast at the request, but Barnabas vows that he will not shoot his own brother. He orders Ben to give him the small lead ball. Barnabas places it in his pocket. On the rooftop, Angélique raises her hands, closes her eyes, and initiates an incantation. Wind begins swirling around her as she calls out for the spirits of chaos to consume her. Quivering, she falls to her knees.

In the garden, Barnabas and Jeremiah prepare to duel. Josette watches fearfully in the distance. Barnabas and Jeremiah face off and turn their backs to each other. Angélique continues her intense ritual. Peter instructs Barnabas and Jeremiah that he will count to ten and that they are then to turn and fire. Jeremiah and Barnabas acknowledge the procedure, and Peter begins to count. Angélique opens her hands to reveal a lead ball lying in her palm. An anxiety-ridden Ben watches as Peter continues the countdown. When Peter reaches the final number, Barnabas and Jeremiah turn to shoot at each other. The lead ball magically flies out of Angélique's palm. The two guns are fired, and Jeremiah falls to the ground. From the edge of the gardens, Josette screams in terror. Angélique demoniacally smiles from the rooftop. A stunned Barnabas drops his gun, and Peter and Ben run to Jeremiah. Josette frantically races to Jeremiah's side. Barnabas stares in disbelief. Josette holds Jeremiah, crying hysterically. Looking up at Barnabas, Josette's eyes flame with hatred. She informs him that he has killed the only man she will ever love. A devastated Barnabas is unable to speak.

At the Old House, Ben steers a horse-drawn wagon carrying Jeremiah's body into the stable yard. Peter sits alongside Ben, and Josette rides in the wagon bed next to her dead husband. Barnabas follows alone on foot. Waiting outside the house are the grief-stricken family members: Joshua, Naomi, André, Natalie, and Abigail. When the wagon stops, Peter asks Josette to allow him and Ben to remove Jeremiah. Barnabas crosses to a distraught Naomi. He tells his mother that he did not intend that Jeremiah die. He informs her that the gun was not loaded and retrieves the lead ball from his pocket. He insists that he could not have killed his brother. Abigail cries out that witchcraft is responsible for Jeremiah's death. She points toward the window where Victoria is watching them. The entire group stares up at a terrified Victoria while Abigail screams out that Victoria is a witch.

𝕮𝖕𝖎𝖘𝖔𝖉𝖊 9.
Original Airdate: March 1, 1991.

Written by Matthew Hall.
Directed by Rob Bowman.

Character List, 1790 Scenes: Barnabas Collins, Naomi Collins, Josette Du Prés, Victoria Winters, Reverend Trask, Natalie Du Prés, Millicent Collins, Ben Loomis, Peter Bradford, Daniel Collins, Sarah Collins, André Du Prés, Abigail Collins,

Angélique, Joshua Collins, Jeremiah Collins, Reverend Amos, Bailiff Henry Evans, Bailiff's Assistant, Prisoners.
1991 Scenes: Barnabas Collins, Elizabeth Collins Stoddard, Dr. Julia Hoffman, Carolyn Stoddard, Willie Loomis, Maggie Evans,Mrs. Sarah Johnson, Phyllis Wicke.

My name is Victoria Winters. A séance held at the great house of Collinwood has sent one woman on a perilous journey into the past...where secrets too terrifying to be written in a family history are threatening to destroy those she left behind. Meanwhile, the family struggles to protect a stranger...the only possible link to the one trapped deep within the past."

In 1991, Phyllis continues to be bedridden with a fever at Collinwood. As she administers an injection, Julia informs Elizabeth and Maggie that if Phyllis' temperature doesn't go down soon, she will die. Elizabeth insists they must take Phyllis to a hospital, but Julia assures her that everything possible is being done. As Phyllis tosses unconsciously, she begins to murmur about a terrible tragedy, speaking Jeremiah's name. Maggie quickly rushes over to the bed and asks Phyllis what is happening and where she is. Phyllis mentions the graveyard and lapses back into unconsciousness. Elizabeth wants to know what Phyllis has just attempted to describe. Maggie responds that Phyllis has spoken of something that is happening in the past.

In 1790, the Collinses have gathered in the family cemetery for Jeremiah's funeral. Reverend Amos delivers the eulogy. Peter looks down to the grave. Abigail fervently absorbs the eulogy. When the Reverend suggests blame should not be placed for Jeremiah's death, Abigail glances towards Victoria, who is standing back behind the family. A composed Daniel holds the hand of a quietly sobbing Sarah. Dressed in black, a mournful Josette holds a faded red rose. Barnabas stands solemnly apart from the rest of the family. The Reverend prepares to complete his speech and signals Ben and a group of laborers to lower Jeremiah's coffin into the ground. Amos scatters dirt on the casket. Josette suddenly falls to her knees at the edge of the grave, calling out to Jeremiah. Before André and Natalie can reach her, Barnabas rushes forward, kneels beside Josette, and calls out to her. She shrieks out in hatred, commanding Barnabas not to touch her. She accuses him of killing her only love. She cries uncontrollably. Barnabas is paralyzed by the power of Josette's wrath. Natalie and André help Josette to her feet. A guilt-ridden Barnabas steps slowly away while Angélique smiles secretly in the background.

Suddenly, the sound of horses' hooves and clattering wheels is heard. A carriage pulls up on the road outside the cemetery, followed by two men on horseback. The carriage door swings open, and out steps Reverend Trask, dressed in black from head to toe. He announces that he has come for the witch. Abigail points to Victoria, claiming that she is the one. Terror-stricken, Victoria exclaims that the accusation against her is not true. Joshua steps toward Trask, calling his behavior outrageous and reprimanding him for disrupting the funeral. Trask reveals that he is acting by permission of the law. He instructs Bailiff Henry Evans and his assistant to take Victoria into custody. Scared to death, a cowering Victoria cries out that the allegations are false. Barnabas comes to her defense, proclaiming that Victoria shall not be taken. But Peter tells Barnabas now is not the time to oppose the charge. As the crowd watches, the bailiff and his assistant escort Victoria to the carriage.

Later that night, Bailiff Evans leads Barnabas down a dimly lit, gloomy basement corridor in the jail. The damp stone walls glisten from the glow of the wall torches. A prisoner screams out from one of the cells, demanding food. The bailiff takes Barnabas to a narrow cell where Victoria sits, huddled in a corner on a bench. When she sees Barnabas, she jumps up and runs to him. She thanks God that Barnabas has arrived and assumes he has come to take her away. Barnabas sadly tells Victoria that he is sorry he is not yet able to secure her freedom. The bailiff informs Barnabas that he will be allowed fifteen minutes with Victoria and departs. Victoria wants to know what will happen to her.

Barnabas divulges that she is going to be put on trial for witchcraft. He reports that the old laws are still in effect which give ammunition for a charlatan such as Trask. Victoria is numb with disbelief. Barnabas encourages her not to worry. He explains that Peter will act as her defense lawyer. Barnabas refers to him as the best advocate in the territory. He also assures Victoria that, with the exception of his Aunt Abigail, the entire Collins family supports her. He points out that once his father is enraged, he can be a formidable force. Victoria inquires as to what would happen should she be found guilty. Barnabas insists that is impossible and asserts it will be a question that need not be answered. Victoria replies that witches are hung. Taking her arm, Barnabas promises Victoria that she will be spared that fate and set free. Victoria tries to look hopeful, but her terrified eyes reveal her overwhelming fear.

At the Old House, Barnabas sits in front of the fireplace, wearily drinking alone. He turns around as Angélique enters. He impatiently asks her if he must bar his door to keep her out. She replies that there is no need for him to be angry. She claims that she has come to express her sorrow over Jeremiah's death, saying she did not have a chance to convey her sympathies sooner. Barnabas thanks her for her concern and informs her that he'd like to be left alone. Angélique seductively sits in front of him. She tells him that she is the only one who truly cares about him and insists that Barnabas knows it is true. He angrily asks how many times he must tell her that he wants nothing to do with her. Angélique responds that Josette hates and despises Barnabas and warns Barnabas that Josette will never change. Barnabas replies that as long as Josette is alive he will never love another. Angélique tells him that he does not mean what he says. She tries to kiss him, but he pushes her away, denying that she knows what is best for him. He orders her to leave. Angélique's eyes flash with anger. She declares that God is her witness and promises that Barnabas will be sorry for rejecting her. She storms out of the room.

In her room, Josette tosses restlessly in bed while Natalie lays tarot cards on a table. Josette declares that she cannot sleep, but Natalie insists that rest will be forthcoming. After turning a final card, Natalie asks Josette if she remembers when she told her she felt bewitched by Jeremiah. Josette inquires if her aunt thinks Victoria is responsible. Natalie replies that she does not but remarks that the tarot cards are insistent. Josette claims that the cards tell only what Natalie wants them to say. Natalie remarks that she wishes that were so. She stares with great concern at the card of the wicked lady.

In Jeremiah's room, Angélique quietly slips inside and retrieves a crumpled handkerchief bearing Jeremiah's initials. She notices Jeremiah's powder horn hanging on the wall and grabs it. Moments later in her room, Angélique pours gunpowder from the horn along the lines of a pentagram sculptured in a clay tablet. She is surrounded by burning candles. She places Jeremiah's handkerchief in the center and begins to recite a spell. She calls out to the spirits of darkness, pestilence and pain. With a dagger, she cuts a slit in the palm of her left hand. Blood oozes out of the wound. Angélique drips blood onto the handkerchief. She resumes her incantation. In the cemetery, a blazing wind whips through the trees. Angélique picks up a flint lighter and begs for Jeremiah to be brought back from the darkness. She commands Jeremiah to rise from the dead to do her bidding. She sparks the lighter, causing the powder in the pentagram to ignite along with the handkerchief. In the cemetery, a storm rages as a hand suddenly reaches up from Jeremiah's grave.

In the Old House foyer, a somber Barnabas sits at the bottom of the staircase. Natalie descends the stairs, reporting that Josette is finally sleeping. Natalie urges Barnabas to be patient, telling him that she feels certain in her heart that Josette loves him. Barnabas thanks the countess, expressing his hope that she is correct. In the woods, a dark figure passes through the foliage. In her room, Angélique is transfixed by the scorched pentagram. The figure staggers inside the Old House. Angélique continues her spell, directing Jeremiah, the zombie, to find his bride. In her room, Josette listens to her music box. Down the corridor, the dead Jeremiah stalks towards Josette's room. Josette hears a noise in the hall and closes the music box. She asks if it is Natalie but receives no response. She walks to the door as the handle begins to turn.

A fearful Josette gasps as the door swings open to reveal the dead Jeremiah, coated with mud. Jeremiah mumbles Josette's name hoarsely and stumbles forward with his arms outstretched. He grabs her and carries her away as she screams. In the foyer, Barnabas, André, and Joshua come running up the stairs after hearing Josette's cries. They rush through the corridor into Josette's room and find she is gone. Natalie, Abigail, Millicent, and Naomi appear in the doorway to witness the discovery. Barnabas rushes out of the room, instructing the other men to follow. Naomi grabs Joshua and asks what has happened. He reveals that someone has taken Josette. Abigail circles the bedroom, waving her hands. She chants to God, claiming that the witch has struck. Abigail begs for the family to be protected from satanic forces. Natalie discovers Josette's locket on the floor. Naomi is stunned, announcing that she had placed the locket on Jeremiah before he was entombed. She wonders if her son was buried alive.

The waves crash against the rocky shore below the cliff at Widows' Hill. Jeremiah carries an unconscious Josette through the woods. Barnabas and Ben follow a path through the trees. Elsewhere, Joshua and André scour the woods. In her bedroom, Angélique sends a supernatural message to Jeremiah, ordering him to take Josette to Widows' Hill and destroy her. Josette awakens as Jeremiah carries her onto the rocky cliff. The wind gusts relentlessly. Josette's cries are heard by Barnabas and Ben, who run out from the woods toward the cliff. Barnabas stares in disbelief when he sees his dead brother hovering over the edge holding Josette. Ben prepares to shoot the zombie, but Barnabas pushes the gun down and moves toward the cliff, begging his brother to release Josette, who begs to be released. A flicker of recognition appears in Jeremiah's dead eyes. He hears Angélique's voice telling him to kill Josette. He moves closer to the edge as Josette continues to scream in terror. Barnabas moves closer, urging Jeremiah to resist whatever evil that has brought him back from the dead. Jeremiah's hollow voice slowly responds. Barnabas is stunned to hear him whispering Angélique's name. André and Joshua come running out of the woods and watch in disbelief. Ben warns them not to move further. Barnabas continues urging his brother not to harm Josette. The wind continues blowing brutally. Jeremiah releases Josette, who runs to safety. Jeremiah screams and plunges off the cliff into the dark ocean below.

As Naomi and Natalie wait in the Old House foyer, the search party returns with Josette. Natalie almost collapses with relief. Naomi plaintively asks Joshua about Jeremiah. Joshua tells her that Jeremiah is now at rest. Millicent and Abigail come downstairs with Daniel and Sarah. Angélique rushes down the stairway to Josette as Millicent takes the children back upstairs. But Barnabas cuts off Angélique, curtly ordering her to stay away from Josette. Angélique insists that Josette needs her help and runs to her. Natalie tells Angélique that Josette should be taken to Natalie's room. As Natalie starts to follow them, Barnabas intercepts her. He privately informs her to keep watch on Angélique and to keep Angélique from going to her room and from being alone with Josette. Barnabas pleads with Natalie to trust him. She wants an explanation but knows there isn't time. She hurries after Josette and Angélique.

Joshua looks toward his sister, who has a disapproving look on her face. Before Abigail speaks, he orders her to keep her opinions to herself, expressing his contempt for her methods of persecution. She turns away in offense after Joshua suggests she could use a drink. Barnabas thanks Ben for his assistance and heads up the stairs. He cautiously enters Angélique's room and looks around. He notices the burnt pentagram slab from Angélique's ritual. He searches further, finding the two clay figures hidden above the wardrobe cabinet. He hears a noise in the hall. Angélique walks up the back stairs. When she enters the room, Barnabas sneaks out by an adjoining door and leaves the room unnoticed. Angélique stares into a wall mirror. Talking to herself, she states that Josette will not be so lucky next time. Barnabas taps on Natalie's door and enters. Lying in bed, Josette exclaims that she will not see Barnabas. She turns her back to him. Sitting at Josette's side, Natalie assures her niece that everything is fine.

In the corridor, Natalie informs Barnabas that Josette is in a frail condition. She apologizes for being unable to keep Angélique from going to her room. Barnabas shows her the two clay dolls. He asks for her evaluation of them and reveals he found them in Angélique's room. Natalie discloses that they are fetishes used for black magic. She notices a fragment of Josette's ribbon on one of the dolls and realizes that the figures represent Josette and Jeremiah. Natalie cannot believe that Angélique would be responsible, but she admits that Angélique's mother practiced voodoo. Barnabas tells Natalie that she does not know Angélique as he does. Guilt-ridden, he insists the entire matter is his fault. Regaining his determination, he asserts that the spell must be broken. He wants to rip the dolls apart, but Natalie prevents him, telling him that Josette would die as a result. She proclaims that only the one who cast the spell can undo it. Barnabas declares he will see to it and starts to go to Angélique. Natalie reaches out to stop him, warning him that Angélique is more powerful than he can imagine. Barnabas, however, is no longer fearful. He rushes off as a frightened Natalie watches.

Angélique lights candles in her room. Suddenly, the door slams open and Barnabas enters. Angélique is startled. Barnabas grabs her hair, pulling back her head. Displaying the clay figures, he makes known his discovery of her tactics. Angélique pretends ignorance. Barnabas orders her to break the spell. Smiling, at first she refuses, then agrees. Barnabas releases her, and she warns that Josette will die. She asks if he would like Josette dead or if he would prefer her alive with the memory of Jeremiah's love. Angélique says there was a time when Barnabas loved her, but he denies ever loving her. He tells Angélique that her schemes have been wasted. He declares his pity for her has turned to hatred and contempt. Holding up the figures, he announces that he'll take them to the bailiff and make certain that

Angélique is hung as a witch. He adds that he and Josette will dance on Angélique's grave. As he prepares to leave, Angélique grabs a dagger from the dresser and lunges at Barnabas, exclaiming that if she can't have him, no one will.

Barnabas evades the dagger and struggles to take it away from Angélique. As she tries to twist it from his grip, she plunges to the floor. As she falls on the dagger, it stabs through her breast. Angélique rolls over; blood is trickling from her mouth. While staring at him, Angélique declares that she is cursing Barnabas for eternity. With a gasp, she dies. At that exact moment, Josette sits up and cries out from the bed in Natalie's room where she has been sleeping. Natalie can see that Josette has been released from the spell. Natalie divulges that Angélique was the one responsible for the bewitching of Josette. She tells a stunned Josette that Angélique was always jealous of Josette and that above all else, Angélique wanted Barnabas. Barnabas rushes into the room. Natalie informs him that the spell has been broken. Barnabas responds that Angélique will trouble them no more. Natalie leaves to notify the others. A tearful Josette asks Barnabas if he can ever forgive her for the grief she has caused. He replies that there is nothing to forgive. He reaches out to her, and they tightly embrace.

In 1991, Willie is finishing a fried chicken dinner in the Collinwood kitchen as Mrs. Johnson fills a sack of groceries for him. She confirms that Phyllis is still very sick. Willie expresses his concern for Victoria and declines his aunt's offer to take lamb stew to Barnabas, explaining that Barnabas hasn't had much of an appetite lately. At the Old House, Willie enters the foyer with the groceries. Barnabas is descending the stairway with Carolyn, who is in a trance-like state. Barnabas tensely asks Willie for a report on Phyllis. Willie admits that the prognosis isn't good. Willie greets Carolyn, but she says nothing as she leaves to go home. Barnabas summons Willie to the drawing room. He pulls out Sarah's diary from the desk and shows Willie that a new entry has appeared in it. Willie reads of Reverend Trask taking Victoria to jail in 1790. Willie panics, asking Barnabas who Trask is. Barnabas replies that Trask was a fanatic witch-hunter. Barnabas insists they must get Victoria back to the present before it is too late. He tells Willie that Julia must convince the others to hold another séance. He commands Willie to bring the doctor so he can speak to her immediately.

At Collinwood, the group has gathered together in the candlelit great hall to conduct a séance. Seated around the table are Maggie, Julia, Elizabeth, Roger, Barnabas, and Carolyn. One chair is empty. Roger again expresses his doubts. Elizabeth tells him they have no choice. Roger sarcastically answers he hopes that if he disappears he'll appear in fifteenth-century Florence. Maggie admits they have no way of predicting what will happen. Barnabas assures Maggie that everyone is aware of the uncertainty involved and prompts her to begin. Maggie instructs the group to place their hands on the table touching each other in a circle. Maggie closes her eyes and starts summoning the ghost of Sarah. She begs Sarah to help bring Victoria back before Phyllis dies. Maggie emphasizes that although they understand Sarah wanted Victoria to go back for a reason, she must return before she is trapped forever in the past.

Suddenly, Sarah's voice speaks through Maggie, warning the group they must stop the séance because something terrible is trying to come back. The front doors fly open as a howling wind gusts through the house, blowing out the candles and knocking Victoria's empty chair into the fireplace. Julia begins to choke. Maggie comes out of her trance and joins the others as they rush to Julia's side. Julia regains consciousness but is disoriented and confused. She reveals that she feels as if something is trying to get inside her. Maggie insists that Julia will be all right, claiming that whatever tried to control Julia wasn't strong enough. Elizabeth leads a shaky Julia upstairs as a worried Barnabas watches. As Julia enters her room, Elizabeth bids her good night, assuring Julia that they'll look after Phyllis. Alone, Julia looks in the wall mirror and smiles. In the reflection is the image of Angélique, grinning evilly.

In 1790, Trask walks down the dark corridor in the jail. His face appears in the window of Victoria's cell, ordering the bailiff to unlock the door. Inside, Victoria jumps to her feet as Trask enters and declares that there are tests to be made. Victoria orders the Reverend to stay away from her. He asks if she will turn him into a lizard or change his blood to maggots. As he reaches to grab her, Peter enters and orders Trask to not touch Victoria. Trask refers to Peter as the devil's advocate and laughs harshly. Peter informs the bailiff that Trask has no business being in the cell and orders him to be removed. The bailiff apologizes and asks the Reverend to leave. Trask smiles at Victoria and advises her that they shall meet again soon. As he departs, he warns Peter that his soul may be in jeopardy for defending Victoria. He tells Peter that he looks forward to dealing with him in court.

Alone with Peter, Victoria thanks him for his efforts and assures him she is not a witch. He replies that he believes her but insists she must tell him her entire true story. Victoria hesitates and then begins to explain her bizarre journey. She reminds him of their first encounter at Collinwood, explaining that she was confused because she comes from the year 1991. She reveals that she works as a governess at Collinwood, the house that Peter has just helped to build in 1790. Victoria admits that the whole thing makes no sense but assures him she has proof. She tells Peter about the Collins Family History which she's hidden at the Old House in her bedroom dresser. She mentions that it was published in 1974 and that she was somehow able to bring it back with her through time. Peter looks at her incredulously. He responds that if the book does exist, he would hesitate to use it in her defense because Trask would twist it to serve his own purpose. Victoria understands but feels the book can convince Peter and Barnabas that she is telling the truth. She tells Peter that she hopes it isn't too late to change what is to happen. Peter asks for an explanation. Victoria reveals that the entire Collins family is in danger. She tells him there is a dark force at work, and she believes she was sent back in time to stop it. A stunned Peter stares at her.

In the dark, rainy woods, Barnabas and Ben finish burying Angélique in an unmarked grave. Barnabas has no final words for her, but Ben speaks out harshly, expressing his desire for Angélique to experience the suffering in hell that she has caused on earth. Ben spits on her grave. Barnabas asks God to have mercy on her soul. In the Old House drawing room, Joshua, Naomi, André, Natalie, and Abigail are assembled. A drenched Barnabas enters and tells them that Angélique is buried. Natalie tells him that Josette is resting in Natalie's room. In the woods, the storm rages as bolts of lightning streak from the sky onto the ground above Angélique's grave.

In his bedroom, Barnabas puts down his wet hat and cape. He is about to leave the room when Josette calls out from behind him. Barnabas is elated, exclaiming that he was on his way to see her. She replies that she could not wait. Barnabas crosses to her and embraces her. They kiss intensely. He breaks away and looks into her eyes. He is stunned at what he sees. Josette's eyes are burning red. Opening her mouth, she reveal two large fangs, which she sinks into Barnabas' neck. They fall to the floor. Barnabas is unable to resist her as she sucks the blood from his body.

Moments later, Josette rises with blood splattered on her lips. Her image is transformed into a large bat, which flies out into the stormy night. Hovering near the ceiling, the ghostly apparition of Angélique materializes. She taunts Barnabas for believing the image was Josette. Angélique exclaims that Barnabas' hell will take whatever shape Angélique chooses. Barnabas' clouded eyes watch Angélique's spirit laugh hysterically and then disappear.

In Natalie's room, Josette paces the room, waiting for Barnabas. Sensing something is wrong, she looks out the window, calls out Barnabas' name, and rushes out of the room. In the corridor, Josette knocks on Barnabas' door. She opens the door and rushes into the bedroom. She finds the delirious Barnabas wounded, lying on the floor with blood streaming from his neck. In a frenzy, she kneels beside him and touches his face. Josette cries out for help and strokes his face, sobbing. She frantically begs him not to die. She tells him they have each other again. Barnabas glances at her, then whispers to Josette that he will love her forever. Josette cries out in anguish as she clutches the dead Barnabas.

Episode 10.
Original Airdate: March 8, 1991.

Written by Linda Campanelli, M.M. Shelly Moore.
Directed by Rob Bowman.

Character List, 1790 Scenes: Barnabas Collins, Naomi Collins, Josette Du Prés, Victoria Winters, Reverend Trask, Natalie Du Prés, Millicent Collins, Ben Loomis, Peter Bradford, Daniel Collins, Sarah Collins, André Du Prés, Abigail Collins, Angélique, Joshua Collins, Reverend Amos, Ruby Tate, Innkeeper, Customer, Man, Workmen.
1991 Scenes: Barnabas Collins, Elizabeth Collins Stoddard, Roger Collins, Dr. Julia Hoffman, Carolyn Stoddard, Joe Haskell, Maggie Evans, Sheriff George Patterson.

My name is Victoria Winters. A terrifying curse has cast its shadow over Collinwood...while an innocent girl huddles in a prison cell awaiting judgement, death roams free, stalking the night...and a tormented family struggles to comprehend its fate. But that fate is already written...and the evil that controls it is relentless."

In 1790, Peter hurries through the darkness up the steps at the front of the Old House. Outside the front door he encounters Ben, who is carrying a musket. He tearfully informs a shocked Peter that he is guarding the house because Barnabas has died. Peter enters the foyer as Natalie rushes down the stairway. She confirms Barnabas' death, attributing it to an unknown animal attack. Peter finds the news impossible to believe. Natalie admits that no one has an explanation. She reveals that a search for the animal is underway. She asks Peter how much more pain the Collins family must endure. He replies that more agony may be ahead.

In Victoria's room, Natalie sits on the bed looking through the Collins Family

History as Peter stands nearby. He has informed her that Victoria brought the volume with her from the twentieth century. Peter reads a portion of the separate journal which Victoria has kept in 1790. He quotes Victoria's comments about being mysteriously thrust back in time. Peter tries to convince the countess that there would be no reason for Victoria to fabricate the materials, insisting that the history book and journal would only work against Victoria in her current predicament. Natalie agrees that Trask would view the items as witchcraft. Peter warns Natalie that the fate of the Collins family is in their hands. Natalie answers that even if Peter is right, the book is incomplete since it makes no reference to Angélique and her schemes. Natalie notes that the book erroneously claims that Barnabas sailed for England following the death of Jeremiah.

Suddenly, Natalie gasps when she reads that Josette died five days after Jeremiah's death by falling off Widows' Hill. Peter tries to assure the countess that the book is wrong about Josette, pointing out that she has already survived an almost fatal experience at Widows' Hill. Frustrated and alarmed, Natalie suggests that the entire book may be wrong. Returning from their search, Joshua and André enter the house, followed by Ben. Joshua plans to organize a hunting party in the morning. André tells him more men are needed. Joshua orders Ben to round up additional help. Joshua accepts Ben's offer to keep guarding the front door until morning.

In the study, Naomi sits silently with her head bowed. Joshua enters and informs her their search revealed nothing. He walks to the fireplace and picks at the dead ashes with a poker. He insists that he cannot accept Abigail's superstitions but admits it seems apparent that an evil force is preying on the house. He questions why the evil did not die with Angélique. An unresponsive Naomi continues to sit quietly. Joshua informs his wife that she should not be alone. She replies that she is alone. Joshua responds firmly that she is not, telling her she must not give up and that she is responsible for the children. Reacting with fear, Naomi asks where the children are. Joshua tells her they are safe, but Naomi exclaims that no one is safe. She stands up and starts for the door. Joshua tries to stop her, but Naomi tells him to leave her alone, exclaiming that she must see the children. Joshua holds her tightly, telling her everything will be all right. She asks him what they have done to deserve the loss of their sons. Crying, she collapses against Joshua. He embraces her, attempting to provide comfort.

Joshua enters the drawing room, where Natalie, Peter, André, Abigail, and Millicent wait quietly. Joshua announces that he has arranged for Collinwood to be ready for immediate occupancy. He does not want anyone spending another night in their present home. He orders that no one is to speak outside the family about what has happened tonight. Abigail asks for an explanation for her brother's request. Joshua sharply tells her that it is no one else's concern. Abigail interrupts him, declaring that the beast that killed Barnabas was a demon sent by Victoria. Peter counters that Victoria couldn't be responsible because she has been locked away in jail. But Abigail insists that since Angélique is dead there is no other explanation. André asks Abigail what motive Victoria would have for bringing evil upon them. Abigail proclaims that Satan needs no motive. Joshua orders Abigail to refrain from furthering her accusations. He announces that he will do everything possible to gain Victoria's release. Abigail warns him to consider his actions. He also states that the beast that killed Barnabas will be hunted down and destroyed. He says there is no need for assistance from outside the family. He wants the people of Collinsport to believe that Barnabas has sailed to England on family business.

Peter and Natalie stare at each other in shock.

Realizing that the family history book revelations are coming true, Peter and Natalie speak privately in the foyer. Natalie feels that she and André must take Josette away from Collinsport immediately to save her life. In the family cemetery, Joshua, Peter and Ben carry Barnabas' casket towards the mausoleum. Inside the crypt, Joshua opens the secret room. He, Peter, and Ben carry the coffin into the chamber. Joshua discloses that he had the secret room built during the Revolutionary War to hide weapons and ammunition. He leans over his son's coffin and prays that he'll meet Barnabas again some day in a better world. Peter bids farewell to Barnabas and follows Joshua out of the room. A tearful Ben speaks, telling Barnabas that it was an honor to serve him. He steps out, and the wall is closed, hiding the chamber.

The next day, workmen busily apply finishing touches to the great hall at Collinwood. Ben assists with bringing in bags and boxes. Millicent enters, demanding her trunks. Ben informs her that her numerous bags are still at the Old House and will be retrieved in a special trip later. Millicent pouts and requests to be notified when Ben goes for them. She states that she wants to be certain he doesn't destroy everything. She hurries away. André comes in, with Natalie following. André informs her that he has completed arrangements for them to sail with Josette from Boston in three days. A relieved countess exclaims that she will notify Josette immediately. At the lily pond, Josette informs Natalie that she will not leave town. She does not want to abandon the Collins family or Victoria. Josette feels guilty that her maid is responsible for the tragedies that have befallen the Collinses. Natalie shows Josette Victoria's journal and the Collins Family History. She hands the books to Josette and instructs her to look at them. Josette reads a few lines and looks at Natalie, stunned. Josette asks how what is written can be true.

In the jail, a somber Victoria reveals to Josette that Peter told her about Barnabas' death. She admits that in the twentieth century there is a descendant of Barnabas' who bears the same name and is very much like the eighteenth century Barnabas. Victoria also confesses that she thought she was falling in love with the Barnabas of 1991. She thinks now it might have been just a fantasy. She believes that she can understand Josette's feelings about the Barnabas of 1790. Josette reminds Victoria that she once told her how she seemed to know Victoria as well as herself. Josette wonders if Victoria is her reincarnation from two hundred years in the future. Victoria answers that she has had the same thought and asks if it is possible. Josette responds by saying she no longer knows what is possible. She says that she must do everything in her power to help Victoria. Victoria, however, insists that Josette must leave town or Josette's death predicted in the history book may come true. A defiant Josette retorts that she is not worried about the book but will stay away from Widows' Hill. Josette claims that by saving Victoria she will be saving herself as well. She vows not to leave Collinwood until Victoria is free. Victoria smiles hopefully.

Inside the mausoleum secret room after sunset, Barnabas' coffin lid flies open as thunder and lightning fill the chamber. Barnabas hisses wildly, with his fangs bared. He emerges from the mausoleum and stands at its entrance. His eyes are burning as he looks out to the wind-blown cemetery. Frightened and confused, his body is overcome by intense urges. He suddenly bolts forward and runs off into the woods with his cape billowing.

At the Old House, Millicent stands in her room, surrounded by trunks. She informs an exhausted Ben to take them to Collinwood. He replies that he will need some assistance. She orders him to get some help, but he responds that it is too late at night. Millicent promptly scolds Ben for talking back to her. She assists loading his arms with bags, and he staggers out of the room. In the woods, Barnabas bares his fangs as the full moon shines above. In the Old House foyer, Millicent descends the stairs, carrying a precarious load of hatboxes. After setting them on the floor, she hears a sound and calls out to Ben. A dark figure appears in the shadows at the far end of the hall. Shrouded in a shadow, the figure approaches. Millicent is overcome with fright when she recognizes the figure as Barnabas. Deathly pale and with eyes burning, Barnabas bares his fangs. Millicent covers her face with her hands and screams as Barnabas grabs her and sinks his fangs into her neck. He lowers the unconscious girl to the floor and feeds on her blood.

He looks up as the ghostly apparition of Angélique suddenly appears over the stairs, laughing diabolically. A stunned Barnabas glances back to a limp Millicent with the two bloodied wounds in her neck. His eyes fill with horror as he realizes what he has done. Angélique teasingly asks Barnabas if he is enjoying his new life. He cries out to her, demanding to know what she has done to him. She replies that since Barnabas would not come to her in life, she has given him eternity to change his mind. She reveals that she intends that Barnabas spend eternity as a lonely beast of the night, feeding on human blood and feared by every living creature. She decrees that anyone who loves Barnabas will die. She tells him that this is her curse and that no one shall undo it. A horrified Barnabas begs Angélique to kill him, but she replies that she loves him too much to kill him. Her demonic laughter echoes throughout the hall before she disappears. Sinking to his knees, Barnabas cries out to God to help him.

At the coach house, Ben loads the wagon with boxes and heads back to the house. He enters the foyer and calls out for Millicent. Seeing her blood-soaked body on the floor, he rushes to her in horror.

In the Collinsport Village, a dense fog floats outside the Deer's Head Inn, as a drunken young woman named Ruby Tate staggers near the entrance. She makes advances to a man, inviting him to come home with her. The man hurries off as she screeches after him. She notices a dark figure with a cane walking slowly toward her and playfully calls out to the man, whose face is shrouded in a shadow. Her smile turns to terror when Barnabas' face emerges from the fog with his red eyes glowing. He bares his fangs and sinks them in Ruby's neck, knocking her to the ground. Upon hearing Ruby's screams, the innkeeper and two customers rush out. Barnabas is hunched over Ruby's sprawled body. Barnabas jumps to his feet, lashing one of the customers with his cane. He then runs off into the fog. The onlookers stare at the dead Ruby, wondering about the identity of the attacker.

At dawn, Barnabas hurries frantically through the woods. The sun is beginning to appear on the horizon. Barnabas howls in agony and rushes to the Old House. He stumbles into the foyer, slams the door behind him, and races to the cellar as he attempts to shield the sun's rays. He staggers into the dark basement and crawls into a corner on the floor.

At Collinwood, Naomi sits at the bedside of a semi-comatose Millicent, wiping her niece's fevered brow with a damp cloth. Millicent speaks Barnabas' name. After Natalie enters, Millicent continues to mention Barnabas' name to the puzzlement of the countess and Naomi. Outside the mansion, Peter, Joshua, Ben, and a group of laborers return from a searching expedition. Peter orders Ben to dismiss the men but to keep them on stand-by. Ben enthusiastically tells the men that they'll have another chance to find Barnabas' attacker. Peter and Joshua enter the house and are appalled to find Trask inside, standing in the great hall with Abigail. Trask sarcastically asks if the men have been out hunting. Joshua informs the Reverend that he is not welcome at Collinwood. Trask reveals that he has heard about the strange attack on Millicent. Joshua gives his sister a disapproving look. Trask says he is aware of her neck wounds and loss of blood.

Joshua denies everything, insisting that Trask's report is nonsense and claiming that Millicent is sick with influenza. Trask replies that an identical assault occurred in the village last night and that a man was seen. Abigail blurts out that it must have been a demon in the shape of a man. Joshua mocks his sister's comment. He is startled when Trask asks to see Barnabas. Joshua defensively asks if Trask thinks Barnabas is the monster responsible for the attacks. Trask responds that, on the contrary, he is suggesting that Barnabas is one of the victims. Joshua is enraged as his sister admits she revealed Barnabas' death to Trask. Joshua berates Trask for interfering with affairs of the Collins family. Trask says he is shocked at Joshua's continued defense of Victoria, insisting that she is the satanic instrument responsible for the deaths of Barnabas and Jeremiah. Joshua orders Trask out of the house. Trask declares that the evil will be stopped with or without Joshua's consent. Peter threateningly repeats Joshua's order for Trask to leave. As he leaves, the Reverend proclaims that the Lord will have His vengeance.

In the Old House basement, Barnabas awakens after sunset. Disoriented, he sits up, hesitates, and rushes out. In the woods outside Collinwood, Barnabas walks through the trees and stares up at Josette's windows. In her room, Josette is dressed for bed. She stares into the dresser mirror. Outside, Barnabas bares his fangs and hisses. Josette walks to a window, opens it, and stares sadly out into the night. Unnoticed, Barnabas looks up at her. Later, Josette lies sleeping as a large bat flutters outside her open window. Seconds later, Barnabas appears in her room. Unable to resist her, his fangs are bared as he leans over her body. Suddenly he hears a sound and turns around to see Millicent in the open doorway. In a trance-like state, she begs Barnabas to take her.

The next morning, Daniel is looking in the woods for Sarah, who is hiding from him. Daniel is stunned to discover Millicent's dead body. The boy's fear overwhelms him as Sarah arrives and screams out at the devastating sight. In the family cemetery, Millicent's casket is carried toward the mausoleum by Peter, André, Joshua, and Ben. Reverend Amos follows them, reading the twenty-third Psalm. Abigail, Natalie, and Naomi stand mourning. In the background, Trask stands alone observing the funeral.

In 1991, it is sunset at Collinwood as Joe drives into the courtyard and sees Carolyn ahead. He honks the horn, gets out of his car and calls out to her, but she ignores him and continues to walk away. Upon catching up with her, Carolyn finally turns to acknowledge him. She displays no interest in seeing Joe. He asks how Phyllis is doing, but Carolyn replies that she doesn't know and turns to walk away. Joe grabs her, and the scarf around her neck loosens to reveal two deep puncture wounds. Joe is startled at the sight. Carolyn angrily pulls away, ordering Joe to stay away from her. She storms off as an agitated Joe watches.

After dark, Carolyn enters the family cemetery. Barnabas waits for her at the mausoleum entrance. She smiles in anticipation as she walks in a daze among the tombstones. Joe crouches behind a tree, out of view. He watches in stunned horror as Carolyn approaches the mausoleum. Barnabas steps out in the moonlight to sink his fangs into her neck.

At the police station, Joe has given the sheriff a full report of what he has just witnessed. Patterson reacts with skepticism, asking if Joe might have merely seen a romantic exchange. Joe impatiently repeats to the sheriff that he found wound marks on Carolyn's neck identical to those on Daphne and himself. Patterson tries to reassure Joe but admits that Barnabas has been at the top of his suspect list since the day he came to town. The sheriff reveals that he's investigated Barnabas' background but found nothing. He comments that no one in England has ever heard of Barnabas. Joe considers that revelation is an indication of Barnabas' guilt, but Patterson responds that there have been no reported attacks since Woodard's death. The sheriff says he needs hard evidence of any wrongdoing. Joe is incensed, exclaiming that Carolyn's life is in danger. He warns the sheriff that if he waits he'll have a dead body as evidence. Patterson tells Joe to calm down and asks him to bring Carolyn to see him. Joe stresses the impracticality of the sheriff's suggestion. Patterson insists he cannot go to Collinwood to confront Elizabeth about Joe's allegation because of the present difficulties. Having lost all patience, Joe angrily heads out the door as Patterson warns him not to do anything stupid and to stay away from Barnabas.

In 1790, André, Natalie, and Josette are gathered in Natalie's room at Collinwood. André and Natalie instruct a hesitant Josette that the three of them must leave for Boston the following morning. In the jail, Josette visits Victoria in her cell, telling her that she doesn't know what to do since her family insists she leave the next day. Victoria agrees that Josette must go away to be safe. She reminds Josette that she must be gone before the date of her death in the history book. With tears filling her eyes, Josette tells Victoria not to worry about her since Angélique's actions have been discovered. She mentions that Peter has assured her Joshua is working on her behalf. Josette warns her about Trask, but Victoria tells Josette not to worry about her, promising that she'll be all right if Josette leaves immediately. Josette asks for an explanation. Victoria reveals that she knows now why she was sent back in time. She refers to their earlier conversation when Josette felt that by saving Victoria she would be saving herself. Victoria insists that by saving Josette now she will be saving herself. She insists it's the only way she can return to the twentieth century. The women hug each other as tears stream down their faces.

In her room at Collinwood that night, Josette is packing. As she searches frantically, Natalie enters, urging her to go to sleep. Josette announces that she is looking for the music box that Barnabas gave her, claiming it is the one item she wants to take with her from Collinwood. She believes she left it at the Old House. Natalie suggests it could be a sign that the box should be left behind. She tells her niece that she must let go of Barnabas. She bids Josette goodnight and leaves the room. Outside the Old House entrance, Josette walks up to the front door carrying a lantern. She slowly steps into the dark foyer and goes to the stairs. She enters her former room upstairs and finds the music box sitting on the mantel below her portrait. The box is open and playing its melody. She closes the lid and suddenly hears her name. She spins around to see Barnabas standing behind her. Stunned, Josette staggers backwards. Barnabas tells her that death cannot keep them apart. Petrified, Josette screams out in disbelief. Barnabas walks toward her, staring with his hypnotic eyes. He begs her to not be afraid, assuring Josette that he won't hurt her. Josette insists that Barnabas cannot be real. As their hands reach out and touch, he sadly assures her that he is real. Josette moves closer to Barnabas and places her hands on his face. He urges her not ask him to explain the curse of his existence. With pain on his face, Barnabas exclaims that it has been a tragic error for him to come to her. He orders her to leave immediately. But Josette does not understand.

She claims that she wants to stay with Barnabas forever. He asserts that he must stay away from her. Josette becomes frightened, and he tells her he must leave forever. She refuses, fearing she would die of a broken heart if she left him. Barnabas informs her that one day in another time she will see a stranger that she has known forever and that stranger will be himself. Josette continues to beg to stay. Barnabas responds that she doesn't know what she is asking. He mentions that his existence is something she couldn't possibly imagine. Josette insists she doesn't care; she will always love Barnabas and wants to be with him forever. Barnabas can resist his urges no longer. His eyes turn red, and he reveals his fangs. Sobbing, he asks if Josette is certain of her decision. He refers to Josette as his bride and sinks his fangs deeply into her neck. Josette moans with pleasure as she surrenders herself to Barnabas completely.

𝔈𝔭𝔦𝔰𝔬𝔡𝔢 11.
Original Airdate: March 15, 1991.

Written by William Gray.
Directed by Mark Sobel.

Character List, 1790 Scenes: Barnabas Collins, Naomi Collins, Josette Du Prés, Reverend Trask, Natalie Du Prés, Ben Loomis, Peter Bradford, André Du Prés, Abigail Collins, Angélique, Joshua Collins, Dr. Roberts, Judge Isiah Braithwaite, Bailiff Henry Evans, Jury Foreman, Jury Members, Court Spectators.
1991 Scenes: Barnabas Collins, Dr. Julia Hoffman, Willie Loomis, Joe Haskell.

My name is Victoria Winters. A transcending evil controls the destinies of two women exchanged in time. In a terrifying past, one of them finds herself on trial for her life... while in the present, the other lies helpless, struggling to survive. Meanwhile, an age-old horror faces extinction as he lies unguarded in his lair."

In 1991, on a cloudy morning, Joe enters the Old House foyer, nervously looking around. Reaching into his shirt, he pulls out a silver cross on a chain around his neck, then descends the winding stairway to the basement. In the darkness, Joe peers into the room where Barnabas' coffin lies surrounded by candlelight. From his coat pocket he retrieves a pointed wooden stake and a hammer. He slowly approaches the coffin and opens the lid. He is startled to see Barnabas lying inside. Joe gathers his strength and raises the mallet in preparation for staking Barnabas. Suddenly Joe cries out in pain. He staggers away from the coffin with a large knife sticking out from his back. He falls to the floor, dead. Suddenly, Julia appears. She wipes her brow with a blood-covered hand. An evil smile appears on her face as she looks down on Joe's body.

Willie enters the foyer carrying laundry. He notices the open basement door and rushes down the stairwell. He finds Julia hovering near the open coffin and inquires as to what she is doing. She turns around, speechless. Taking a few steps toward her, Willie glimpses a mound on the floor and asks Julia what it is. Julia stares maniacally at him and angrily screams out in French. She reaches down and pulls the bloody knife out of Joe's back and charges toward Willie. Willie moves backward and tries to fend off Julia's attack. He twists her arm, causing the knife to drop to the floor. She continues to call out derogatory and threatening French words. Willie slams her against the wall. Her head hits the stone and knocks her to the ground unconscious. In a panic, Willie rushes over to Joe's lifeless body and discovers the stake and hammer lying nearby. Although shocked by Joe's death, Willie is relieved to find that Barnabas is unharmed, still asleep in his coffin.

That night in his room, Barnabas surmises that Joe must somehow have seen him with Carolyn. He instructs Willie to bury Joe in the woods, regretting the need to place him in an unmarked grave. Willie shakes his head sadly, commenting that Joe was a nice guy. Badly shaken, Julia sits on the sofa, drinking a brandy. She reports that she has no memory of assaulting Joe. The last thing she recalls is being in her lab at Collinwood. Willie answers that Julia seemed insane and tried to slash him with the knife. He reveals that she was screaming in French. Barnabas translates two of the words that mean "to kill." Julia replies that she does not know French. Barnabas mentions that Angélique speaks French. He's certain that she is the one responsible, commenting that Angélique is the one who cursed him. He mentions the second séance when Julia felt as if something were trying to get inside her. The implication is that Angélique has controlled Julia, who shudders at the thought. Barnabas warns that Phyllis is the one in danger now, since her death would also ensure Victoria's death. Julia wonders why Angélique would want the two women to die. Suddenly she realizes that Angélique and Barnabas are former lovers. Barnabas bitterly informs her that Angélique has destroyed everyone he's ever held dear. He instructs Julia to go to Maggie, believing that as the medium for the séance, Maggie might be able to undo what Angélique has done to Julia.

In 1790, it is early morning as Natalie enters Josette's room in Collinwood. She is alarmed to find that the bed has not been slept in and quickly leaves the room. Outside the Old House, Natalie, André, and Joshua rush to the front door in a panic. Joshua comments that he should burn the Old House to the ground. The trio hurries through the upstairs corridor into Josette's room. They discover Josette lying on the bed with her eyes closed and hands folded over her chest. Natalie cries out to her niece as André wails in despair. They are overcome with relief to find that Josette is still breathing. Joshua urges them to return Josette to Collinwood immediately.

At sunset, Barnabas' hand emerges from his coffin as the lid creaks slowly open inside the secret room of the mausoleum. At the Old House Barnabas excitedly enters Josette's dark room. He softly calls out her name in confusion when he finds the bed empty. At Collinwood, Josette lies unconscious in her bed. Suddenly she awakens. André, Natalie and Naomi rush to her side. Natalie assures Josette that she is all right. Frightened, Josette asks what she is doing there. She asks where her lover is and tries to sit up, but Natalie restrains her. Natalie asks Josette if she can tell them what happened to her. André reminds a confused Josette that she was attacked. She thrashes about, calling out Barnabas' name. Naomi gently responds, saying that Barnabas has gone. Josette insists that Barnabas is waiting for her and anxiously exclaims she must go to him. André tries to calm her, but Josette is frantic, begging to be allowed to go to Barnabas. She turns toward the window. Natalie looks outside and reports that she sees nothing. Outside, Barnabas stares at the house with his raging eyes and bared fangs.

In the jail, an alarmed Victoria has been informed by Peter of the attack on Josette. Victoria is concerned to hear that Josette will now be at Collinwood on the fifth day after Jeremiah's death. Peter assures her that someone will keep constant watch over Josette to prevent the history book prediction of her death from coming true. He confirms that he will withhold the history book from Victoria's trial the following day. He has given the book to Natalie for safekeeping. Despondent, Victoria wonders how she can be persecuted when people should realize Angélique was responsible. Peter replies Victoria is being accused because she is alive and Angélique is dead. Victoria exclaims that she could not have committed the evil deeds because she has been in jail. But Peter responds that Trask will use that fact against her and try to convince the jury that she has the power to perpetrate evil from behind bars. Victoria discloses that the same type of attacks had been happening in Collinsport in 1991 that have been occurring in 1790. She asks Peter if he knows what a vampire is. Peter urges her to put such thoughts out of her mind, fearing that Trask will use them against her in an effort to link her with demonic practices. But Victoria continues her commentary, pointing out that the victims have received neck wounds and been drained of their blood. Peter orders her to stop talking of vampires, insisting that as her lawyer he will take care of her defense.

In the Collinsport courthouse, Abigail sits in the witness chair, interrogated by Trask as she testifies against Victoria. A room full of villagers watches. She mentions how Victoria appeared the same day that Phyllis vanished from the overturned carriage. Abigail accuses Victoria of being a child of the devil. She glares at Victoria, who sits at the defense table with Peter. Seated behind them in the front row of the spectator pews are Joshua, Naomi, and Natalie. Peter rises angrily to object to Abigail's statement. Presiding Judge Isiah Braithwaite orders her to stick to the facts. Trask strides to the prosecution table and holds up Victoria's twentieth-century dress. He asks Abigail if she has seen the dress before. She confirms that Victoria was wearing it upon her arrival. Trask displays the dress to the jury, astonishing them when he points out the zipper. Peter protests, exclaiming that the age of invention is at hand and implying that Trask is not aware of the latest inventions. Trask interrupts and proceeds to reveal the washing label's odd symbols. He hands the garment to the jury to inspect. Abigail replies that Victoria gave strange explanations as meanings of the symbols, one of which, "machine tumbled," Abigail equates to the overturning of Phyllis' carriage. Peter abruptly stands and voices his objection as Abigail smiles contentedly. Trask asks Peter for his explanation of the symbols. Peter replies that they are simply the marks of the maker, leading Trask to respond that the maker is Satan. A loud murmur fills the court. The judge demands order, and Peter again insists that Trask's inflammatory judgments be restrained.

Trask assures the judge that he can substantiate his claims. He picks up a cloth bag from the prosecution table and pulls out the Collins Family History. Victoria and Peter are devastated to see it. Abigail announces that Victoria arrived with the book. Natalie rises and angrily accuses Abigail of stealing the book. Trask replies that Natalie had no right to withhold it from the court. Growing impatient, the judge requests an explanation. Trask reveals the title of the volume and submits it, along with pages from Victoria's journal, as evidence for the prosecution. Peter objects, but the judge, although weary, allows Trask to quote from Victoria's diary. Trask reads Victoria's claim of traveling backward in time two hundred years and her feeling that she must keep her secret from being known. Joshua and Naomi react with amazement. The court is filled with startled discussion. Victoria frantically tells Peter that she must explain what has just been read. Peter feels otherwise, but Victoria is adamant, insisting she has no choice. Trask confronts Victoria, asking if she denies writing the journal. Peter rises, protesting that Victoria is not on the witness stand. The judge supports Peter's complaint. Trask begs forgiveness, insisting he thought Victoria would want to explain. Victoria jumps to her feet, accepting Trask's challenge. Peter tells her he will not allow her to proceed, but Victoria is determined.

Sitting in the witness stand, Victoria confirms that she wrote the pages in the journal. She admits that she is from the twentieth century, causing the courtroom spectators to gasp. Joshua and Naomi are stunned. Peter lowers his head in despair. Braithwaite demands order in the court. Glancing at the judge and jury, Victoria exclaims that she realizes the story sounds incredible and how she herself finds it hard to believe. Trask opens the history book and informs the previously stolid jurymen it is dated 1974. They are startled, and more mutterings are heard from the crowd.

Victoria acknowledges that the book is proof of her journey through time. Trask responds that, on the contrary, the book is not from the future, but about it. He insists that it is a demonic volume of the Collins family fate as preordained by the devil. The judge commands order in the noisy room. Trask instructs the jury members that Victoria is an instrument of Satan, claiming that she was sent to the unsuspecting Collinses to make certain that the evil events written in the history book came true. Peter stands and cries out his objection, but Trask asserts that he will prove his claims. He informs the judge that he has studied the history book closely and has compiled a list of predictions that have already come true. The judge overrules Peter's objection, granting Trask permission to read the list. Expressing his gratitude, Trask approaches the jury as he mentions the predicted deaths of Jeremiah and Millicent.

As the Reverend speaks Barnabas' name, Peter bounds to his feet and proclaims that the book did not predict Barnabas' death but instead stated that he traveled to England. Trask retorts that the overseas trip was a fabrication instigated by Joshua in an effort to hide the horrible circumstances surrounding Barnabas' death. Trask tells the judge that the lie about Barnabas can easily be proved. Joshua stares viciously at Abigail. She looks back defiantly at her brother. Trask notifies the jury that the history book forecasts more deaths. Peter begs the judge not to allow Trask to proceed, but the Reverend convinces Braithwaite to grant him permission to continue.

Trask reads the prediction of Josette's fall from Widows' Hill, prompting another uproar from the crowd. He then reveals a passage that claims Sarah will die from a fever. As another outburst occurs among the spectators, a sobbing Naomi stands and cries out, asking Victoria why she is hurting the family. She accuses Victoria of killing her sons. Tearfully, Victoria replies that Naomi knows she wasn't the one responsible. Joshua rises beside his wife, assuring her that they do not know what to believe. Trask interrupts, insisting that the truth is known. He points an accusing finger at the quivering Victoria, exclaiming that she is the source of the tragedies. Trask declares that Victoria is a witch. Victoria frantically shouts that she hasn't done anything. She begs to be believed. The judge pounds his gavel in an effort to quiet the loud audience. Victoria fights to hold back her tears.

In the drawing room at Collinwood that night, a somber Naomi apologizes for her outburst in court, blaming Trask for frightening her. Peter assures her that Victoria understands what happened. He tells Naomi it will be their turn in court tomorrow. Pacing the floor, Joshua doesn't understand why the existence of the history book was kept from the family. Natalie explains that they were uncertain how much of it to believe and did not want to unnecessarily frighten anyone. Naomi sobs as she refers to the remaining predictions of Josette's and Sarah's deaths. Joshua places his arm on his wife's shoulder and tries to convince her that the events will not happen. Natalie agrees, asserting that they must guard Josette safely through another night to break the terrible chain of events.

In her room, Josette sleeps restlessly while Natalie attaches a cross to the wall above the bed. She instructs André to put another one in the window. Peter and Joshua enter. Joshua frowns at the sight of the crosses. In the corridor, Peter follows Natalie. He wants to know the purpose of the crosses. Natalie asks him if he has heard of vampires. In amazement, Peter asks if everyone has gone mad. Natalie points out that the pattern is always the same, including deep bites and a loss of blood. Peter divulges that Victoria also attributes the attacks to a vampire. Natalie is determined they must protect Josette for the next two nights.

In Josette's room, André keeps a watchful vigil through the night. Outside, Barnabas approaches the house. When he spies the cross in Josette's window, he bares his fangs as his burning eyes rage. Josette suddenly awakens and cries out. Her father and aunt rush to her side. She stares at the window and calls Barnabas' name. Natalie hurries to the window but informs André she sees nothing outside.

The following day at the courthouse, Peter calls Joshua as his first witness for the defense. The bailiff swears him in. Later, Joshua sits on the witness stand testifying on behalf of Victoria. He reports that she was an excellent teacher and that everyone, the children included, regard her highly. He insists that the tragedies were brought about by Angélique. When Peter asks Joshua to reveal who Angélique was, Trask rises and objects, claiming that the woman is dead and has no bearing on the proceedings. The judge informs Trask that he will decide if that is the case and requests Peter to resume his questioning. Later, Natalie sits in the witness chair. Answering Peter's questions, she discloses that she witnessed Angélique's witchcraft, referring to the voodoo dolls used to manipulate Josette and Jeremiah. The countess divulges that Angélique was in love with Barnabas. Again Trask tries unsuccessfully to object. Natalie stresses that jealousy was Angélique's motive. The judge smiles approvingly, and observers in the court laugh as Natalie's comment that Trask knows very little about women.

Later, Ben testifies that Angélique put him under her spell but admits he doesn't remember how it was done. He does recall the straw doll which Peter holds up, telling the court that it was found in Angélique's room. Ben explains that he believes Angélique was responsible for putting a lead ball in the gun that killed Jeremiah. Trask complains to the judge about the accusations against the deceased Angélique. He mentions that two more attacks occurred the previous evening and sarcastically asks if Peter thinks Angélique is striking from the grave. Peter responds that he does believe Angélique's power is still alive, insisting the thought is no more outrageous than Trask's suggestion that Victoria has committed witchery from her jail cell. Suddenly, the proceedings are interrupted by a woman's voice.

The crowd is stunned as Angélique walks down the center aisle. Staring in disbelief, Ben rises from the witness chair and screams out that Angélique is dead. He tells the judge that he buried her and exclaims that she is a witch. Angélique approaches the front of the room, displaying a look of bewildered innocence. She asks Ben how he can say such a thing. Ben leaps from the chair and runs toward her, calling her a witch. The judge hammers his gavel as the bailiff and an assistant restrain Ben. Ben is dragged out of the court screaming. Victoria and her supporters stare in disbelief. Angélique claims to have been away for a few days and says she has done none of the terrible things that have been said about her. Trask instantly addresses the jury, ridiculing the claim that Angélique has risen from the dead. Insisting that Angélique is innocent, Trask defiantly points toward a terrified Victoria and announces that everyone knows she is the witch. The judge again hammers his gavel, repeating his request for order in the court. Victoria trembles with fright.

In her jail cell, Victoria is visited by Peter, who reports that he has been unable to find Angélique; she vanished after leaving the courthouse. Victoria is certain the jury will find her guilty. Peter urges her not to think negatively. He tells her the jury has retired for the evening and that a verdict is expected in the morning. Victoria wonders why Angélique hates her so much. Peter replies that everything Angélique has done seems to stem from her feelings toward Barnabas. Peter mentions that Josette was a rival of Angélique's and suggests Angélique also considered Victoria an adversary. Victoria exclaims that Barnabas is dead.

In Josette's room at the Old House, Barnabas approaches Josette's portrait as the music box plays in his hand. He speaks to the portrait, saying that he and Josette can no longer be kept apart. He vows that tonight they shall be together for all eternity. He begs Josette to come to him. In her room at Collinwood, Josette sleeps as Natalie and Naomi keep watch. Believing the history book, Natalie tells Naomi that she's certain everything will be fine if they can keep Josette safe until midnight. Naomi departs to check on the children.

At the Old House, Barnabas continues to summon Josette. Becoming tired, Natalie falls asleep in her chair. Responding to Barnabas' call, Josette awakens, slips out of bed and crosses to a trunk. She hears Barnabas telling her that they will be together for eternity. After lifting out her wedding gown, she murmurs to him that she is ready. Confirming that it is ten minutes before midnight, Peter and André enter the room from the hall. They stare in horror at Josette's empty bed. André frantically wakes Natalie, asking where Josette has gone. Natalie jumps to her feet in terror.

The Old House foyer is filled with flickering candelabra as thick mist seeps in from outside. Barnabas waits at the top of the landing. Josette enters below as if in a trance, wearing her long white gown. Barnabas calls out her name and holds his hand out to her. She slowly ascends the stairs. Suddenly, Angélique's image appears to Josette. Angélique's voice echoes in Josette's head, telling her that if she becomes Barnabas' bride she will join him in eternal damnation. Angélique causes Josette to see visions of Barnabas as a vampire attacking his victims. Realizing something is affecting Josette, Barnabas calls her name. She says nothing as Angélique continues to fill her head with warnings. Josette sees an image of herself as a vampire. Barnabas walks up to her and touches her on the shoulders. Regaining her sense of reality, Josette shrieks, demanding that Barnabas let go of her. She runs screaming from the house, leaving Barnabas stunned. He races after her.

The waves crash against the rocky shore below the cliff at Widows' Hill. Josette races through the woods. She stumbles to the ground but gets up and keeps running. Barnabas chases after her. Josette gets closer to the cliff and looks back to see Barnabas running toward her. She lets out a scream, and Barnabas cries out for her not to go there. She reaches the edge of the cliff, hesitates, then jumps to the sea below. A heartbroken Barnabas falls to his knees, wailing, and stares down at the rocky shore.

In Victoria's cell, a grim-faced Natalie sits next to a sobbing Victoria. The countess comments that no matter what they do they seem powerless to control fate. She tells Victoria that they are leaving and returning home with Josette's body.

Victoria informs her that she will miss her friendship. Touching Victoria's face, Natalie fights back tears and remarks how much like Josette Victoria is. Peter appears in the doorway and notifies them it is time for the verdict. Victoria silently bows her head.

In the courtroom, the jurymen settle into the jury box. Trying to comfort her, Peter takes Victoria's trembling hand. Joshua, Naomi and Natalie watch nervously. An anxious Trask sits at his post while Abigail looks on. The bailiff orders quiet in the room. The judge asks the jury if they have reached a verdict. The foreman stands and confirms they have. The judge requests the bailiff to deliver the verdict to his bench. The foreman hands a piece of folded paper to the bailiff, who brings it to the judge. He opens the paper and reads it, expressionless. The judge asks the defendant to rise. Victoria stands unsteadily with Peter at her side. Slowly the judge announces that the jury has found Victoria guilty of witchcraft. The entire courtroom erupts. A shattered Victoria stares in disbelief. Peter is stunned. Natalie jumps to her feet and cries out that Victoria is innocent. A triumphant Trask emits a smile. The judge hammers his gavel, loudly commanding order in the court.

After the room quiets, Braithwaite asks Victoria if she would like to make a statement. Tearfully, she pulls herself up and declares that she is innocent. Joshua, Naomi and Natalie watch, paralyzed with shock. The judge resumes his procedure. He announces that, in accordance with Massachusetts law, in three days at dawn Victoria will be hung by the neck until dead. Trask and Abigail exchange satisfied expressions. He asks God to have mercy on her soul. A murmur envelopes the room. A trembling Victoria stares at the judge in overwhelming terror.

Episode 12.
Original Airdate: March 22, 1991.

**Written by Linda Campanelli, Matthew Hall, M.M. Shelly Moore.
Directed by Mark Sobel.**

Character List, 1790 Scenes: Barnabas Collins, Naomi Collins, Victoria Winters, Reverend Trask, Ben Loomis, Peter Bradford, Daniel Collins, Sarah Collins, Abigail Collins, Angélique, Joshua Collins, Dr. Roberts, Judge Isiah Braithwaite, Bailiff Henry Evans, Nurse, Minister, Hangman, Guards, Villagers.
1991 Scenes: Barnabas Collins, Elizabeth Collins Stoddard, Victoria Winters, Roger Collins, Dr. Julia Hoffman, Willie Loomis, Maggie Evans, Phyllis Wicke, Angélique.

My name is Victoria Winters. The thread of time is unraveling, the hours grow short, and a young woman awaits her execution two hundred years in the past. Her lifeline to the present lies helpless in the great house of Collinwood. But an evil force plots to sever that lifeline... and the executioner stands waiting for his victim."

In 1991, the evening fog surrounds Maggie's studio. Inside, Julia violently screams out in French as Maggie pins her down on the bed, attempting to exorcise from her the evil spirit sent by Angélique. The possessed Julia fights Maggie, then becomes still. Julia quietly calls out Maggie's name, and the two women embrace, realizing Julia has been freed of Angélique's possession. Later that night, Julia is resting on the bed. Maggie hypnotically looks into the mirror. Staring back at her in the mirror is the grinning image of Angélique.

In 1790, Joshua and Peter visit Victoria inside her jail cell. Taking her hands, Joshua urges Victoria to have faith. He notifies her that he and Peter are leaving immediately for Portland to ask the governor to overturn the decision. Joshua departs from the cell, leaving Peter and Victoria alone. They look at each other tenderly; Peter assures Victoria that he will have obtained her stay of execution the next time they meet. Victoria is teary-eyed as Peter kisses her. After Peter departs, Victoria gloomily contemplates her future.

At night, a storm hovers over Collinwood, as Naomi descends the massive stairway. She pauses as she hears Barnabas' voice telling her that he needs her. A confused Naomi stares at Barnabas' portrait. Barnabas' voice begs his mother to come to the Old House. After Naomi rushes out of the house, the apparition of Angélique materializes over the stairs, laughing evilly.

Carrying a lantern, Naomi approaches the dark exterior of the Old House. In the upstairs corridor, she notices a dim light and a sobbing sound coming from Josette's room. In the room she walks slowly and is shocked beyond words to see Barnabas crouched on the floor in front of the burning fireplace, weeping softly. A surprised Barnabas turns around as his terrified mother backs up, crying out to God. Barnabas moves toward Naomi, trying to calm her. Tears stream down her confused and frightened face. Barnabas reaches out to his mother, assuring her that it is really himself. Naomi faints in Barnabas' arms.

A roll of thunder is heard outside Collinwood as Sarah and Daniel rush into Naomi's room, jumping on the bed. Sarah tells her brother that she saw their mother go to the Old House. Abigail enters and asks the children why they are not in bed. Daniel replies that Sarah had a dream about Naomi. Sarah says that Naomi is in danger, insisting they must go help her. An intolerant Abigail assures the children it was only a dream and orders them back to bed. She stares curiously at Naomi's empty bed after the children leave.

As the storm draws closer, Abigail hurries up the dark stairs to the front of the Old House. She notices a light coming from a second floor window. Upstairs, Abigail enters Josette's room, where she finds Naomi sitting in a chair, staring blankly. Abigail crosses to her and asks what she is doing there. Naomi says nothing. Suddenly Barnabas enters from the dressing room, and Abigail shrieks in terror. Calling Barnabas a demon, she demands that he stay away from her. She races for the hallway, but Barnabas chases after her, begging her not to run from him. In a trance, Naomi sits alone, uncomprehending. Abigail cries for help as she hurries down the corridor. Barnabas catches her on the staircase, telling her to stop screaming, but Abigail continues to cry out hysterically. Barnabas' vampiristic urges take over as he bares his fangs. He rages, asking his aunt why she never listens. He opens his mouth widely and sinks his fangs into her neck. Abigail screams in terror. Barnabas lays her limp body on the floor. Suddenly he hears a scream. As blood spills from his mouth, he looks toward the base of the stairwell. Daniel and Sarah are staring up at him, frozen with terror. His eyes filled with anguish, Barnabas calls Sarah's name and descends the stairs. The screaming children dash for the door. Barnabas begs them not to run away. Barnabas is alone in the house when the laughing apparition of Angélique appears above the dead Abigail.

Taunting Barnabas, Angélique reminds him of the curse she placed on him. She tells him how everyone who loves him will be lost. A tormented Barnabas runs out into the storm as the ghostly image disappears.

Barnabas races through the rain-soaked woods calling out for the children. Farther ahead, Daniel and Sarah rush through the wind-blown trees. Barnabas continues to chase after them. He runs past a hollow where the children huddle. Noticing that Sarah appears ill, Daniel puts his arm around her to keep her warm. She shivers violently and begins to cry. Daniel tells her that they'll be all right. The rain continues to pour down. In the morning, the children remain nestled together when Ben finds them during a search. Hearing Ben's call, Joshua and Peter rush to them. Joshua feels Sarah's forehead and discovers she has a fever. Daniel deliriously speaks in fragments, mentioning the Old House, Naomi, Abigail, and Barnabas. Joshua instructs Peter and Ben to get the children home and to summon Dr. Roberts. He tells them that he is going to the Old House.

Joshua enters the Old House foyer and calls out to his wife. As he looks up the stairs, he is shocked to see Abigail's bloody body lying on the stairs. He kneels to her and cries out to God. He hears a humming noise from upstairs, calls out for Naomi, and ascends the stairs.

He enters Josette's room and discovers Naomi humming to herself as she sits in a chair. As if nothing has happened, she smiles and tells him she was wondering where he was. Puzzled, Joshua walks toward her, asking Naomi if she is all right. Naomi calmly assures him that she is fine and mentions she has been cleaning Josette's room. Joshua realizes that his wife is incoherent. When he asks her if she knows what happened to Abigail, Naomi responds that nothing has happened to Abigail. She asks if the children are with Victoria. Joshua again asks her about Abigail, urging her to concentrate. He tells Naomi that his sister has been badly hurt. Naomi replies that Joshua said the same thing about Barnabas but insists Joshua was wrong. She says that Barnabas is coming to dinner. She happily comments that Barnabas and Josette are a lovely couple. After a pause, Joshua plays along with his disoriented wife. Brokenhearted, he places his arm around her and suggests they take a look at the new house.

In the children's room at Collinwood, Dr. Roberts examines Sarah as she lies in bed, perspiring from fever. Joshua and a nurse stand by. Daniel rests in the adjoining bed. In the corridor, the doctor warns Joshua that unless the fevers are broken soon the children will die. Joshua is devastated. The doctor explains that he has prescribed a purgative which the nurse will administer every three hours. He apologetically states that nothing else can help Sarah and Daniel. He then asks if Joshua is certain he doesn't want to move Naomi to a facility for the insane. Joshua insistently responds that Collinwood is Naomi's home.

In Victoria's jail cell, a troubled Peter gives a drink of water to a pale and somber Victoria. He assures her that the governor will act in her favor, telling her that Joshua is certain of it. Peter says that the rash of new attacks is further proof that other forces are involved. They both agree that Angélique is undoubtedly involved. Peter reminds Victoria of their conversation about vampires. He reveals that the countess believed Josette was attacked by a vampire. He also discloses that in her delirium Josette kept repeating Barnabas' name. Victoria stares in fascination as Peter tells her that the dying Millicent also spoke of Barnabas as did Daniel when he was found. Victoria comments that vampires are allegedly immortal. Peter confirms the legend.

In a state of shock, Victoria informs Peter that there is a man from her own time who is very much like Barnabas and who claims to be a descendant of Barnabas. She also reveals that he has the same name, and that she thinks he was falling in love with her. A stunned Peter looks at Victoria as she speculates on the possibility that she may be Josette's twentieth century reincarnation. She mentions that she and Josette believed it was possible. Victoria realizes that is why Angélique wants to destroy her. Peter and Victoria think that Barnabas is a vampire.

After dark, in the children's' room at Collinwood, the nurse looks after the worsening Sarah and leaves to retrieve water from downstairs. Barnabas appears behind the French door curtains. He immediately crosses to Daniel's bed and looks down at his young brother, who unconsciously turns his head. Barnabas asks Daniel if he can hear him and touches his brow. Suddenly, Sarah groans loudly, and Barnabas goes to her side. Kneeling at Sarah's bed, Barnabas clasps his sister's hand, calling to her. Suddenly, Sarah's eyes open weakly. She gazes at him with a frightened look. Barnabas begs her not to be afraid, assuring her that he would never hurt her. Sarah whispers, asking if it is really Barnabas. He reassures her. Sarah tells Barnabas that she is not afraid and conveys her love for him. Barnabas expresses his love in return. He kisses her hand. He wants her to promise that she and Daniel will get well. Sarah asks her brother if he can hear the angels that are calling for her. A terrified Barnabas exclaims to Sarah that he will not let her go. Barnabas takes her in his arms as she promises him she will always love him. She asks him never to forget her and dies in his arms. Barnabas' face is filled with pain as he hugs his dead sister. He tearfully lowers her to the bed and departs.

In Victoria's cell the next day, Peter has informed a misty-eyed Victoria of Sarah's passing. Peter remarks that the history book has claimed another victim and fears that Daniel will be next. Responding to Peter's comments, Victoria asks him to repeat himself. Peter adds that Daniel is the last male heir of the Collins family. Victoria excitedly exclaims that she now knows why she was sent back in time. She declares that it is Angélique who is trying to change history in an attempt to destroy the Collins family forever. Victoria realizes that if Daniel dies, then all the people she knows in 1991 will cease to exist and there would be no place for her to go back to. Peter continues the revelation by pointing out that Angélique's plan would prevent Victoria from ever meeting Barnabas in 1991. Victoria wants to know what is being done to save Daniel. Peter replies that the boy is being treated with warm blankets and purgatives. Victoria frantically informs Peter that Daniel should be wrapped in sheets soaked in alcohol and ice. She urges Peter to depart for the local icehouse.

In the children's room at Collinwood, Peter pours chunks of ice into a basin containing alcohol. Daniel lies feverishly in bed as Joshua and the nurse watch. The nurse nervously complains to Joshua that the wet sheets can only make Daniel worse. She insists that the doctor must be informed. Joshua replies that Dr. Roberts has already given up on the boy. He angrily tells the nurse that he will not allow his son to die and orders her out of the room if she doesn't want to help. The offended nurse turns away. Peter brushes Daniel's body with a sheet of cold mixture. With a strained face, Joshua assists. He and Peter step into the corridor. Joshua declares that he is going to the Old House to close it permanently. He instructs an apprehensive Peter to stay with Daniel.

In Josette's room at the Old House, Joshua holds a lantern as he looks sadly at Josette's portrait. Later, he stands in the corridor outside the room and finishes boarding up the doorway. He descends the stairway to the foyer. Suddenly he hears Barnabas calling to him from the darkness. Joshua stares aghast as Barnabas emerges from the shadows. He cries out to his son and raises his musket. Barnabas solemnly instructs his father to shoot if he must but warns him that it will not help. Joshua stares in horror. He tells Barnabas that he must be the one responsible for the deaths of Josette, Abigail, and Millicent. Barnabas quietly confirms his father's accusations. Barnabas tells his father that Angélique has cursed him and his entire family for all eternity. Overcome with emotion, Joshua reaches out to Barnabas, and the two men embrace. Barnabas declares that Angélique must be stopped. Joshua agrees but informs Barnabas they have only until dawn to prevent Victoria from hanging. Barnabas is stunned at the news. Joshua reports that the governor had promised him to intervene, but Joshua has had no reply. Joshua discloses that Trask and Abigail spoke out against Victoria during the trial. Barnabas begins describing a plan to his father, insisting that Joshua must find Ben and tell him everything.

Later that night, Ben escorts Trask up the stairs leading to the Old House entrance. Ben has led Trask to believe that Abigail must see him immediately. He has told the Reverend that he must come to the Old House because Joshua has banned Trask from Collinwood. An intoxicated Trask enters the foyer and calls out for Abigail. After no response, he turns around and finds that Ben is gone. The front door slams shut. Desperately he tries to open it, but it won't budge. Trask calls out to Ben, demanding an explanation. Suddenly, a hand grabs the reverend by the throat and swings him around. Trask is horrified to find himself staring face to face with Barnabas. In the drawing room, Barnabas drags a protesting Trask to the desk and slams him into the chair. Barnabas orders him to write a letter to Judge Braithwaite clearing Victoria of the charges against her. A terrified Trask frantically writes as Barnabas dictates to him.

In the basement, Trask stands quivering as Ben chains him to a wall. He cries out, begging to be released. Later, Ben has constructed a brick wall in front of the Reverend, with a small opening in front of his face. Begging for his freedom, Trask decries that he will make a public confession and leave town. Barnabas informs him that his signed statement is already being delivered to the judge by Peter. Ben puts another brick in place, leaving Trask with just a small peephole. Trask exclaims that Barnabas will burn in hell. Barnabas peers through the small hole and says goodbye to the reverend. He cements the last brick in place, leaving the screaming Trask in total darkness.

At the Collinsport Inn, Peter visits the judge and delivers Trask's confession. Peter assures Braithwaite that the letter is genuine. The judge wants to know where Trask is. Peter replies that he has vanished. The judge is not surprised and says he will gladly act on the letter. He says he has always considered Trask a charlatan. An elated Peter thanks the judge excitedly and departs. After Peter is gone, Braithwaite looks again at the letter, but the writing has disappeared. Angélique appears behind him and informs him that there is no letter. She walks toward the judge and places a spell on him, causing Braithwaite to forget Peter's visit and Trask's letter.

In the family cemetery, Joshua meets Barnabas and Ben outside the mausoleum. He informs a relieved Barnabas that Victoria will soon be free. Barnabas starts to enter the mausoleum. Joshua is hesitant, but Barnabas insists that the time has come. Joshua sadly follows his son, leaving a tearful Ben alone to keep guard. Barnabas and Joshua enter the secret room. Joshua asks for God's help, wondering how he can carry out the task at hand. Barnabas assures Joshua that it is the only way. He tells his father that the real Barnabas is gone and what Joshua sees before him must be destroyed. He makes Joshua promise to end his suffering and hands his father a wooden stake and mallet.

At dawn the next morning, Ben paces anxiously outside the mausoleum. In the secret room, Joshua looks inside the coffin and stares at Barnabas who lies sleeping. With trembling hands, he places the stake over Barnabas' heart and raises the mallet. Outside the mausoleum, Joshua staggers out, distraught. He informs Ben that he could not bring himself to kill Barnabas. Ben wonders what they are going to do. Joshua asks him for his help. In the secret room, Barnabas lies sleeping as Joshua and Ben slide the heavy stone lid to cover the sarcophagus. The men then wrap thick iron chains around the coffin. Joshua asks Barnabas to forgive him and prays that God will have mercy on Barnabas' soul.

At Collinwood, Daniel lies in bed, wrapped in a cold damp sheet as the nurse wipes his face. Joshua feels his son's forehead, noting that Daniel still has a fever. At the jail, Peter waits with a tense Victoria in her cell. He assures her that she will be released shortly. The bailiff opens the door for Judge Braithwaite to enter. He informs Peter that the governor has turned down the request to release Victoria without explanation. Victoria and Peter stare at each other in shock. Peter reminds the judge of their visit last night when the judge assured him that he would stay the execution on the basis of Trask's letter. A perplexed judge looks at Peter as if he is insane. He insists that he hasn't seen a letter and did not meet Peter the previous night. Peter grabs the judge and exclaims that Braithwaite is lying. But the bailiff pulls Peter away. A disbelieving Peter stares at the badly shaken judge. He tells Peter that, although his strain is understandable, his conduct is inexcusable and that Peter will answer for it. Braithwaite angrily leaves the cell as the bailiff restrains Peter. Peter begs the bailiff to listen to him, insisting that there has been a misunderstanding. The bailiff apologetically replies that there is nothing he can do. He leaves the cell, locking it behind him. Peter continues to cry out to the bailiff. A despondent Victoria stares silently at Peter.

In the prison courtyard, preparations are underway for the hanging at the gallows. In the jail cell, Peter speaks emotionally to Victoria, insisting that what awaits cannot be the end. He promises that someday, somehow, he'll find her again. They embrace tightly. Victoria tenderly speaks Peter's name as the minister enters. The bailiff follows, notifying Victoria that it is time for her to go to the gallows.

In 1991, a violent storm rages over Collinwood. In her bed, the unconscious Phyllis Wicke thrashes about. Maggie sits at her side, watching with a strange look. She slowly crosses to the mirror and stares into it. Staring back from her reflection is the grinning face of Angélique, who vows that Victoria will not return to the twentieth century.

In 1790, the bailiff and a guard lead Victoria out of the prison with her hands shackled. She is followed into the courtyard by Peter and the minister.

In 1991, Maggie turns off Phyllis' life-support machine. Maggie stares emotionless as Phyllis gasps for air.

In 1790, Peter kisses Victoria. He is restrained by guards as the bailiff leads her to the gallows. She faints but is revived and taken up the steps to the hanging platform. She stares through the open noose.

In 1991, Phyllis continues tossing about and gasping for air while Maggie watches. The beeping on the heart monitor stops, indicating that Phyllis is dead.

In 1790, the minister asks Victoria if she has a last request. She shakes her head, indicating that she has nothing to say. She looks down at Peter, who is watching from below with tear-filled eyes.

In 1991, Julia enters Phyllis' room. She extends a greeting to Maggie, who only stares in a trance-like state. Realizing something is wrong, Julia dashes to the motionless Phyllis and tries to revive her. Roger and Elizabeth rush into the room.

In 1790, the hangman places the noose around Victoria's neck. She stares silently as the minister asks God to have mercy on her soul. Suddenly, Peter screams out and charges up the stairs to the gallows, fighting the guards.

In 1991, Julia desperately rummages through her bag and retrieves a bottle of adrenalin.

In 1790, Peter is shot in the back by a guard and falls down the steps to the ground. Victoria cries out in horror as the crowd surrounds the dying Peter.

In 1991, Julia fills a syringe as Barnabas enters the room.

In 1790, the bailiff orders the hangman to proceed quickly. Peter looks up at Victoria as the hangman places a black hood over her tear-streaked face.

In 1991, Barnabas watches intently as Julia plunges a syringe into Phyllis' chest.

In 1790, the hangman reaches for the lever to release the trapdoor underneath Victoria.

In 1991, Julia continues to administer Phyllis' medication.

In 1790, the hangman pulls the lever, and Victoria's body drops through the open platform.

In 1991, Phyllis struggles to breathe. The violent thunderstorm causes the lights to go out momentarily. When the lights come back on, Phyllis is gone, and everyone stares in shock at Victoria lying in her place. Elizabeth rushes to sit on the bed alongside the disoriented Victoria, who is gasping for air. Victoria cries out, wanting to know where she is. Elizabeth informs her that she is safe at home. Julia tells her that she's back at Collinwood in her own time. Tears form in Victoria's eyes as she hugs Elizabeth, thanking God for her return.

In 1790, the minister and bailiff watch in horror as the hood is removed from the hanging victim, and Phyllis is found hanging from the rope dead instead of Victoria. At Collinwood, a bed-ridden Daniel looks at his father, smiles, and calls out to Joshua. Joshua optimistically exclaims that the boy's fever has broken.

In 1991, a jubilant Victoria continues to cling to Elizabeth. Maggie appears to have been released from Angelique's trance. Barnabas fearfully glances at Victoria. Upon noticing his presence, Victoria jolts backward. Observing the reaction, Julia glances at Barnabas with concern. Still staring at Victoria, Barnabas is consumed by the fear that she may have learned his secret during her adventure in 1790.

Postscript

After her return from 1790, Victoria was unable to clearly recall her experiences from the eighteenth-century. She did, however, retain fragmented memories which alternately fascinated, puzzled, and haunted her. She resumed her romantic relationship with Barnabas, who remained fearful that Victoria's knowledge of the horrors from 1790 would someday resurface and jeopardize their future together.

(Based on story projections for a second season.)

Cast List

1991 STORYLINE

LYSETTE ANTHONY Angélique
BRUCE BARBOUR Deputy
BARBARA BLACKBURN Carolyn
Stoddard
MICHAEL BUICE Local Tough (a.k.a.
Muscles)
MICHAEL CAVANAUGH Sheriff
George Patterson
BEN CROSS Barnabas Collins
STEVE FLETCHER Deputy Jonathan
Harker (a.k.a. Paramedic #2)
JIM FYFE Willie Loomis
STEFAN GIERASCH Dr. Michael
Woodard
JOANNA GOING Victoria Winters
JOSEPH GORDON-LEVITT David
Collins
EDDIE HAILEY Deputy
RIF HUTTON Paramedic #1
EDDIE JONES Sam Evans
J.B. AND THE NITESHIFT Roadhouse
Band
CHARLES LANE Antique Shop
Proprietor
BASIL LANGTON Reverend
VERONICA LAUREN Sarah Collins
JULIANNA McCARTHY Mrs. Sarah
Johnson
HOPE NORTH Gloria
GEORG OLDEN Gardener (a.k.a. Boy
#1)
ELY POUGET Maggie Evans
JEAN SIMMONS Elizabeth Collins
Stoddard
REBECCA STAAB Daphne Collins
BARBARA STEELE Dr. Julia Hoffman
ROY THINNES Roger Collins
WAYNE TIPPIT Dr. Hyram Fisher
MICHAEL T. WEISS Joe Haskell
ELLEN WHEELER Phyllis Wicke

1790 STORYLINE

LYSETTE ANTHONY Angélique
BARBARA BLACKBURN Millicent
Collins
RICHARD BURNS Customer
MICHAEL CAVANAUGH André
DuPrés
BEN CROSS Barnabas Collins
BRENDAN T. DILLON Judge Isiah
Braithwaite
JOANNE DORIAN Nurse
RALPH DRISCHELL Dr. Roberts
APOLLO DUKAKIS Reverend Amos
RICHARD EVANS Customer
JIM FYFE Ben Loomis
STEFAN GIERASCH Joshua Collins
JOANNA GOING Victoria
Winters/Josette DuPrés
JOSEPH GORDON-LEVITT Daniel
Collins
EDDIE JONES Bailiff Henry Evans
VERONICA LAUREN Sarah Collins
JULIANNA McCARTHY Abigail
Collins
COURTENAY MCWHINNEY Crone
SHAWN MODRELL Ruby Tate
ADRIAN PAUL Jeremiah Collins
JEAN SIMMONS Naomi Collins
BARBARA STEELE Countess Natalie
DuPrés
ROBERT S. TELFORD Innkeeper
ROY THINNES Reverend Trask
DICK VALENTINE Jury Foreman
DONALD WAYNE Minister
MICHAEL T. WEISS Peter Bradford
LAUREL WILEY Girl

Production Credits

PILOT (EPISODE 1)

ALLIED WEATHER SERVICE Weather Reporting
HOWARD ANDERSON COMPANY Titles, Opticals & Mastering
MARK ANDERSON 2nd Assistant Cameraman
DEBORAH AQUILA New York Casting
DR. STEVEN ARNOLD Cast Doctor
ROY BARNETT Electrician
JOHN BENTLEY Assistant Prop Master
LARRY BIRD Set Designer
BILL BLUNDEN Associate Producer/Film Editor
JOHN BOYD Re-recording Mixer
ED BURZA Men's Costumer
STEVE BUTLER Assistant Film Editor
CFI Film Processing
STEPHEN J. CANNELL PRODS. Sound Effects Editorial
CHAPMAN CRANE Cranes/Dollies
CLAIRMONT CAMERA Camera Equipment
JEFF CLARK 1st Assistant Cameraman
PAUL CLARK Greensman
GENE CLINESMITH Transportation Coordinator
BOB COBERT Music Composer
SHIRLEY CUNNINGHAM Women's Costumer
DAN CURTIS Series Creator/Executive Producer/Director/Writer
PAUL DAFELMAIR Men's Costumer
MICHELLE DARRINGER Insurance
KAREN DAVIS Women's Costumer
DE FOREST RESEARCH Script Research
BOB DELLA SANTINA 1st Assistant Director
DISC CASTING SERVICE Extras Casting
LANCE DODSON Property Master
STEVE DORSCH Script Supervisor
CARL DUBLICLAY 2nd Assistant Director
EASTMAN KODAK Film Stock
PAUL ECKER Paint Foreman
ERIC ERZINGER Production Assistant
JOHN FARROW Location Manager
STEVE FEKE Supervising Producer/Writer
ED FOWLES Construction Foreman
LABEN FREEMAN Craft Service
ROGER FROST Set Dresser
ALFONSO GORIS Greensman
JOHN GRAY Special Effects
GREYSTONE PARK RANGERS Security
LAURA LEE GRUBICH Hair Stylist
JEANNIE GUNN Set Decorator
MATTHEW HALL Technical Advisor

SAM HALL Creative Consultant
ROBERT W. HARBIN Casting Director
FRED HARPMAN Production Designer
MARK HARRIS Film Editing Apprentice
DEANN HELINE Production Associate
LORRAINE HENDRICK Teacher
NORM HENRY Line Producer/Unit Production Manager
DAN HILAND Re-recording Mixer
STEVE JARRARD Lead Man
BRIAN JOHNSON Dolly Grip
JOJO JORDAN Stand-In (Jean Simmons)
HEATHER KAY Stand-In
RUTH KENNEDY Executive Assistant
STEVE KING Best Boy
BRIAN KINSEL Stand-In
JIM KRUCKMEYER Electrician
LIONEL LA VALLE Boom Operator
JAY LACK Grip
CHRIS LEDESMA Music Editor
GUS LEPRÉ Hair Stylist
DIETRICH LOHMAN Director of Photography
TOM MARSHALL Transportation Captain
MARY MATTHEWS Stand-In
WENDI MATTHEWS Casting Assistant
DR. GERALD MICHAELSON Cast Doctor
MICHELSON'S FOOD SERVICE Catering
BILL MILLAR Optical Effects
STEVE MILLER Set Dresser
JOHN MITCHELL Cable
PAT MITCHELL Sound Mixer
JOHN MOIO Stunt Coordinator
MOLE RICHARDSON Electric Equipment
DEE MONSANO Make-up Artist
MONY MONSANO Make-up Artist
MARK MOORE Camera Operator
CRAIG NYCZ Paint Foreman
ART PASSARELLA Labor Foreman
ROCCO PASSARELLA Construction Coordinator
JIM PIERSON Production Assistant
DOLORES PLEVIAK Executive Assistant
HALL POWELL Writer
BARBARA RILEY Negative Cutter
CLIFF ROGERS Production Accountant
TINA ROSENBERG Assistant Production Accountant
ERIC RYLANDER Special Effects
ERIC SAMSELL Grip
STEVE SARDANIS Art Director
RICHARD SARSTEDT Stand In

170

MIKE SCHWARTZ Electrician
B. TENNYSON SEBASTIAN II Re-recording
    Mixer
CHUCK SEFTON Chief Lighting Technician
CHUCK SERECI 2nd Grip
FRANK SERECI Grip
ROSE TOBIAS SHAW London Casting
WENDY SHEAR-TERLINDEN 2nd 2nd
    Assistant Director
LYNN SMITH 2nd Assistant Cameraman
SONY PICTURES STUDIOS Re-recording
DR. ARNOLD STEVE Cast Doctor
JANET STOKES Art Director
SUPERIOR BACKINGS Original Portraits
BILL TAUB Writer
TEDDY'S ANSWERING SERVICE Stunt
    Answering Service
HECTOR URRUTIA Electrician
JEFF VERDICK Transportation
WALKER LOCATION SERVICES Police Permits
ART WALLACE Developer of Certain Characters
WARNER BROTHERS SCRIPT Mimeographs
WARNER HOLLYWOOD STUDIOS Set
    Soundstages
LARRY WARWICK Production Designer
MARCIA WARWICK Production Coordinator
ALICE WESTON Production Secretary
WESTSIDE STUDIO SERVICE Sound Equipment
BILL WHITESIDE First Aid
DR. STEVEN WITLEN Cast Doctor
BILL WITTHANS Key Grip
TERRY YOUNG Insurance

SERIES (EPISODES 2-12)

AM TELECOMMUNICATIONS Telephone
    Service
KEN ABRAHAM Production Assistant
ACTIVE LOCK+ALARM Locksmith
ADOLF-GASSER, INC Cine-Crane
DAN ALLEN Horse Wrangler
TOM ALTOBELLO Assistant Props
AMERICAN BARRICADE Traffic Cones
HOWARD ANDERSON COMPANY Titles,
    Opticals & Mastering
DONNA BARRISH Wardrobe Supervisor
CHARLES BATEMAN Electrician
DENIS BENARDELLO Head Painter
MONICA BIELAWSKI Assistant Production
    Coordinator
VAUGHN BLADEN Honeywagon
BILL BLUNDEN Associate
    Producer/Supervising Film Editor
BRUCE BOLT Crewcab Construction
BOLTING TRUCKING Shipping
JON BOORSTIN Co-Producer/Writer
RICHARD BORIS Greens Foreman
STEVE BOUCHARD Prop Maker
ROB BOWMAN Director
JOHN BOYD Re-recording Mixer
SUE BOYD Assistant Hair Stylist
BREUNERS FURNITURE RENTAL Furniture
NIC BROWN Chief Lighting Technician
TODD BRYANT Production Assistant

DEENA BURKETT Main Title Design
LES BUTLER Assistant Film Editor
STEPHEN BUTLER Film Editor
CFI Film Processing
LINDA CAMPANELLI Writer/Executive Story
    Editor
TIM CASTAGNOLA Paint Laborer
TONY CASTAGNOLA Laborer Foreman
CENEX Extras Casting
CHAPMAN/LEONARD Dolly
BILL CHERONES 2nd 2nd Assistant Director
CINELEASE Grip/Electrical Supplies
LEON CLEMONS Grip
GENE CLINESMITH Transportation
    Coordinator
TREY CLINESMITH Driver
BOB COBERT Music Composer
JOE COLE Best Boy Electrician
BILL CONDIT Production Van
MICHAEL COO Key Grip
ANTHONY COWLEY Production Designer
DIANE CROOKE Set Costumer
BARBARA CROW Assistant Production
    Accountant
BRAD CURRY Drapery Person
DAN CURTIS Series Creator/Executive
    Producer/Director/Writer
GREG CURTIS Special Effects Coordinator
TRACY CURTIS Production Assistant
DAVID DITTMAR Make-up Assistant
STEVE DORSCH Script Supervisor
TIM DRURY Boom Operator
DAN DUGAN 1st Assistant Director
EASTMAN KODAK Film Stock
EAVES-BROOKS COSTUME CO. Period
    Costumes
CHRIS EGUIA Property Master
TONY EGUIA Assistant Props
VERONICA EGUIA Assistant Props
MITCHELL EL-MAHDY Set Medic
ALEC ELIZONDO 2nd Assistant Camera
    Operator
CHUY ELIZONDO Director of Photography
JOHN FARROW Location Manager
STEVE FEKE Supervising Producer/Writer
JENE FIELDER Body Make-up Artist
S. MICHAEL FORMICA Unit Production
    Manager
FUJI Film Stock
JERRY GEBR Portrait Artist
TOM GEBR Lead Man
CHRIS GEISSER Cook
GARY GERO Animal Wrangler
JAN GLASER Casting Associate
JOHN GOODWIN Make-up Assistant
ALFONSO GORIS Greensman
JOE GRAHAM Dolly Grip
CHARLES GRAY Swing Crew
GARY GRAY Set Dressing
WILLIAM GRAY Co-Producer/Writer/
    Executive Story Editor
BRUCE GREENFIELD 2nd 2nd Assistant
    Director

171

DR. MORRIS GREENSPOON Special Eye
Contacts
GREYSTONE PARK RANGERS Security
HP OFFICE SUPPLIES Office Supplies
BARBARA HALL Production Coordinator
MATTHEW HALL Writer
SAM HALL Writer
MARK HARRIS Film Editing Apprentice
ANNE HASCHKA Assistant Film Editor
DEANN HELINE Production Associate
LORRAINE HENDRICK Teacher
HERMAN HERNANDEZ Cook's Helper
HOFFMAN TRAVEL Travel Agent
MEG HOFFMAN Assistant Production
Accountant
CRAIG HOLT Assistant Film Editor
MARGARET HUSSEY Writers' Assistant
ALEX JACHNO Electrician
JIMMY JONES Crewcab/Starwagon
JOJO JORDAN Stand-In (Jean Simmons)
EDWARD KALPAKIAN 2nd 2nd Assistant
Director/Production Assistant
HEATHER KAY Stand-In
JOHN KEATING Production Assistant
RUTH KENNEDY Executive Assistant
BRIAN KINSEL Stand-In
TIM KIRKPATRICK Set Decorator
MARK KLINE Best Boy Grip
CHRIS LEDESMA Music Editor
KEN LEE Make-up & Wardrobe Transportation
DAN LESTELLE Craft Service
LIGHTNING BIKES Messenger Service
STEVE LLOYD Driver
DR. ROLAND LOUDERMILK Chiropracter
PAUL LYNCH Director
SCOTT A. LYNK Construction Foreman
LISA MAGDALENO Secretary
MARSHALL/PLUMB Script Research
TERRY MARSHALL Electrician
TOM MARSHALL Transportation Captain
ED MASSARELLA Driver
ARMAND MASTROIANNI Producer/Director
MARY MATTHEWS Stand-In
ROGER MATTMULLER Fuel Truck
LUCIE MAZMANIAN Assistant Production
Accountant
PAUL McAVENE Wardrobe Assistant
MICHAEL MEANS Assistant Production
Accountant
MIKE MEINARDUS Special Effects Assistant
DR. DON MICHAELSON Doctor
DR. GERALD MICHAELSON Doctor
MICHELSON'S FOOD SERVICE Caterer
BILL MILLAR Special Visual Effects/Main Title
Design
DARIN MILLER Swing Crew
JOHN MITCHELL Cableman
PAT MITCHELL Sound Mixer
TOM MITCHELL Cableman
M.M. SHELLY MOORE Writer/Executive Story
Editor
ED NIELSON Camera Operator

DEBBIE NODELLA Production Accountant
NORTH HOLLYWOOD ICE CO. Dry Ice
CHRISTOPHER S. NUSHAWG Set Designer
MICHAEL O' CORRIGAN Supervising Sound
Editor
PAGENET Pagers
DEE-DEE PETTY Hair Stylist
JACK PETTY Make-up Artist
JIM PIERSON Production Assistant
MIKE PINEGAR 1st Assistant Camera Operator
PLAZA FLORAL GROUP Florist
DOLORES PLEVIAK Executive Assistant
RON PONIEWAZ Star Suites
PRICE POINT SUPPLY Polaroid Film
POST GROUP Post-Production Services
SCOTT PROPHET Dolly Grip
BARBARA RILEY Negative Cutter
WALTER ROBLES Stunt Coordinator
ROCKY MOUNTAIN MOTION PICTURES
Camera Equipment
ALBERT G. RUBIN Insurance
BRYAN RYMAN Production Designer
BROOKE SARTORIUS Assistant Props
B. TENNYSON SEBASTIAN II Re-recording
Mixer
CRAIG SEITZ Production Assistant
SELIG CHEMICAL INDUSTRIES Fogging
Compound
ED SHAVERS Assistant Props
MITCH SIMMONS Paint Foreman
MARY JO SLATER Casting Director
MARK SOBEL Director
SONY PICTURES STUDIOS Re-recording
SPARKLETTS Water Service
CHARLES SPILLAR Electrician
DEBORAH SQUIRES Women's Costumer
STAR EXECUTIVES Security
JOHN J. STEPHENS Re-Recording Mixer
EDWARD F. SUSKI Re-recording Mixer
ANNE SWEETING Art Department Coordinator
JOHN SYRJAMAKI 2nd Assistant Director
TECH-FX Video Assist
TYPEWRITERS UNLIMITED Typewriters
JAN VAN UCHELEN Assistant Hair Stylist
JEFF VERDICK Transportation Co-Captain
LAURIE VIERA Production Coordinator
ART WALLACE Developer of Certain Characters
ROSALIE SAMPLIN WALLACE Costume
Designer
WARNER HOLLYWOOD STUDIOS
Grip/Electrical Supplies/Set Soundstages
WENDY WASSALL-ENGALLA Casting
Assistant
JEFF WATKINS Craft Service
GARY WATTMAN Best Boy Grip
RICK WELDON Construction Coordinator
TERRY WILLIAMS Film Editor
ROSALYNDA WOLD Men's Costumer
YATES SUPPLY COMPANY Masks/Chemicals
GREG YEFFETH Grip
GALE ZIMMERMAN Electrician

MGM TV PERSONNEL

ANN ASHCRAFT Production & Planning Manager
LEE BARTLETT Production Counsel
JANIS FINKLE Development Manager
LES FRENDS Administration V.P.
DAVID GERBER Chairman/Chief Executive Officer
LORI GERSON Creative Services Manager
ANDREW GONZALES Post Production V.P.
SUSAN HARBERT Series Programming V.P.
RICHARD S. KAUFMAN Music V.P.
RON LEVINSON Current Programming V.P.
LYNN LORING President
TOM MALANGA Finance & Administration Sr. V.P.
JULIE MANN Legal
CINDY MARVIN Publicity Assistant
CAROLYN MASKIN Production & Planning Manager
JACKIE MILLER Estimating Associate Director
GAYLE MNOOKIN Post-Production Associate Director
MARISSA O'LEARY Business Affairs Manager
MARK PEDOWITZ Business Affairs & Administration Sr. V.P.
BRUCE POBJOY Post-Production Sr. V.P.
TERILYN RAWSON Creative Affairs V.P.
KIM REED Publicity, Promotion & Advertising V.P.
CHRISTOPHER SEITZ Production Sr. V.P.
LORNA SHEPARD Business Affairs V.P.
MARCIA SPIELHOLZ Business & Legal Affairs V.P.
RON VON SCHIMMELMANN Production V.P.

Collectibles

The continuing popularity of *Dark Shadows* has prompted the release of memorabilia based on the 1991 revival.

HOME VIDEO & T-SHIRT

Episodes 1-12 available individually. Episode 1 features 15 minutes of additional footage not seen on television. Full-color Barnabas T-shirt (pictured) also available.

MPI HOME VIDEO
15825 ROB ROY DR.
OAK FOREST, IL 60452

COMICS & POSTERS

Regularly issued comics featuring new adventures as well as adaptations of the television series' storylines. Posters of illustrated cover paintings also available.

INNOVATION
3622 JACOB ST.
WHEELING, WV
26003.

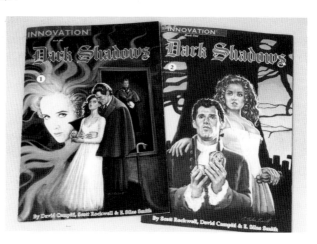

MODEL KIT

A realistically detailed resin model kit of Barnabas Collins in 1790. Includes a cemetery scene base.

ACTION KITS INTERNATIONAL
P.O. BOX 7201
GRAND RAPIDS, MI 49507

WATCHES

Limited edition collector watches of Barnabas and Angelique in uniquely designed display boxes.

ABBELARE
419 N. LARCHMONT ST.
SUITE #108
LOS ANGELES, CA 90004

FAN ORGANIZATIONS

For *Dark Shadows* information, and details on the annual *Dark Shadows* Festivals, please send a self-addressed, stamped envelope to:

DARK SHADOWS
P.O. BOX 92R
MAPLEWOOD, NJ 07040

For information on the current events *Dark Shadows* newsletter and fan publications, please send a self-addressed, stamped envelope to:

SHADOWGRAM/WORLD OF DARK SHADOWS
P.O. BOX 1766
TEMPLE CITY, CA 91780